W9-CBU-417

KILLDEER
MOUNTAIN

KILLDEER MOUNTAIN

A NOVEL

DEE BROWN

THORNDIKE PRESS • THORNDIKE, MAINE

Library of Congress Cataloging in Publication Data:

Brown, Dee Alexander.
  Killdeer Mountain.

  Large print ed.
  1. Large type books. I. Title.
[PS3503.R79533K5 1983b]   813'.52   83-9163
ISBN 0-89621-469-9

Large Print edition available through arrangement with Holt, Rinehart, Winston, A Division of CBS Educational & Co.

Cover design by Christy Rosso.

KILLDEER
MOUNTAIN

By chance — far more than by my own efforts — did I learn the story of Charles Rawley, if indeed it is his story and not that of Drew Hardesty and Kathleen Hardesty, or Nettie Steever and Blue Sky Woman. You must judge for yourself what happened, as I have tried to do, from such evidence as participants and witnesses of these curious events were willing to give.

In a way the story is a puzzle, solved in most part, perhaps. During some phases of it — in particular the ending of it, if there is an ending — I was one of the observers. But the heart of the matter rests within the memories of others, and because each of us sees or feels or uses the senses in differing degrees from all other human beings, inevitably there are conflicts in the tellings. The world we view is a complex mirror that tricks us with false images so that what we believe to have happened to us or to others may or may not have taken place as is fixed in our memories.

I have set down what was told to me at different times by several men and women. Some of the narrators were merely on the periphery of events, and they may have misinterpreted what they saw and heard. Others were directly involved, yet because they were so close to the action their vision of the meaning of what was occurring may have been blurred. And some attempted to conceal truths that others revealed either accidentally or intentionally.

I have tried to fit these varying images and sometimes twice-told tales together so that the puzzle is no longer a puzzle. Life itself, however, is a mystery, and not one of us is always who or what we may seem to be.

1

I swung myself down from the seat of the canvas-covered freight wagon, the steady rain streaking my face when I looked up to take my leather bag from the driver's hand. "It's over there," the driver said. "Other side the stables."

Daylight was almost gone, but I could read the irregular white lettering along the side of the building: LIVERY FEED & SALE STABLE. I hurried on through the rain that pattered upon my wide-brimmed hat and was soaking my linen duster. STEEVER HOUSE, the sign read, in the same uneven characters that were painted on the wall of the livery stable. Built of logs and rough planking, the hotel was two floors high but not much wider than the length of the wagon I'd been riding in all day. It appeared to be leaning against the rain-laden wind. No lights showed in the windows, and when I reached the wooden sidewalk, I saw a shingle sticking in a crack between the double doors. The word *Closed* was scrawled in shoe-blacking across one side of the shingle.

Swearing aloud, I turned and started back toward the livery stable. A large man wearing an India-rubber poncho that could have been military issue loomed out of the darkening weather, halting a few steps in front of me. "Looking for lodging, mister?" the man asked. His voice was disembodied, the sounds rolling as though he were speaking inside a cave. I attributed this to the atmosphere, but nevertheless felt an eerie sense of unease.

"I was hoping to stay the night at the Steever House," I told him.

"Closed," the man replied.

"How much longer?"

"Some days, I expect. They left this afternoon, Miss Nettie and her both, to go upriver to that new fort." He paused and then said slowly as though the words he spoke held some secret significance: "They were sent for." He shook rivulets of rain from his shiny black sleeves and stepped closer. He was peering at me, wanting to see more clearly, and in doing so revealed for the first time his own face illuminated by flashes of distant lightning. His eyes were set in deep sockets so that I could discern no glint in them. A short heavy beard covered the sides of his face except for a long ugly scar from ear to chin that was like a

10

burned brand on his left cheek.

"I said they left," he added offhandedly in his hollow voice, "but they're still down there on the steamboat. It's tied up for the night because of the storm."

He made a slight gesture toward his right, and I turned so that I could see the indicated black fringe of cottonwoods slanting away from the settlement. "The boat landing's down there?" I asked.

The man nodded. "You could sleep back here in the stables," he suggested mildly.

"Thanks, but I'll try the boat." I shifted my bag to the other hand and started down the sloping road toward the river, my boots sinking to the ankles in mud.

I cursed the weather and the *Saint Louis Herald.* In my mind I composed a scorching letter to the editor whom I'd worked for during three years of war. As soon as the fighting was finished, he'd had the gall to send me up the wretched Missouri River in search of more stories of conflict and gore. Oh, I'd seen worse than this Dakota weather and the greasy eating places and bug-ridden inns along the river, far worse I'd seen and endured from Shiloh to Vicksburg and Chickamauga and Atlanta and following Sherman to the sea. But I was past thirty and ready to settle down in Saint Louis

11

and marry that pretty German girl out there at Belle Fontaine. She wasn't going to wait around forever while I gallivanted back and forth across the states and territories of the Republic.

A gust of wind splashed raindrops against my neck, and a cold wetness seeped down my collar. But before I could raise more self-pity for my miseries, the lights of the steamboat at the landing came into view. Below a pair of tall smokestacks, running lanterns along the side of the pilothouse cast a glow upon a recently varnished nameplate. "The *Roanoke!*" I yelled out, after a moment of refusing to believe my first stroke of good luck in weeks, and went sliding and splashing down through the muck to a crude platform of logs that was the loading dock.

I called to the startled deckhand posted on a packing box nearest the gangplank: "Is Captain Enoch Adams on board this boat?" He roused up from a half sleep, unwilling to accept that anyone would appear out of such weather in so lonely a place to board the *Roanoke.* He told me that Captain Adams would likely be on the saloon deck and then he let me come aboard, offering a gunnysack to wipe the mud from my boots. As I climbed the companionway the sound of music became audible, a melodeon.

Someone was playing "There's a Good Time Coming," and when I reached the entrance to the central lounge, a strong baritone voice sang out the last stanza. I stowed my bag against the wall and stood there a moment, letting my eyes grow accustomed to the yellow lamplight. The melodeon player was a young woman in a scarlet-and-white-striped dress, her back to me, very slim-waisted, her reddish hair netted and decorated with a bunch of artificial purple violets. Standing beside the melodeon and looking fondly down at the young woman was a lieutenant colonel in a neat new blue uniform. For a moment her face was in profile as she exchanged a few words with the lieutenant colonel, and then she began playing spiritedly again, accompanying herself in a fine mezzo-soprano:

> *Some folks like to sigh,*
> *Some folks do, some folks do.*

Although the lounge was crowded, there were the usual three or four passengers moving around the edges of the attentive audience. A stout thick-necked man crossed between me and the melodeon, blocking my view of the young woman. The lieutenant colonel joined her in the chorus:

13

Long live the merry merry heart
That laughs by night and day,
Like the Queen of Mirth,
No matter what some folks say.

The face of Captain Enoch Adams, clean-shaven except for a drooping moustache, his hair grayer at the temples than when I'd last seen him in Saint Louis, suddenly materialized before me. "Sam," he said, offering his hand, "I had no idea you were at Bell's Landing." Neither his voice nor his looks conveyed any hint of surprise at my unanticipated presence, but I'd learned during the war that the captain rarely showed any reaction to the unexpected, or revealed any emotion publicly. When he was master of the late lamented *Effie Deans,* I'd made three wartime journeys with him, and although we'd endured a number of surprising, indeed dreadful experiences, I never saw him exhibit any evidence of excitement except possibly an occasional brightening of the color in his otherwise mild blue eyes when events were at their most perilous.

The nearest he ever came to betraying his feelings toward me was one evening on the Tennessee River when he suggested that I call him Enoch instead of Captain Adams, but he'd been through a very trying day and had consumed more than his usual one glass of bourbon. After all, he was old enough to be my father, and I could never bring myself to address him other than by his title.

"The editor of the *Saint Louis Herald* put me here, captain," I explained. "May God forgive him."

"I suspected as much. You'll be wanting shelter against the weather, I suppose."

"Judging from the crowd," I said, "you must be filled up. If so, I'll sleep below."

He turned and pointed a thumb and forefinger at a rosy-cheeked Irish lad who was wearing a sort of brass-buttoned uniform to indicate that he was the *Roanoke's* steward. The music of the melodeon had stopped and the audience was beginning to disperse.

I could not hear what Captain Adams said to the steward, his words being drowned out by the sudden laughter of the young melodeon player. She had pressed between the captain and me and was crying out in a husky, almost breathless voice: "You *did* say that I might invite someone to accompany me to the captain's table this evening, did you not, Captain Adams?"

The captain's manner changed instantly. The old rascal almost simpered, but he was not quite as far gone as the fawning lieutenant colonel. "Why, yes indeed, Miss Kathleen," he stammered.

"Then I've chosen Colonel Harris for my table escort."

"Lucky fellow, you, colonel." The captain smiled at Harris, and then winked at her. "I'd hoped that I'd be your choice," he said softly, as he regained his composure.

"Why, sir, you're the host," she objected. Her red-and-white dress twirled as she spun half around, her green eyes looking into mine.

The captain turned back to me. "Sam, I want you to have the privilege of knowing our loveliest and most accomplished passenger. Mrs. Kathleen Hardesty. Mr. Samuel Morrison." I thought her response was something special for me, but I soon came to know that she had a way of making her eyes lock into the eyes of whatever male happened to be exchanging looks with her. After I'd managed to murmur a word or two, our eyes unlocked, yet she continued to survey me with as intent a scrutiny as I've ever received from a woman. It was as if I were being measured, although I was flattered to hear her husky voice saying: "I greatly admire journalists, Mr. Morrison, they are such *interesting* gentlemen."

There was about Mrs. Hardesty an odor of peppermint, which was just right for her. As she swept away from the captain and me, her red-and-white-striped dress enveloping her lithe figure gave her the appearance of a peppermint candy stick. She glanced back at me once with those measuring green eyes and went off with the lieutenant colonel in the direction of the ladies' staterooms.

Captain Adams and his steward put me up in the last available cabin, both apologizing for its crowded condition. It was half filled with tins of imported biscuits bound for some Scottish fur trader at one of the forts upriver. The captain had stored them in the empty cabin to keep them dry.

"If I hadn't had this stateroom," he explained, "I would've stacked them in my quarters. Old McLeod can't abide a soft biscuit, and they would dampen down below."

The steward made a neat row of the tin boxes along the upper bunk and placed the remaining ones along the wall opposite, leaving me just enough space to get to the washstand and crawl into the lower bunk. "Your bed will be made during the dinner hour," the steward promised.

"Yes, and you'll dine at my table, Sam," the captain added. "About twenty minutes from now."

After they'd gone I washed up and chose my

least-soiled shirt from the bag. For a few moments the sound of rain drumming on the hurricane deck made me sleepy, but then I thought of Miss Peppermint and her green eyes and of how I would soon be looking into them again at Captain Adams's dining table.

Fortuity, a deviation from our usual routines, the accidental crossing of pathways — what remarkable effects they have upon us bungling human beings. Chance had saved my life more than once during the war, and on this night, when I might have been enduring the discomforts of a dreary livery-stable loft, chance had closed the Steever House and brought me that mysterious stranger in the India-rubber poncho to tell me in his hollow voice of the presence of a steamboat at Bell's Landing. And chance had somehow brought me Miss Peppermint, only she was not *Miss* Peppermint, she was *Mrs.* Kathleen Hardesty. And why Mrs. Kathleen and not Mrs. John or Thomas or Something-or-other Hardesty? And what was she up to, being so cozy with Lieutenant Colonel Harris?

I suppose I was a bit giddy for lack of decent food during the past day or two. Anyway when I stepped out of my cabin into the aromas of soups and fishes and roasts, I dismissed Mrs. Peppermint partially from my mind and thought mainly of feasting. And do not the wise men say that food and romance are complementary?

On the *Roanoke* the lounge between the gentlemen's cabin and the ladies' cabin was used as a dining room as well as a dance floor. The captain's table was forward, opposite the melodeon and nearby the pantry door. Captain Adams was already seated, with Mrs. Hardesty and Lieutenant Colonel Harris on his left and two empty chairs on his right. He motioned me to the chair at the end opposite him, so that Mrs. Hardesty was very close to my right elbow, the table being an undersized one as are most dining tables on small steamboats.

Mrs. Hardesty was frisky and exuberant, chattering about the stormy weather and how positively exhilarated she was by lightning and thunder. She was stopped only by the approach of the captain's remaining two guests, and when I rose to greet them I received another pleasant surprise.

They were Dr. Konrad Lieber and his wife Emilie, acquaintances from Saint Louis. Lieber was an excellent physician and an accomplished musician, a violinist. He must then have been in his mid-forties, but his sandy, neatly trimmed beard showed no trace of gray. When he was a young boy he and other members of his family had emigrated from Germany to Saint Louis, but he had returned to that country for his medical education. Later he had married into one of the wealthy fur families of Saint Louis, the Chenaults. Although Emilie Chenault Lieber was reserved in manner and rather plain in appearance, with her mouse-colored hair parted in the middle and rolled into a tight bun at the back, beneath the surface she was quite jolly and agreeable, and a woman of some passion. Before the war the Liebers held weekly musicales in their home overlooking the Mississippi River, and I had been fortunate enough to be invited to several of them. Indeed, it was at the Liebers' that I met that pretty German girl from Belle Fontaine, whom I intended to make my wife if the editor of the *Herald* would only cease sending me to wars and frontier imbroglios.

As Lieber settled into the chair nearer me, he remarked in an exaggerated jesting tone that he often used: "Captain Adams gave Emilie and me fair warning that you had come aboard." He spoke English with a slight accent that thickened only when he became angry or excited.

"We're pleased that you've joined us, Mr. Morrison," Emilie Lieber said, leaning closer to her husband so that I might hear her soft voice above the clatter of the diners. "I suppose your newspaper is sending you upriver to compose a piece about the commemoration at Fort Rawley."

"Beg pardon, ma'am," I replied, "but I must confess my ignorance of a fort named Rawley or a commemoration."

"And you a newspaper writer!" Mrs. Hardesty cried out, and laughed teasingly into my right ear. "You're supposed to know everything."

Captain Adams defended me. "Our scribbler has been out on the Plains in pursuit of the Indian treaty makers and the nefarious railroad builders. The first that any of us heard of this memorialization was after you left Saint Louis, Sam."

"Do I receive an acquittal this time?" I asked Mrs. Hardesty, but turned quickly away from her bottomless green eyes. "Rawley, Rawley? Isn't he that big wartime senator from Ohio?"

"Yes, but it's his son who is being honored." Dr. Lieber brushed his fingers across the close-clipped sandy beard on his chin. "I was the army surgeon at Fort Standish when Major Rawley was there. The War Department is naming the replacement fort in his honor. They insisted that I be there for the occasion."

Out of my memory of the war I recalled

something about Senator Rawley's son. At the time I had been following the Union army in Tennessee, but I'd read about Charles Rawley and Fort Standish in a packet of newspapers that came from Saint Louis. A battle with the Indians somewhere in Dakota. Killdeer Mountain. Senator's Son Charged with Cowardly Conduct Under Fire. That was how I remembered it.

"Wasn't he court-martialed?" I asked Lieber.

"No, no, it never came to that. An inquiry only. He later redeemed himself entirely."

Emilie Lieber smiled at me. "Konrad is always the modest one. Everybody credited him with restoring young Charles Rawley's faith in himself. You should see the letter of thanks he received from Senator Rawley."

Lieutenant Colonel Harris was pouring wine into our glasses. "The commemoration surely is worthy of your reportorial pen, Mr. Morrison," he said. "I was sent from Washington by President Johnson to represent the White House."

"Ah, yes," Captain Adams agreed. "Several of the high and mighty of our Republic will be there, Sam."

"Are they aboard the *Roanoke?*" I peered at the tables across from us.

"A few. But the main party is on the *Deer*

Lodge. They left three days ahead of us. I'm told that Senator Rawley and his entourage occupy half the staterooms aboard the *Deer Lodge.*"

I shook my head. "Being past due in Saint Louis, I was planning to take the next boat downriver. But if President Andrew Johnson – and everyone else – Surely you're not bound for Fort Standish, or Fort Rawley, are you, Mrs. Hardesty?"

"I am indeed." Her face grew serious for the first time since I'd met her.

"Don't tell me you were sent for. By the Rawleys?"

"No, but I expect to meet them." Something hard had crossed the surfaces of her green eyes, limiting their depth. I caught a faint odor of peppermint as she continued firmly: "No, Mr. Morrison, I am journeying to Fort Rawley to recover the bones of my late husband and return them to Kentucky."

Before we finished dinner I learned that Kathleen Hardesty's husband had been killed in an encounter with Sioux Indians somewhere near old Fort Standish. I also learned to my surprise that she was not one of the Saint Louis passengers. She had come aboard the *Roanoke* at Fort Rice only three days ago. What she was doing at that rude and windy post of cottonwood-log huts, she did not say. I suppose no one had asked her, neither Lieutenant Colonel Harris nor Captain Adams nor Dr. Lieber. They were all enchanted by her, content to leave some mystery around her, and so I must confess, was I. Emilie Lieber was not enchanted; it was easy to determine from her eyes and her manner that she was quite wary of Mrs. Peppermint.

After dinner I went to my cabin for a cigar, and noticing that the rain was no longer beating on the hurricane deck I opened the door to the narrow promenade between the cabins and the deck railing. The air was fresh and electric, but utterly windless. Swift-dancing lightning filled the southwestern sky, outlining a boiling mass of approaching clouds. The storm was giving us only a respite. I lit my cigar and started on a brisk turn around the saloon deck, trying to work the kinks out of my wagon-cramped leg muscles. When I reached the companionway to the main deck, I continued aimlessly down the steps. The deckhand on guard at the gangplank was still lounging on the packing case, a lantern burning beside him. He was half upright, his shoulders against a burlapped bundle. He was looking intently at something on the riverbank.

Under a bright play of lightning, I made out the shape of a man standing just beyond the loading dock. Drops of moisture on his black India-rubber poncho winked like shiny beads.

"He must be drunk," the deckhand commented.

"How long has he been there?"

"Ever since the rain stopped. Maybe half an hour. I halloaed him a time or two, but he never even moved a muscle. He just stands there looking at the *Roanoke.*"

He was that hollow-voiced hollow-eyed man who'd told me the boat was at the landing, that Miss Nettie and *her* both were going upriver to that new fort. They were *sent* for, he had said with emphasis. I had forgotten about that. So they too had been summoned to Fort Rawley for the commemoration. I wondered who Miss Nettie and *her* were.

The first thunder of the squall line rumbled along the river, and the trees along the bank caught a sudden sweep of wind. When the lantern's wick began sputtering, the deckhand lifted the square-sided light and extinguished the flame. Almost continuous lightning now flooded everything with a phosphorescent glow. The man in the poncho stood motionless like a black statue. He could see me as plainly as I could see him, and I was certain that his sunken eyes were fixed on me. For a few seconds then, as the storm roared down upon us, the world turned to solid darkness. I kept my gaze upon the riverbank, but at the next flash of lightning, the black shadow had vanished.

"He's gone," the deckhand said. "I was beginning to think he was not human."

Rain was swirling in on the wind. I turned and ran up the steps to the saloon deck, shivering, and clamping my jaws tight to keep my teeth from chattering.

2

In keeping with the after-dinner custom on passenger boats in those days, the males retreated to the gentlemen's cabin for cigars and brandy, while the females gathered in the ladies' cabin to do whatever it is that females do when they are together. I found Captain Adams and Dr. Lieber at a table in the gentlemen's cabin with the *Roanoke*'s pilot, Henry Allford. Captain Adams and Allford had been together on the *Effie Deans* during most of the war, and although I had never warmed toward that acerbic pilot, I respected his remarkable ability to get a steamboat past sandbars, snags, and sawyers in flood or shallow waters. Allford was bald except for fringes of reddish hair above his ears; his facial expression at all times portended doom just ahead.

After we'd exchanged greetings I remarked to Allford that the refurbished *Roanoke* was quite an improvement over the wartime dilapidation of the old *Effie Deans*.

"The owners spent several thousands re-outfitting this boat, I'm told," he replied gloomily. "A crystal chandelier over there in the ladies' cabin, those red plush divans out there in the central lounge, carved woods in here and elsewhere, as you must have noticed. I suppose you know they were restoring the *Effie* this spring at a Saint Louis dock when she caught fire and burned beyond redemption. Were you ever aboard her before the war, Morrison? Splendor, pure splendor."

"No, only during the war. But I can attest to her sturdiness during that run we made in the Gulf of Mexico."

The pilot clucked his tongue deprecatingly. "Only a bit over a hundred miles from the mouth of the Mississippi to Mobile Bay," he said. "But sheer foolishness, utter foolishness. Except for the Sound, we had no charts of any kind. By the time we reached Montgomery, the Rebels had given up the 'cradle of the Confederacy' to Wilson's cavalry."

"And the war was over," Captain Adams added. "All the same, I believe we set a record with the *Effie Deans* from the spring of '64 to spring of '65. Above eight thousand miles, was it not, Henry?"

"Eight thousand, two hundred and seventy-six miles," Allford answered gravely.

"The *Effie Deans,*" Dr. Lieber said softly as he poured a few more drops of brandy into his glass. "Named I believe for one of Sir Walter Scott's heroines. My God, was not that the boat Major Rawley came up on?"

"She was indeed," the captain said, turning to face me. "Sam, you should have been along with us on that trip. When we left Saint Louis we had near on to three hundred men packed aboard. Galvanized Yankees, they were."

"Galvanized Yankees?"

"Yes, they'd been Confederate soldiers. The lot we had aboard came from prisons in the East and Illinois, I believe. Mostly farm boys from Virginia, Kentucky, and the Carolinas. From what I gathered, they had been crowded for months into Union prison camps in the most uncongenial places. No trees, no shade of any kind, nothing to look at but high board fences and the sky. Sleeping on the ground without even a handful of straw between them and hard-packed sand. You can understand why, when offered, they'd take an oath of allegiance to the Union and join our army to fight Indians out here in the West. God knows, each man may have had a different reason — a determination to survive by any means, disillusionment with the war, a secret avowal to desert at first opportunity."

"Plenty had that last scheme in mind," Allford said. He pulled a plug of Daniel Webster chewing tobacco from the pocket of his jacket, opened a long-bladed knife, and trimmed a thin shaving into his lower lip. He stared mournfully up at a brass cabin lamp affixed to the paneling. "Gen'l Ulysses Grant figured some would skedaddle at first opportunity. He was against the whole design, but President Lincoln was for it, and so Grant went along, providing they were shipped out here in the West."

Captain Adams's corroborating nod was almost imperceptible. Moisture in the air had brought his graying hair to a wild curl so that it splayed over his ears from the sides of his cap. "Six men escaped before we left the Saint Louie wharf," he said. "Major Rawley was so furious he made me hold the boat another day so that he and his young officers could comb the city in search of the deserters. He confiscated every set of irons he could find in the Saint Louie jail and shackled men at random — right out on the main deck in full view of the riverfront. I told him it was useless to search for the runaways. You know, Sam, how uncontrolled that river town was in sixty-four."

"So Rawley was in command of the converted Rebels," I said. "Were his officers all good Union men?"

"Decidedly. You can imagine what would have happened if − But he and his officers were all so damned young! Green as grass in June."

"Unfledged," the pilot agreed, and aimed an accurate jet of brown tobacco juice into a brass cuspidor that rested quite close to my left boot.

"I met some of them later at Fort Rice," Dr. Lieber said. "But I knew none well except Major Rawley. Young, yes, but he impressed me as being earnest and willing to learn."

"A spoiled swellhead," Captain Adams retorted. "A windjammer!"

Lieber looked surprised. "I saw none of that in him at all. Quite the opposite in fact."

"Well, you knew him later on. Perhaps that near brush with the Angel of Death − the surprise Indian attack − losing all his squad and his own life almost − out there on the Malpais. Ordeals can change a man."

"On the Malpais?" I asked. "I understood that Rawley lost his men at Killdeer Mountain."

Lieber glanced at the captain, deferring to him, and then when he realized that he was to reply, the doctor said: "Killdeer Mountain came afterward. What happened on the Malpais could have happened to any officer.

31

He was taken completely by surprise, by superior forces, and was overwhelmed."

"It was pride that did it," Captain Adams declared. "All young men believe themselves to be immortal, but Rawley had gone beyond that. He thought he was indestructible because of his inborn superiority. He believed that God had gifted him, chosen him. He told me such, more than once. That forced march of his across the Malpais was meaningless, totally unnecessary. The officers at Fort Standish later admitted so in my presence. What do you think, Lieber?"

Dr. Lieber replied slowly, his accent slightly heavier than before. "The relief march was unnecessary, yes, but Major Rawley did not know it was unnecessary when he left the *Effie Deans*. He expected that his ten men might be needed to save Fort Standish from being overrun. He did not know about our fortifications, how strong they were."

"I assured him there was no great danger there in the short run," the captain said. "Others on board, who knew the fort, supported me. We all warned him that on the Malpais there could be more danger for him and his platoon than for the defenders of the fort. He refused even to listen. No, he wanted to make a dashing show, to aggrandize his own image of Major Charles Rawley. He gloried in himself. I had seen it growing in him from the day we left Saint Louie. He came to me that first afternoon and laid down the rules. A pink-cheeked boy, what was he, twenty-two? His battalion staffed with a dozen other pink-cheeked boys. Except for Rawley, from Ohio, not one, I think, had ever ventured far from the Atlantic shore, certainly never crossed the Alleghenies westward. *He* was in command of the *Effie Deans* now, he told me with a bold directness. I was to obey his orders, as if I were one of his junior officers."

A dry humorless chuckle came from Allford. "I heard Enoch's response through my thin cabin partition. Like a whip cracking, his voice was."

Captain Adams had got out his large curved-stem pipe and was tamping rough-cut into the bowl. "I let him know the boat was my command, but that I would cooperate with him in all matters which did not endanger the safety of the vessel. He seemed to respect me after that. Actually came to me for advice once or twice, the way a spoiled son will do when he runs up against a hard block. Sometimes he listened, sometimes he didn't. He did not listen to my advice about the court-martial."

"How was that?" I asked.

Captain Adams turned to glance up at the fanlight above our heads. "Sounds like hail," he said. The rattling of ice against the curved window became a counterpoint to the clicking of poker chips at the table behind us. Rain streaked the dirty glass with runners that reflected orange light from the brass cabin lamp. The captain drew deeply from his pipe, and puffed a ring into the blue swirl of smoke suspended from the ceiling. Tobacco pungency mingled with whiskey aroma.

"That court-martial was inevitable, I suppose. In spite of all Rawley's precautions — doubling the guard, hourly night inspections, threatening harangues — one or two or more of the Galvanized Yankees would be missing almost every morning at reveille. They just slid off the deck into the Missouri waters, risked their lives, but I'd wager most of them made it to shore. Then one night, just after we'd steamed past Independence — with all those former Rebels having their last look at civilization as we passed — houses, people in citizens' clothing, horses and buggies, women in white dresses, whatever — it was too much for them. That night almost a dozen got away. There was an alarm, they made great splashes when they dived, and Rawley and his young officers fired off their pistols. Their chances of hitting anyone in that black water were about as likely as shooting a catfish in the dark."

The captain stopped for a minute to relight his pipe. Hail still tapped capriciously against the fanlight. "Next morning he came to see me – d'you remember, Sam, we'd built a large compartment of heavy planking on the rear of the main deck to store war supplies – gunpowder, ammunition, and such – when we were operating below Memphis?"

"With cotton bales around the outer walls," I recalled.

"Yes, we'd got rid of the cotton bales, but the compartment still served as a hold. Well, Rawley wanted to know if I would open it so that he could lock some of his men in there each night to discipline them. I took him down and showed him how full-packed it was with his battalion's supplies – tents, blankets, uniforms, dry rations, arms, ammunition. I told him he'd do well to get twenty men in there. 'I'll double that number,' he snapped back. I pointed out that the weather had been exceedingly warm, and that if he locked the compartment hatch the men would suffer not only from the heat but also from bad air. His only reply was a shrug."

After a long pause, Captain Adams recounted how Rawley had had all the ammunition moved up into the staterooms where his officers were quartered, and that night had crowded forty men into that musty place below. Long before daybreak they were yelling and pounding and pleading to be let out for air. Rawley and Adams had a row over that, and Adams finally persuaded him to open the hatch and post night guards.

"It was during all the racket, I suppose, that one more man went over the side. He was reported missing at reveille."

Rawley was surprisingly calm when he visited Adams's cabin to inform him of this. "I must set an example," was how he put it. "I must shoot one of my men for desertion." Seeing the consternation on Adams's face, he went on hurriedly, trying to explain that surely Adams must understand the necessity for this. Unless the desertions were stopped, he would have no command left aboard the boat by the time they reached Fort Standish. Adams reminded him that "to prove desertion he must seize a man in the act," and he had had no luck at that.

"He informed me that a few of them talked of nothing else. His officers had overheard them, and the talkers were a bad influence on the others. He could make good soldiers of most of these Rebels if he could put such a fear of desertion in their minds that they would no longer think of it. I asked him why he was telling me all this. When he was unsure of himself he had a manner of twisting an ear with his thumb and forefinger. He did so then, scuffing his boots on the floor of my cabin the way a young boy will do in the presence of an overbearing elder. 'So you will understand what I am doing,' he replied slowly.

"He pointed out that I was not a military man, and might misunderstand the action he planned to take. He was telling me this so that I would be prepared for it.

"I did not know what to say, so I said nothing, and he excused himself hastily, blundering against the corner of my bunk as he turned to leave. That night we had a heavy rain, not windy like the storm we're having now, but a steady downpour. The poor devils who slept on the exposed decks had to crowd under what shelter they could find. I'm not a light sleeper, but several times I awoke to hear them cursing and moving about. An ideal time for going over the side, I thought to myself, and at dawn I dressed and went up to the pilot-house to watch morning roll call. Henry was there, his head poked out the window, curious as I to see how many would be reported missing."

"I was certain," Allford said, "some names would not be answering."

"But not a man was absent," Captain Adams declared with an emphatic slap of his hand against the tabletop. "I was looking right down at Major Rawley, a big solid youngster he was, always dressed in his best uniform for reveille – fancying a wide-brimmed black hat instead of the cap he wore at other times. I expected to see a smile of satisfaction on his face when the last report of 'All present' sounded, but instead his expression was quite grim. He shouted something to one of his lieutenants. I could not follow the immediate proceedings, but after a moment or so a tall man stepped forward from one of the squads and stood stiffly at attention facing the major."

Adams had taken notice of this man before, a muscular towheaded fellow, hair fine as cotton. He always seemed to be in company with another man half his size, who Adams described as "rat-faced, with a long twitchy nose and his crooked teeth squeezed in to the front of his narrow mouth, popeyes set too close together, and small pointed ears curved in to his skull." When they were together, and that was most times, their relationship appeared to be one of prince and commoner, the towheaded soldier tall and proud in the foreground, the rat-faced runt obsequious and deferential in the background, regarding the prince in an almost worshipful way.

"That morning as I looked down from the pilothouse at the forward squad of men on the hurricane deck, I could see the rat-faced soldier in the rank just behind the towheaded one who had been ordered to step forward. All of us within earshot of Major Rawley's voice were listening to his words, spoken in those rotund oratorical tones they say won fame for his father, the senator."

Rawley cried out, so that all the assembled men on deck could hear him plainly, that Private Noah Burkett was under arrest "for violation of the Seventh and Twenty-first Articles of War." Private Burkett was to be placed in irons until such time as a court-martial could be convened for his trial. Adams could plainly see from Burkett's face that he had not the slightest notion what Major Rawley was accusing him of.

"That face of his was almost childlike. Ringed with fine yellow hair, it was like the face of a child scolded for some reason so obscure it could not be fathomed. But the face of the runt directly behind Burkett was almost feral in its anger, the narrow curve of the teeth bared in a snarl directed at Rawley, or at

Rawley's back I should say, because he had turned away, leaving two of his young officers to take custody of Burkett."

As Adams was quick to explain, none of the enlisted Galvanized Yankees was armed then, not even the noncommissioned officers — their weapons were all locked in that deck hold. The plan was to first test them by mixing them with loyal troops in the forts upriver before issuing arms to them. In any case, the two officers had no trouble with Burkett, big and muscular though he was. It was learned afterward that he had been a blacksmith in Kentucky, one of John Morgan's raiders captured in Ohio.

Adams was not surprised to have another visit from Rawley later that morning. He asked him to come down to the gentlemen's cabin to witness the court-martial of Private Noah Burkett. Of course Adams wanted nothing to do with it, but Rawley pled so fervently — he wanted a responsible outsider, someone who could testify if necessary that the accused had been fairly tried, had been served with adequate defense counsel.

"He went on and on — he assured me that he and his subordinates all had read the Articles of War thoroughly. Lieutenant Mayes, he said, was the only one of them who had any knowledge of civil law, and Mayes had been assigned to defend Burkett."

In the gentlemen's cabin they had placed three chairs in a semicircle, facing out from the bar, with one of the round gambling tables in front of them. Two smaller tables were pushed to the sides for the defending and prosecuting officers. A young lieutenant wearing spectacles sat at a fourth table with a sheaf of ruled foolscap, several pens, and an inkwell for recording the proceedings. Adams had never witnessed an army court-martial before, and it was quite plain that none of the young participants there had ever witnessed one either. They had nothing to go by but a single well-worn copy of *Army Regulations* that they kept passing back and forth. Except for Major Rawley, who seated himself in the middle chair as president of the court, they were all ill at ease.

When they brought the prisoner in, the major read the first charge, a violation of the Seventh Article of War, which stated that any soldier "who shall begin, excite, cause, or join in, any mutiny in any company in the service of the United States during wartime shall suffer death, or such punishment as by court-martial shall be inflicted." The second charge was absenting himself from his company without leave.

"From where I was seated Private Burkett's

41

face was in profile," Captain Adams said, "but I could see that he was as puzzled by the charges as was I. Mutiny was a vague term to him, but when he heard the accusation that he had been absent without leave, his wide brow wrinkled and he started to speak, but Rawley banged on the table with a saber knot he was using for a gavel and ordered him to be seated."

The first witness was the sergeant of Burkett's platoon, a lean, swarthy fellow, eyes dancing about from one officer's face to another.

"You know the kind, he'd tasted a wee bit of power and wanted more — the sort who would sell out his own brother for a step up in the world. He willingly allowed the prosecutor, a little pink-cheeked lieutenant named Hollister to lead him like a sheep with a ring in its nose. 'Yes, sir, more'n once I heard Private Burkett say he was going to pull foot,' the sergeant whined in that hill-country nasal tone he had."

Hollister pressed him to tell him just how Burkett had said it. The man replied: "He said he would be damned if he didn't leave this boat first opportunity that he got."

"Well, they went over every word, repeating everything, time and time again. They called the captain of Burkett's company, a slow talker he was, measured his words carefully.

Although Lieutenant Hollister got him to say that Burkett was a poor soldier, a very hard man to get along with, he failed to trap the captain into supporting the sergeant's testimony that Burkett had been overheard threatening desertion."

Captain Adams closed his eyes and sighed, an expression of distaste appearing upon his face at the memories he was recalling. "It was next day before they came to the second charge against Private Burkett – of absenting himself from his company without leave. The main witness for the prosecution was the lieutenant of Burkett's platoon. Can't recall his name at the moment, but he appeared to be about seventeen or eighteen. He had sandy hair – was trying to sprout a beard but it looked more like the down on a young gosling. Wispy. Off-duty he sang a lot, high tenor voice. During the evenings when they were drinking at the bar, Rawley was always asking him for a song. This lieutenant testified that on the night of the heavy rain one of his most trusted Galvanized Yankee corporals had come to him with the information that Private Burkett was going to leave to desert.

"Lieutenant Mayes, the defense counsel, wanted to question this corporal, who turned out to be a Dutchman. You, Doc Lieber,

43

might've made out what the corporal was trying to say, but his enunciation was a bit thick for my ears. Lieutenant Mayes repeated the phrases several times, and about all that the Dutch corporal's testimony amounted to was that he had heard Burkett say if anybody wanted to desert he did not give a damn when they went and he had as lief they would go one time as another.

"The prosecutor, Hollister, then took the wispy-bearded lieutenant in hand and led him along the path he wanted to take him about as easily as he had led the swarthy sergeant. He asked him if he had personally observed Private Burkett on the night in question. The man replied that he had, several times. After the corporal had informed him of Burkett's threat to desert, he went to his deck quarters and found him lying down, apparently asleep. This was, according to his testimony, about eleven o'clock P.M.

"The next time the lieutenant recalled seeing him was three o'clock A.M. He was making his rounds when he found Private Burkett down by the gun on the starboard side. He gave no reason for being there, according to the lieutenant, who then quickly added that from his own observation Burkett appeared to be awaiting an opportunity to leave the boat."

"And this wasn't questioned by the defense counsel?" I asked.

"Indeed it was. Mayes immediately leapt into the breach, forcing the lieutenant to admit that rain was falling heavily at three A.M. But when Mayes then suggested that Burkett might have left his deck quarters to find better shelter in the gun bay, the lieutenant stood by his original opinion. He also went on to say that having ordered Private Burkett back to his assigned quarters, he saw him again, after the rain ceased falling, in several different places on the boat — 'evidently with the intention of deserting.' "

"And the defense counsel was content to leave the matter there?"

"Not quite. He chose this time as an opportunity to bring in a Private Tharp, who had been in close company with Noah Burkett throughout the rainy night. Private Tharp as you may have guessed was that rat-faced little man — always in Burkett's shadow. Tharp testified that he and Burkett had moved their blankets several times during the night, trying to keep dry. He declared that he had been with him all the time. Prosecutor Hollister was smart enough to bring out the relationship between Tharp and Burkett, hinting that one would be inclined to lie for the other, that it was like spouse testifying for spouse. Whether the members of the court believed Tharp's statement, I don't know. I didn't think it mattered because to my mind there was no case against Private Burkett, and I was sure then that he would be set free of all charges."

Captain Adams reached for the brandy bottle. "Yes, that was pretty much the extent of the testimony against Noah Burkett, the soldier Major Rawley had chosen to make an example of. To crush all thoughts of desertion among the others."

"But surely," I protested, "they couldn't convict a man on testimony that consisted almost entirely of hearsay and supposed intentions? I doubt if there was an enlisted man in the armies of the Union or Confederacy who did not at least once in his term of service cry out in anger or frustration that he would be damned if he did not leave the blasted ranks at first opportunity."

"True," Allford the pilot agreed somberly. "But next morning I had to guide the *Effie Deans* through a thicket of snags to bring her in for a landing so Major Rawley could stage his death show."

Dr. Lieber appeared to be even more appalled than I at what the captain and the pilot had told us. "Charles Rawley never made mention of this to me," he said, his soft-spoken words heavy with his native accent. "Surely he did not actually permit execution of this man, this Burkett?"

"They found him guilty on all charges and specifications," Captain Adams said, "and 'in the best interests of the Army and his battalion' sentenced him to be shot to death by musketry in the presence of his battalion."

"Without waiting for a review from the major's regimental commander?" I asked.

"As Henry just said, we landed the next morning," Captain Adams replied. "The sentence was carried out that afternoon." He rolled the brandy in his glass and bent to inhale the aroma.

"When Rawley came to my cabin and asked me to land the boat, I was quite surprised, and when he told me why, I was dumbfounded. I did not know the rules, the command channels for putting a court-martialed soldier to death, but I was certain that some higher endorsement was necessary for legality. I suggested as much to Rawley, but he waved his arms in a gesture of dismissal and said something about the irregularity of his situation — no regimental commander was in miles of the *Effie Deans* — weeks must pass before communications could be exchanged, and time was of the

essence if he was to stop the incessant desertions. No, he would take the responsibility,
and then he reminded me that he had my
assurance that the trial had been fair toward
Private Burkett. 'The man was given a fair
trial, yes,' I yelled at him in anger, 'but the
sentence is abhorrent. Mutiny I never heard
mentioned but once, yet you are convicting
him of that high crime because someone heard
him say he was going to desert at the first
opportunity. And you convicted him of being
absent without leave when he never left the
boat.'

"Rawley shook a finger at me. 'I warned you,
Captain Adams,' he said, 'that you would not
understand the military action I have been
forced to take — for the good of the battalion.'
He gave me a chilling look. 'You will bring the
boat in for a landing, sir.' "

Dr. Lieber leaned forward, elbows on the
table, resting his bearded chin in his hands.
"Quite out of character, I must say, for the
Major Rawley I came to know."

"You knew him afterward, as I've pointed
out," Captain Adams said caustically. "I will
admit that his later actions may have been
atonement enough. But that day, it was plain
to see that what he was doing disturbed him
not in the least. He was so certain it was the

right thing to do. And we all know, don't we, gentlemen, of the deadliness of righteous men?

"Well, Henry piloted us in to a landing place on the Iowa bank, somewhere above Council Bluffs. I should've refused to permit the stop, but Major Rawley and I had that spoken agreement over a handshake – the *Effie Deans* was my command, but I would cooperate in all military matters that did not endanger the boat. As soon as we touched bank and the plank was run out, Rawley sent a squad ashore to dig a grave. A few minutes later he marched the entire battalion off, and formed them into three sides of a hollow square, with the fresh grave in the open side. They had a drum corps of sorts – two drums – and with a slow beat and slow tread, the firing squad and Noah Burkett marched into position. Burkett, with his wrists manacled behind, stood facing the firing squad, his back to the open grave.

"From where I was, I could hear only snatches of Major Rawley's address to the silent battalion. It was a warm early summer's day, but an erratic wind had come up to sweep away the haze and scatter voice sounds. The calls of distant meadowlarks were sometimes clearer to my ears than Rawley's broken phrases. Burkett's tall muscular form was lonely against the horizon. He wore no blindfold, no hat, and his yellow hair was brightened by sunlight and the contrasting backdrop of clean blue sky.

"Suddenly a series of quick loud commands broke the silence. I saw the men of the firing squad raise their weapons, and the rattle of carbine fire was like the sound of tearing canvas. Tiny puffs of pearly smoke lifted and vanished in a sky filled with frightened birds, the whirr of their beating wings mingling and then fading with the echoes of gunfire. I realized that Burkett was no longer visible; his body had fallen into the open grave. I saw one of the officers move toward it with a gray blanket. The heavy wool billowed in the wind, and then he let it drop over the dead man. As he stepped back, the gravediggers came forward and began shoveling earth into the shallow pit. The battalion was already moving, formed into long files, returning to the *Effie Deans*.

"I don't believe Major Rawley left any sort of marker there; he certainly allowed no time for it. Since that day, I've passed the place beside the river five — no, six times, and I always have it in my mind to stop and go ashore to leave a marker, a name scratched on a stone at least. He must have had kin in Kentucky."

Some of the poker players at the table behind

us broke into laughter. A chair scraped against the floor, and one of the men swore in disappointment.

"Incredible." Dr. Lieber's voice was almost a whisper. "That so sensitive a man, as he showed himself to me, could be so insensitive."

At that moment our attention was drawn to movement outside the open door of the gentlemen's cabin — a dozen yards or more across the waxed flooring of the lounge. Two women, one large and buxom, the other slender, had come out of the corridor that led from the family staterooms. The slender one was Indian, hardly more than a girl, her glossy black hair parted in the middle. She wore a red blanket shawl over a black woolen dress. The white woman I judged to be well past thirty; her hair was almost as dark as the Indian's. After they sat upon one of the plush divans facing us, what struck me about the pair was the aura of pensiveness that cloaked them. Even at the distance that separated us, I could see sadness in the Indian girl's eyes, and as for the white woman, her face bore the marks of some past anguish that reminded me of the faces of soldiers I had seen after bloody battles, survivors who forced themselves into a reckless affirmation of life rather than a passive acceptance of its scourges.

"Who are they?" I asked Captain Adams, whose gaze also was upon them.

"Oh? Why, of course, you would not know them. The white woman is Nettie Steever. Runs the hotel up there in Bell's Landing. I believe the little redskin was also rescued from Canada by Major Rawley."

Miss Nettie and her both, the hollow-voiced man in the poncho had said to me earlier in the evening. *They were sent for.*

Damn this Major Rawley, I thought, he's mixed himself into the lives of all these people! Yet I know nothing of him really, except the differing opinions held by Dr. Lieber and Captain Adams.

"The girl is Towanjila," Lieber was saying. "Blue Sky Woman. She was the daughter of Spotted Horse, as bloodthirsty an old chief as ever roamed these Dakota lands. Charles Rawley brought both women back with him when he captured Spotted Horse."

"Hold on a moment," I begged him. "Captain Adams just left me with Rawley aboard the *Effie Deans*, after the execution of an apparently innocent man — to halt desertions. Did the desertions stop?"

"Oh, there were no more desertions," Captain Adams assured me. "Whether it was from fear of Rawley or fear of Indians, I don't know. I suspect the latter. The boat's crew told them plenty about the hostile Sioux. By then we were well into Sioux country."

"Why," I asked, "did Rawley take only ten men with him to cross the Malpais?"

"All he had left after General La Prade sent one of his colonels to meet us at Dutchman's Landing. When we stopped there to take on wood, the colonel was waiting with La Prade's orders in his hand. La Prade was in command of this whole district, and was trying to put together an expedition to guard a large wagon train bound for the Montana gold fields. The scheme was a darling of the Washington politicians — they were running out of gold to pay for the war — anyway La Prade grabbed the whole battalion of Galvanized Yankees, leaving Major Rawley with only the ten men to reinforce Fort Standish. La Prade's colonel gave Rawley his choice — I heard him tell the major to select ten of his meanest soldiers because they'd have mean work to do at Fort Standish.

"Before turning his battalion over to La Prade, Rawley assembled the companies beside the landing there at the Dutchman's. He gave a little farewell speech, telling them of the important duty they had been chosen to perform, and asserting his confidence in their bravery and perseverance. Then he walked along the ranks, halting from time to time to motion a man to fall out, until he had chosen his squad of ten. I was mightily surprised, I can tell you, when I saw him choose Tharp, Private Tharp, that rat-faced scrub with the crooked teeth, the late Private Burkett's constant companion. Tharp, to be one of the chosen ten — I couldn't figure it. Maybe Rawley did not know of Tharp's hatred for him, maybe he did. I don't know. Anyway during the few days between the execution of Burkett and our arrival at Dutchman's Landing, I'd seen Tharp's eyes watching Rawley more than once, usually staring at the major's back — well, you know, if looks could kill —

"We'd hardly got started upriver again when we ran into low water. Henry can tell you about the vagaries of the upper Missouri — a few days between snow melts, and the boats just sit below the sandbars, waiting it out for a rise."

Allford wiped his chin with a white-starred blue bandanna. "I knew we'd never make it past Devil's Shoals at the big bend below Fort Standish," he began. "In low water the eddies there fill with every sort of clamjamfry and build the sand high and hard. Major Rawley came up to the pilothouse three or four times a day for a look at my charts. When the *Effie Deans* nosed in at the big bend, and I passed the word we'd have to wait for a rise, the major already knew what he was going to do. We were sixty miles by Missouri waters from Fort Standish, but across the Malpais the distance was about thirty. He'd drawn a map from my river charts, and estimated he could make a forced march to Fort Standish between daylight and dark. I warned him the country was mighty rough, and Enoch cautioned him about the hostile tribes. But nothing we could do. He handed out rifles and cartridges and marching gear to his ten men, and next dawn they started. Last I ever saw of any of them." Allford turned his melancholy face toward the open door. A chattering chorus of feminine voices had suddenly filled the outer lounge. The women were returning from the ladies' cabin.

"We must join them," Captain Adams said, knocking the dead ashes from his pipe into his hand and dropping them into the cuspidor.

Kathleen Hardesty in her peppermint-stick dress was frisking across the waxed flooring, her green eyes shining in the glow of the wall lamps. Now that I knew she was a widow, I suppose I regarded her in a different light. She stopped beside the two women on the sofa — Nettie Steever and Towanjila — and began speaking in her animated way to the white woman.

The four of us at the table in the gentlemen's cabin arose almost simultaneously, pushing our chairs back. "Storm's passed, I think," Allford said with an upward glance at the fanlight. "Enoch will be wanting the *Roanoke*'s paddle wheel in motion at first daylight, so it's off to bed for me." The smile that broke fleetingly across his gloomy features was an incongruity. "Enjoy your dancing, gentlemen."

I followed Captain Adams out, but instead of joining the growing throng I turned toward the steps that led down to the main deck. Mrs. Hardesty was already testing the melodeon, and a fiddle player and banjoist were tuning up beside her. She must have caught the motion of my passing from the corner of her eye. Her head turned suddenly; she smiled provocatively and said something to me, but I could not hear the words above the rising gabble.

Before I reached the bottom step, fresh air enveloped me. I took several deep breaths to clear the fumes of the gentlemen's cabin from my head and lungs. The deckhand at the gangplank was snoring beside his lantern. I turned in the opposite direction and was surprised to see stars in the western sky. I walked past the boilers, feeling the warmth of their banked fires, and went on beyond the roustabouts' cabins to the big paddle wheel at the stern.

The increasing starlight, reflected on small waves racing across the surface of the river, made the night more luminous. I was standing with my hand gripping a chain, staring across the rippling water at the silent and forbidding Dakota landscape, when the lapping of waves against the boat grew suddenly louder. I looked straight down. Beside the paddle wheel something had surfaced. In a more southern clime I would have suspected an alligator, but the swimmer was a human being. The shadow of an arm rose grasping for a hold, the fingers sliding and slipping off the wet slimy wood that supported the paddle wheel. Whoever it was began to struggle, breathing hard — frustrated, angry, frightened. I kneeled, then lay flat on the deck's edging, reaching down a hand. The swimmer caught my fingers quickly and I managed to pull him aboard. I had already guessed who he was — that hollow-voiced, hollow-eyed man who had told me earlier that evening of the presence of the *Roanoke*. I now saw the eyes in those hollows; they were somewhat glazed but fixed on me with a haunted intensity. He wore no poncho now; the drip-drip from his soaked clothing and his heavy breathing were the only sounds above the lapping of the waves.

"Why?" I asked him.

He drew in a deep draft of air. "I wanted to come aboard unseen."

"You could've used the plank. The guard's asleep."

"I did not know that." He shrugged. "So I failed."

"What do you want? Free passage?"

He nodded.

"You'll likely be caught by daylight, and thrown off," I said.

"That's my affair."

He was beginning to shake from the cold.

"You'll freeze in those wet clothes."

He stood fully erect for the first time since I'd helped him aboard. "I'll dry out by the boilers."

"Suit yourself," I said, turning my back and starting to walk away from him.

He called softly after me: "I don't want — don't want them to know I'm aboard. You won't report me?"

I glanced back at him. He was trying to wring water from the sleeves of the clinging shirt. "No," I told him. "Why should I?"

His responding thanks was unsubstantial, a fading echo of the night.

3

I danced with Kathleen Hardesty, two square dances in fact. A trio of loud-playing self-styled musicians from the steamboat's crew — violin, guitar, and banjo — had replaced her and the softer-toned melodeon. She was a vigorous young woman and liked to dance in close engagement with her partners. If I had any illusion that she was favoring me with her subtle tactile communications, this was quickly dispelled when I watched her tripping later with Lieutenant Colonel Harris.

As our second dance ended, I was both relieved and regretful that she chose to sit out the next. She led me to one of the small tables pushed against the wall, and after I obtained mint drinks for us from a passing waiter, she began questioning me about my personal history.

For politeness' sake I gave her a basic fact or two, but then insisted that my profession required me to turn the tables and question her instead. "Back in the States it is not unusual for wives and other relatives to travel to battlefields and recover their dead," I said. "But for you to come out here alone for that purpose — to the wildest of the western territories — you provoke my newspaperman's instincts."

"I loved Drew Hardesty," she replied simply. "It is my duty to see that what remains of him should lie in Kentucky."

"I would have judged you to be from north of the Ohio River," I said. "Instead of Kentucky."

She explained that she was Kentucky-born but that her family had moved to Cincinnati before the war. Her father had been a merchant there, later doing business as a supplier to the Union army. The contracts had brought him a small fortune. "Because of my marriage to Drew Hardesty," she went on, "he left little of his fortune to me, the wife of a Confederate soldier." She paused to sip from her julep glass. "If Papa had known before he died that Drew, after being taken prisoner, decided to become a Galvanized Yankee, swearing allegiance to the Union, and then was killed in a blue uniform — it might have made a difference. I don't know."

Her husband had been captured during the foolish raid that General John Morgan led across the Ohio River in '63. "Drew's folks in

Kentucky think it's awful that he forswore his loyalties to the South," she said, "but Lieutenant Colonel Harris assures me there was nothing dishonorable about a Rebel becoming a Galvanized Yankee."

Lieutenant Colonel Harris, showing his horse teeth in a wide grin, suddenly appeared beside her chair. "I believe I heard my name mentioned," he said. "If so, Mrs. Hardesty, I hope you were granting me permission to dance with you."

"In a minute," she replied after turning to smile up at him. "Please join us, sir."

With a brief nod to me, Harris took the chair between us. I resented his presence, not so much for his inane remarks but because he had broken off the conversation between Kathleen Hardesty and me. The more I learned about her, the more she interested me.

After Lieutenant Colonel Harris swept her off into the next dance, Captain Adams paused briefly beside the table. "As usual, Sam," he said, "there's a lamentable shortage of female partners for dancing. Might I introduce you to one or two who are sitting out this one?"

"I would like to meet Nettie Steever. I have not seen either her companion or herself on the dance floor."

I followed him around the edge of the

dancers to the divan where the lady hotel-keeper sat with the young Indian woman. Both seemed to be magnetized by the moving crowd and the music, and Captain Adams had to call Nettie Steever's name more than once to gain her attention.

At first she seemed indifferent to my presence. Towanjila, the Blue Sky Woman, was so shy (and apparently lacking in English vocabulary) that I quickly gave up trying to convince her that she might enjoy dancing with me. With honest brusqueness Nettie Steever also refused me. "In my business," she said in her heavy contralto, "dancing is work. I have nothing to gain by dancing on the *Roanoke.*"

"Then you never dance for pleasure, Miss — or is it Mrs. Steever?"

"Call me Nettie," she said. "No, dancing gives me little pleasure. But if you were a guest in my hotel, I would dance with you." Her dark glancing eyes fixed sharply upon me. "What line are you in, Mr. Morrison?"

I explained that I was a newspaper correspondent. "Perhaps you've seen copies of my paper, the *Saint Louis Herald?*"

"I never learned to read," she answered. "The only use I have for newspapers is to wrap things in, and kindle fires." She ended with a rather coarse laugh, as though she enjoyed putting down my pride.

I decided to take a different tack, which was really the reason I'd wanted to meet her. "Captain Adams was telling me about Major Rawley," I began. "What was he like?"

"Who?" she asked, although I'm sure she understood the name. She crossed her legs, and before her full black skirt covered her feet again I noted that she was wearing men's shoes, heavy brogues.

"Major Rawley," I repeated. "Is not your past association with him the reason why you are journeying up to the fort for the commemoration?"

"The major? A decent sort, he was."

"He rescued you from Canada, did he not?"

"Yes, he did that." She was watching the dancers again.

"How long were you a captive of the Indians?"

Her dark brown eyes stared at me for a moment, and then she smiled with what appeared to be good humor as she replied: "I do not wish to talk of those times, or remember those times." At the moment I could think of nothing to say in reply, and the Indian girl took advantage of the lull in our conversation to lean close to Nettie Steever and speak softly to her in Lakota. The older woman nodded, then said to me: "Towanjila wishes to go. You will excuse us, Mr. Morrison." They arose and turned toward the portieres that led into the ladies' staterooms.

Across from me was the open door of the almost deserted gentlemen's cabin. I could see the back of Dr. Lieber's aristocratic head; he appeared to be dealing out cards. He was playing solitaire.

"Ah, Morrison," he said when I came around him. "You've had enough of that frontier shuffle and gallop?"

"For the while. Surely your wife is not out there in the mob."

"No, no. Emilie is not feeling her best, although I think she might've come out for something more sedate than this crowd prefers."

"I'm sorry. Would you care for a brandy?"

He nodded. I got two brandies and sat watching his game until he finished the hand and laid the pack of cards aside. "You seem rather restless tonight, Sam Morrison. At loose ends."

"I've decided to stay aboard and go upriver to the commemoration ceremonies. You and Captain Adams put this Major Rawley into my head," I said, "and I can't get him out."

"Yes, Rawley has that effect. A strange and complex young man." Lieber tasted the brandy. "Compassionate, too, I would say, yet hard and determined at times. Ready at one moment to cast everything away, then suddenly filled with iron resolution."

"You and Captain Adams differ in your perceptions of him."

"Yes, curiously. But we knew him at different times under different circumstances. Enoch has told me that Charles Rawley despised the Indians, considered them savages, worthy only of extinction. Yet I had many talks with Rawley about the different tribes. He'd read Parkman and Catlin and seemed to share their sympathetic outlooks."

"You first saw him at Fort Standish?"

"Yes, when they brought him in. He was suffering a sort of delirium from a blow against the side of his head. Very nasty wound. Later he told me that a warrior had struck him with a lance. An inch difference would have finished him."

"Just what happened out there on the Malpais?"

Dr. Lieber sighed. He had told the story often enough, perhaps was weary of it. He said that Colonel Herrick, in command at Fort Standish, conducted the investigation and wrote the report but that he had helped a bit with the medical terms. They were some days finding the bodies — the weather was hot and rainy — the corpses were in an advanced state of decomposition — and had been stripped of everything. Colonel Herrick ordered his men to dig a pit and cover the remains as speedily as possible. Then with Major Rawley's help, the colonel and Lieber reconstructed the incident.

The Galvanized Yankees were less than a dozen miles from the fort when they were attacked without warning by a mounted party of fifty or more well-armed warriors. "One of the Sioux subtribes, I judged from the arrowheads," Dr. Lieber said. "I collect them, you know. On foot, with no experience in prairie Indian warfare, Rawley and his men had no chance. That he survived, you might say was an oversight on the part of the Sioux."

After he was brought to Fort Standish, Rawley's physical recovery was quite rapid, but his mind evidently had suffered a severe shock. To Lieber he seemed disoriented. Several times he'd wander off on foot into the prairie round about the fort, as if challenging the Indians to return. Colonel Herrick expressed the opinion that Rawley might be inviting death because of some guilty feeling over losing all his men yet surviving himself.

Two or three times the colonel had to send a sergeant out with a led horse to bring Rawley back in. When Dr. Lieber would suggest to Rawley that he be more cautious, he would always reply with some remark about the beauties of the grassy plain — the wild strawberries and high bush blueberries, the calls of the killdeer, the soaring eagles, the hovering kestrels. "And biting flies and myriads of mosquitoes," Lieber would retort. "Not to mention the deadly Sioux. You are not yet a well man, Major Rawley."

A sudden change came about in Rawley soon after the arrival of a company of Volunteers from Minnesota. Colonel Herrick had arranged with his political friends in Saint Paul to enlist this company of cavalry. A goodly number of the Volunteers were war dodgers who had come there from the East, but with the enforcement of the draft in Minnesota they evidently reasoned that chasing Indians in Dakota was safer than being shot at by rebels in the South. Few of them had any military experience, but they were well equipped and rode the best government-issue horseflesh. When Herrick discovered that Major Rawley was an excellent horseman, he put him in command of the greenhorns from Saint Paul. "This seemed to make all the difference in the world in Rawley's attitude," Lieber said. "I think he actually *enjoyed* the horse drills he put the men through for hours every day."

Late in June unexpected orders came from General La Prade. Herrick was to leave a skeleton force to garrison Fort Standish, and march both his infantry and cavalry companies to Burdache Creek for a rendezvous with La Prade's main column. In addition to the escort troops guarding the wagon train to the Montana gold fields, La Prade was assembling a punitive expedition against the Sioux.

Colonel Herrick was delighted by the news. He was one of those "political" colonels created by the Civil War. When he accepted his commission he had expected to go East and win fame, glory, and promotions, but instead the War Department assigned him to the frontier. During three years of service Herrick had seen little action. He'd missed the Santee Sioux uprisings back in Minnesota and his name had appeared in no dispatches to the Saint Paul newspapers. Fearing the war would end before he could gain any military reputation to aid him in his political ambitions, Herrick had been trying for months to stir up the Teton Sioux. Undoubtedly one of the results was the massacre of Major Rawley's little squad of inexperienced infantrymen.

Dr. Lieber and Rawley heard about the garrison's new orders from Herrick, who informed both men that they were to march with him to Burdache Creek. "I was surprised by Rawley's response," Lieber said. "He appeared to be quite uncomfortable with the orders, and in that quiet manner of his asked Colonel Herrick for permission to command Fort Standish in the colonel's absence. 'Oh, don't be foolish, major,' Herrick replied. 'This is a great opportunity for you. You are needed to command the cavalry troops in the field. Besides I should think you'd be spoiling for blood revenge, to even the score with those devils who slew your men out there on the Malpais. Your father, the Senator, considers the incident a blemish on your fine record.' Rawley made no reply to that, but over the next few days as the garrison prepared for the march I observed that he was growing more uneasy.

"He actually came to me for a physical examination, evidently hoping that I might find something wrong with him."

"Had he fully recovered?" I asked.

Dr. Lieber hesitated a moment. "I believed so. Although his eyes sometimes held a strange hollowness in them. I could detect no reason for this."

I was startled by his remark. "And his

voice?" I asked. "Was it sometimes hollow-sounding?"

Lieber looked puzzled. "Come to think of it, possibly so. At times. Why?"

"Nothing. I saw badly wounded men like that during the war." But when I made my reply I was thinking of that strange man I'd helped bring aboard the *Roanoke*. I realized that although he had reminded me of those wounded soldiers, this was not the only reason I couldn't shake the haunting memory of his eyes, his voice.

"Well, there was nothing I could do other than pronounce him to be in good health and perfectly sound in body. A few days later we marched out, in very good order I thought, considering the inexperience of most of the men. Colonel Herrick rode in the advance with his mounted scouts, a handful of veterans and half-breeds who'd been with him at Fort Standish for many months. Major Rawley and the cavalry company followed at a short interval, and far in the rear were the infantry and our wagon train of supplies."

Rawley invited Dr. Lieber to ride with him, offering one of his spare mounts, and the doctor was glad to leave the uncomfortable ambulance to the care of his hospital steward. Late on the third day of the march, they reached General La Prade's camp on Burdache Creek, an enormous assemblage of tents and wagons extending along a level bench beside the cottonwood-bordered stream. A lieutenant from the quartermaster's rode out to direct Colonel Herrick to a bivouac site.

While they were moving into position, the colonel asked Rawley and Lieber to join him in a visit to General La Prade's headquarters tent. He suggested that Rawley might wish to learn how his battalion of Galvanized Yankees was behaving. Overhearing the colonel's remark, the quartermaster's lieutenant volunteered the information that General La Prade had left the Galvanized Yankees back at Fort Rice. "I reckon the gen'l figgered the white-washed Rebels wasn't to be trusted escorting anything to the gold fields," he added.

Herrick laughed and said that he was sure Major Rawley would agree with General La Prade's judgment of the former prisoners of war. "Yes," Rawley replied, and then begged off accompanying the colonel to the general's tent. His face was rather haggard, pale around the lips, his eyes unnaturally bright. He braced himself as though he feared he might fall from his saddle.

Herrick was impatient to be on his way. After advising Rawley to restore himself, perhaps take a dose of the tonic Dr. Lieber had prepared for him, the colonel turned his horse and led Lieber along the creek toward a large tent with a flag flapping above it. Mounted in front of La Prade's tent was a trio of drying human heads, dark-skinned with long black hair. They had been fixed to a crosspiece at the top of a pole, and as Lieber later learned had been carried that day at the head of La Prade's column.

They found the general relaxing with a sketchbook and crayon, which he laid aside to welcome them. Instead of a uniform, La Prade wore dark blue corduroy, the only mark of his rank being a single silver star on the front of his wide-brimmed black hat. "I trust that matters have been quieter around Fort Standish," he said, "since Major Rawley's unfortunate encounter with the hostiles."

"Very quiet, sir," Colonel Herrick replied.

"Yes, the warlike Sioux have left this part of the country and are massing up around Knife River." La Prade studied the colonel's face as though he meant to sketch it, and then continued in the tone of a lecturer addressing a schoolboy. "Spotted Horse is the trouble-maker, collecting warriors from all the subtribes of the Sioux to drive us from their country. My scouts tell me the hostiles are determined to resist navigation on the Missouri and stop the passage of immigrants across the plains to the Montana gold fields. They're being well armed by the *métis,* half-breed traders from the British settlements to the north. We must destroy the warriors now before they grow too strong for us."

"My men are eager to do battle with them," Herrick said.

"Caution is the word, Colonel Herrick, until we close with the main force. Spotted Horse is a cunning tactician. He knows we're coming and he's filled the land between us and the valley of the Knife with war parties. They're skillful at decoying, artful at setting ambushes." With a lazy gesture he pointed toward the outside front of his tent. "Look there at those three Sioux heads on the crosspole. The Sioux entrapped and killed one of my bravest captains yesterday. His sergeant paid them back in full measure. After the sergeant and his men killed the Indians, he cut their heads off with a butcher knife and packed them into a gunnysack. Brought the bloody things back to me with his captain's body. I ordered him to impale the heads on poles and assign a man to parade them in advance of the column until they begin to stink. Put panic fear into the hearts of the enemy out there. Terrorization.

That's what war is, would you not agree, Surgeon Lieber?"

While Lieber was telling me this, quoting La Prade's words as he remembered them, his face revealed his revulsion, and he said he was certain that the general sensed his feelings at the time. "I was surprised that he directed his philosophical question to me," Lieber remarked as he lifted his brandy glass. "I agreed with La Prade that intimidation through terror certainly must be a useful weapon in combating an adversary, but confessed that as a medical man I felt quite helpless in attempting to deal with the damage that prolonged fear could have upon a human being's mind. I cited Major Rawley as an example. La Prade immediately wanted to know the major's condition, and was surprised to learn that Colonel Herrick had allowed him to come along as commander of a Volunteer cavalry company. He told Colonel Herrick quite bluntly that Rawley should have been left at Fort Standish, adding that neither the major nor his battalion of Galvanized Yankees at Fort Rice was ready for field duty. He rose abruptly from his folding chair as though signaling the end of our visit, and in a somewhat biting tone reminded Colonel Herrick that the young major's father, Senator Rawley, was one of the most powerful men in Washington."

When Colonel Herrick and Dr. Lieber returned to their bivouac area, twilight was deepening. Lieber was admiring the rose-colored western sky changing into a dark purple when he noticed a mounted sergeant approaching at a rapid trot. The sergeant was Joseph O'Hara, whose patrol had found Major Rawley half conscious after the massacre on the Malpais. Lieber had noticed before that O'Hara took a sort of proprietary interest in the major, and the young Irish sergeant was now very concerned about him. "Colonel Herrick, sir," he said after saluting. "Major Rawley has not returned."

"Returned from where?" Herrick demanded.

"He told me he was going out on the plain to try to sight a buffalo herd. He rode off toward the north. I kept him in view until a few minutes ago. He'll never make it back before dark now, sir."

Herrick swore loudly, then ordered Sergeant O'Hara to organize a search party. "We should've left Rawley at Fort Standish," he said to Lieber. "General La Prade was correct in his estimate of him. He's either foolhardy or featherbrained or both."

It was midnight before Sergeant O'Hara found Major Rawley and guided him back in.

The ambulance wagon in which Lieber lay half asleep was near enough to Colonel Herrick's tent for him to hear the colonel giving Rawley a stern reprimand, but the doctor had heard Herrick heap much worse abuse upon young officers for much lesser offenses. As he drifted off to sleep Lieber suspected that General La Prade's pointed remark about old Senator Rawley's power in government weighed heavily upon Herrick's mind. As this power was of the same species that the colonel hoped eventually to win for himself, he was not inclined to challenge it.

When the column moved out the following morning, General La Prade assigned Colonel Herrick's command to the rear, where it was responsible for the immigrant train bound for the gold fields. This train consisted of more than a hundred covered wagons carrying two hundred men, women, and children with their goods and supplies. In addition there were twelve pieces of artillery, a herd of three hundred beef steers to provide meat if no buffalo were found, and another hundred or so wagons hauling army supplies. In the lead was La Prade's main column of soldiers, some mounted, some on foot. As the trail had dried under a hot July sun, a choking cloud of dust rolled from front to rear of the train.

Colonel Herrick sent Rawley's cavalrymen far out on the flanks, the colonel accompanying the horsemen on one flank himself. Dr. Lieber also would have preferred riding with the cavalry, but duties kept him near the ambulance in the event of accidents or illnesses among either soldiers or civilians. Most of the time he walked beside the slowmoving wagons, usually wearing a muslin towel over the lower half of his face to screen the dust from his lungs.

One of the difficulties faced by the wagon drivers was keeping closed up in column, a condition of march that General La Prade insisted upon enforcing with military severity. After a nooning halt on the second day, Lieber was surprised to see the general trotting his horse out of a dust cloud. Although the doctor was wearing the towel over half his face, La Prade's keen eyes recognized him. "Surgeon Lieber," he called out as he pointed to a mule-drawn immigrant wagon struggling at a snail's pace about fifty yards to the left, "why is that vehicle not closed into its proper line of march?"

Because of the constant dust Lieber had not noticed the wagon, and he told La Prade so. La Prade squinted through the swirl of yellow powder at the plodding mules. "Another of those draft shunters, I'll wager," he cried. "They're running away from fighting in the war, yet they curse and ridicule my expedition and the officers of my command." He held his horse steady while he wiped his face with a handkerchief.

"Appears to be a woman driving," Lieber said.

La Prade squinted again. "So it does. Maybe we'd better have a look." He rode on ahead, and Lieber did not overtake him until after the general had halted the canvas-topped wagon, dismounted, and climbed into the rear. Just as Lieber came up, a man in dusty frontier jeans was hurled out upon the ground from the wagon's tailgate, followed by a red-faced and angry General La Prade. The man on the ground pulled himself up, staggered to his knees, arose again to glare with bloodshot eyes at La Prade. His gray-streaked hair was long and greasy, his beard short and unkempt. He was obviously quite drunk. Paying no heed to his muttered threats, La Prade quickly looped one end of a rope around the man's middle and fastened the other end to the rear of the wagon. Then he strode down the length of the vehicle and in a calm voice asked the woman her name.

Lieber could not hear her reply. The general mounted and rode forward then and with his quirt slapped the lead mule into faster motion. "Keep closed up in column!" he yelled at the woman, "and if your drunken husband can't stay on his feet, cut him loose and let him lie out here until he is sober again."

Dr. Lieber paused for a minute or so; then he motioned toward the thinning crowd of dancers outside the gentlemen's cabin. "The woman in the wagon was Nettie Steever, and quite handsome she was then. That was only two years ago, Morrison, yet the Nettie Steever you were talking with a few minutes ago, out there, looks a dozen years older. Chance, destiny, fair winds, ill winds, who knows what they will bring to us at any given moment to change the direction and intensity of our lives.

"Major Rawley got to know her much better than I. The cavalry night camps adjoined those of the immigrants, and after Rawley met Nettie, he made a point of bedding down every evening near the Steever wagon. He would help her gather buffalo chips for the cooking fire. The husband, a brute of a fellow, was indifferent to Rawley while sober, but when he was drinking he showed his jealousy in mean little ways. One evening, when we were camped on Heart River, they almost came to blows after Steever struck Nettie during a drunken rage. I believe that sooner or later there would have been a physical clash, perhaps fatal, to one or both of the two men. But before that could happen, La Prade ordered the immigrant wagons corralled for several days while he led the soldiers on ahead to seek battle with the Sioux.

"Although La Prade's scouts warned of a heavy concentration of Indians on Knife River, the general left a goodly number of soldiers behind to guard the immigrants. Major Rawley asked Colonel Herrick to volunteer his cavalry company for this duty, but the assignment went to some mounted infantrymen, Iowans as I recollect. We left the grumbling immigrants in their wagon corral near the head of Heart River, and made a two-days' forced march toward the north.

"My God, the weather was hot, Morrison. A hundred and five degrees one day, a hundred and ten the next. The wide prairie showed not a sign of life except an occasional hawk and myriads of grasshoppers and winged stinging ants. Twenty or more horses and mules died from exertion, and the men began suffering from diarrhea, dysentery, and something we called mountain fever. The water we found to drink was the worst sort of alkali, sulphate magnesia probably. Within a few hours after drinking it, the symptoms were like typhoid. I dosed the victims with quinine, sometimes mixed with a little brandy, and advised them to restore their strength by swallowing as much beef tea as they could get down — but, pshaw, Morrison, you don't want medical reports, do you? You want me to get us to Killdeer Mountain."

Dr. Lieber's fingers tapped a soft military beat against the tabletop. "I can never forget my first view of that chain of high hills filled with rocky ravines, some thickly timbered. Along the base of this range the tipis of the Sioux were assembled, the most formidable array of Indians that any of the veteran scouts had ever seen.

"Killdeer Mountain. Not named for the variety of plover that bears the name, but Tahkakate, the place where they kill the deer.

"What happened there changed the lives of many of us, but none so much as Major Charles Rawley's." Dr. Lieber gazed out the wide door at the dancers who were now waltzing to the soft strains of the melodeon. "Almost every one of us has a Killdeer Mountain in our past that we would give almost anything to expunge. A misdeed, a shame, or an act of mercy that results in the reverse of the effect desired. I believe Rawley later settled his

Killdeer Mountain account, and more. That's why I'm going up to old Fort Standish to honor him."

I was only half listening to Dr. Lieber's soliloquy on the meaning of Killdeer Mountain. My mind was on that hollow-voiced stranger I'd pulled out of the waters of the Missouri. Was he the man Dr. Lieber had been telling me about?

Mist on the fanlight indicated a drop of temperature outside, and my stranger was soaked to the skin. Although there was something alien about him, I felt responsible for his presence, perhaps the same sort of obligation that Dr. Lieber's Sergeant O'Hara bore for Charles Rawley after saving the major's life.

"Excuse me, sir," I said, and pushed my chair back.

"Yes, of course. It's late," Lieber bobbed his head apologetically.

He was saying something about looking in on his wife, Emilie, but I did not linger. I was suddenly eager to go down to the main deck and see how my half-drowned wretch was faring.

4

I found him crouched very close to one of
the boilers, a black shadow in the starlight,
and he was singing to himself in a hoarse
whisper:

Pretty Kathy Martin
Tiptoe fine,
She could not get a man
To suit her mind.
Some were too coarse
And some too fine,
She could not get a man
To suit her kind.

When he saw me he stood quickly erect. I
could smell steam, heavy with a fusty wool
odor, rising from his damp clothing.

"You don't believe you saw me," he said.
"You don't believe I exist, do you?"

"I can see you now," I replied.

"You said nothing to anyone about my being

aboard?" he asked quickly.

"No."

He shivered slightly in the strong flow of chill air off the plain.

"You're not drying out," I said. "That boiler's barely warm."

"The fire's banked, yes. But they'll be stuffing wood in the firebox before daylight."

"You'll freeze to death meanwhile." I did not like him at all; I had to force myself not to turn away from what he was. I had the odd feeling that he was only part of what he had once been, and that if I did not keep myself in his presence what remained of him would disappear. "Look, there's a spare bunk in my stateroom, dry blankets."

For the first time his face revealed a sudden show of emotion, perhaps painful embarrassment, perhaps a fear of something he preferred not to reveal.

"At daylight anyone can see you here," I said.

He said nothing for several moments, and then turned his head away from me as though he wanted his spoken words to be private, a communing with himself. "I *must* see their faces," he said distinctly. "After all, what I tried to do was done for them."

He had stopped shivering as he looked away.

Something kept me from asking him what he meant.

"No one is about," I assured him. "Those who are not dancing have gone to their staterooms for the night. We can reach mine by the outside passage."

He looked directly at me then. His sunken eyes were like two black holes. "All right. I'll go with you."

His catlike footsteps followed me along the planking, making less noise than the lapping of river water against the sides of the boat, and then up the companionway to the saloon deck. When I made the turn into the outer promenade, I thought I saw a shadow move between me and the stern. But it was gone quickly like a floating wraith and I nearly dismissed it as a fragment of mist or fog. The man's strong hands gripped my shoulders, powerfully, stopping me dead in my tracks. He had seen the shadow too, I knew, and so I stood motionless and silent until he released me. Without a word then I led him to my stateroom door.

After I lighted the wall lamp, I saw his face clearly for the first time. Without the heavy beard the scar on his left cheek might have been repellent to some, but his eyes drew my attention away from that forbidding aspect of his face. I was quite surprised by the man's eyes, having imagined them as being insensitive, with no more life in them than a dead man's. But their expression had changed. In the lamplight they regarded me with a lively and somewhat kindly expression. Later I was to perceive in them also an ashen sadness, a resignation that comes only to those who have struggled against great odds and lost.

I thought he would express pleasure over the warmth and coziness of the stateroom, but he said nothing, merely glancing at the tins of biscuits on the upper bunk and along the wall. There was no expectancy about him. It was as though what he had intended to happen had already happened. I began lifting the tins down from the upper bunk to make room for him there, stacking them on top of those along the wall. He tried to help, but his fingers were stiff from dampness and cold and he kept dropping the containers. The odor of damp wool emanating from his presence was annoying. I jerked a blanket from the bunk and handed it to him. "Hang your wet clothes over the pipes there and wrap this around you. You're beginning to smell like a sick hound."

Half a laugh choked and hung in his throat, but he was soon in the blanket and resting in the upper bunk. In repose he looked almost human, and much younger than I had taken him to be earlier. His eyes followed me when I began rearranging the biscuit tins again so as to allow more floor space for us.

"Why did you do this?" he asked quietly. "Offer me refuge here?"

"Inquisitiveness," I replied. "When you spend your life tracking down stories for a newspaper it gets to be a habit. You want to go to that damned commemoration at Fort Rawley, yet you don't want to be seen. I'm curious as to why. Are you without funds? Do you fear someone on this boat? Or is it something else? Why does going to Fort Rawley mean so much to you?"

He drew himself into a sitting position, folded his bare arms outside the blanket, and spoke almost boastfully: "You're a newspaperman, are you? Well, I should be an honored guest. I'm the only survivor."

I stood facing him. "Survivor of what?"

"The massacre on the Malpais." His mouth twisted in an odd way. "I could tell them the truth." He paused. "I could tell you the truth."

"But there were no survivors other than Major Rawley. And he died in the fire at Fort Standish." I was no longer sure of myself, but I repeated: "There were no others."

"I tell you I was there," he insisted.

His voice had grown too loud, and a strange

light shone in his deep-set eyes. Perhaps he is a lunatic, I thought.

"They're all buried out there on the Malpais," I said, "except for Major Rawley."

"No! Listen to me. I tell you I was there. I've told no one, not even Nettie, of what happened out there. Listen to me."

To judge by this man's manner and appearance, I told myself, he is surely mad. Yet after he began to talk, with a singular calmness — and in tones so soft that sometimes I had to step nearer to understand — there was a remarkable lucidity in his tale. I was more than skeptical, yes, but he wanted to talk, to talk with the fervor of a man who has been in forced containment for days on end and who at last has found a willing listener. If I did not believe him, he said, I should have a look at the battalion roster, still at Fort Rice. I would find the name he had enlisted under: Alex Selkirk. His real name did not matter. He was no one of importance, he assured me.

I interrupted him. "I believe you are of importance. You're Charles Rawley, aren't you?"

His mouth opened slightly. Incredulity showed clearly in his face, and then he laughed. "That was a shot in the dark, wasn't it? No, I'm not Rawley. Rawley's long dead.

But I knew him. Before the war. We weren't friends, more rivals than friends. But in rivalry we saw something of each other. He'd organized a militia company across the river in Ohio, and we had one in the Kentucky blue-grass. Our companies sometimes competed — races, drills, joustings, that sort of thing. Rawley hated to lose. He'd take advantage, any way he could. He was no gentleman."

He went on a bit more about Rawley, his ruthlessness, his cruel streak. Selkirk had gone hunting with him once, and that was enough. "I liked the chase," he said, "the suspense, the outdoor smells, the sun and wind. I hated the kill. Rawley was bored by the chase. He took pleasure only in the kill, gloried in it, and he could be brutal at it."

After the war started, Selkirk had seen no more of Rawley. Selkirk's Kentucky militia company went right into General John Morgan's Confederate cavalry regiment, while Rawley's was disbanded, most of the members going into Union regiments. Not until Morgan's raid across Ohio and Indiana in 1863 did Selkirk give any more thought to Rawley. "Somehow I had the feeling that I might meet up with him in an ambush or a skirmish, and I thought how ironic that I who hated to kill was trapped in a warrior's role that he would take pleasure in. We never faced each other, of course, until after I was captured and shipped down to Saint Louis to board the *Effie Deans.*"

He had been afraid to leave the *Effie Deans,* he admitted, but from the time of the first desertions at Saint Louis, he had thought constantly of leaping over the rail on some dark night. After they passed Independence, he had actually approached the rail two or three times late in the nights, but the guards had grown more alert by then, using their bayoneted rifles to send him back to his blankets. Then had come the court-martial and execution of Private Noah Burkett, a chilling and dispiriting event that brought him to a decision to delay any escape attempt until after the battalion reached its destination and he was safe on land. Sooner than he expected his feet were on the ground. At Dutchman's Landing, he had been completely surprised when Major Rawley chose him from the ranks for that ten-man platoon destined for Fort Standish. "I thought he picked me because of my size, my height," he told me. "But the very next man he motioned to step forward was a bony little runt named Tharp. Mean murdering little bastard, he was."

Soon after the *Effie Deans* was forced to a

standstill by low water at Devil's Shoals, Major Rawley announced his plan to leave the steamboat with the platoon and cross the Malpais to Fort Standish. And for the first time since his capture in Ohio, Alex Selkirk or whoever he was found himself in possession of a rifle and forty rounds in a cartridge box. Perhaps because Selkirk was the tallest of the ten Galvanized Yankees, Rawley informed him that he was to act as sergeant during the march. From the moment at first dawnlight when they started across the Malpais, desertion was foremost in his thoughts. That action was also in the minds of most of the others, especially in the malign brain of Private Tharp.

They had no trail whatever to follow. Major Rawley kept always in the lead, repeatedly consulting his map and compass. Around mid-morning they entered an eerie country of fantastically shaped hills, dull yellow with very little vegetation. They had filled their canteens with river water, but Rawley gave them no instructions concerning the use of it, and during the half-hour he allowed them for a noon rest, they drank most of it.

Because these men had been confined in prisons and on the steamboat for many weeks they were unfit for a long march. Four or five of them like Selkirk were cavalrymen and had always disdained to march on foot. Even over level land with a road to follow they would have had difficulty in covering the thirty miles to Fort Standish between daylight and dark. On the uneven surface of the Malpais, with its gulches and sharp-bluffed hills and stony passages, the task would have been arduous for seasoned infantrymen.

Heat and thirst, feet rubbed raw, heavy packs and wool uniforms – these began to tell on them in the early afternoon. Rawley felt the punishment, too, but not until his uniform was soaked with sweat did he order jackets removed and rolled into packs. He was too late in warning the men to conserve the water in their canteens.

Although Rawley exchanged few words with his acting sergeant, the latter knew that his commander was desperately hoping to find water. Occasionally Selkirk could hear the young major cursing to himself, damning the fate that had brought him to this wilderness, railing against the savage Indians who made it necessary for him to endure such misery.

At last the country began to flatten. They left the yellow hills behind, but shimmering sunlight on the almost grassless plain created mirages before them – little sparkling pools, cool lakes of dark water. When Rawley first sighted one of these mirages, he ordered the platoon forward at double time only to see the sheen of moisture vanish suddenly just as it seemed within reach. Two or three times more they were deluded, and then upon sighting a strip of green grass bordering a stream they refused to accept it as real until they saw and heard wild ducks lifting from the water.

After they had stumbled forward, falling to drink from the creek, Rawley spoke to Selkirk of their prospects for reaching Fort Standish that day. "Maybe twelve, fifteen more miles I figure it," he said. "We might do it by nightfall. If we all bathed in this creek we should be refreshed enough to complete the march. Tell the men to stack their arms and then strip and jump in. You act as guard until they're out and then take your turn."

Rawley walked a few yards upstream. He undressed and removed a locket and chain that he wore around his neck, placed it carefully on a hump of grass, and then waded into the stream. He was floating in the cold current with only his head above the surface by the time the men dived in, noisily cursing and splashing. After five minutes or so the major stepped out on the bank and began drying his legs with his underwear. He pulled on his long cotton drawers, and signaled Selkirk to order the men out and take a quick turn in the creek himself. Selkirk found the water to be stinging cold. He washed himself and floated on his back, feeling the cold penetrate his flesh. He could see Rawley seated on the creek bank, still in his underdrawers, letting the sun and wind dry the upper part of his body. The major seemed reluctant to leave that green and liquid oasis to resume march across the dry barren plain. When Rawley reached for his undershirt and began putting his arms into the sleeves, Selkirk rose up and started walking toward his own clothes on the bank, stepping from side to side to avoid fresh mud left by the other bathers. A sudden breeze chilled him and he noticed the high grass waving and bowing under its force. When he looked up, he saw one of the men standing at the rifle stack. At first he thought nothing of it; the man was dressed, wet hair plastered against his skull, random damp spots on his dark shirt. He was Private Tharp.

As Selkirk buckled his trousers, he watched Tharp draw a cartridge from his box and insert it into the weapon. Major Rawley had strictly forbidden the loading of arms without an order from him, and Selkirk was about to yell at Tharp but in that same instant Tharp raised the rifle, aimed upstream, and fired.

The detonation was startling, from the first explosion of powder to the reverberating waves of sound that seemed to grow in force and extent, ringing and thundering in Selkirk's ears, persisting it seemed to him interminably, although the sound could not have continued for more than a few seconds. Wild ducks and snipe, startled from their feeding, filled the sky; a pair of snowy white cranes wheeled above his head, so close he could see the black tips of their wing feathers.

Except for the soaring birds, everything seemed to stop. Selkirk had to force himself to turn his head so that he could look upstream, only to see Major Rawley turning his head to stare at him. The major had been shot in the back by Private Tharp, and the expression on his face was incredulity. *The simplicity of that poor devil Rawley,* Selkirk thought in a flash. *How dangerous it is for him and us!* Rawley could not comprehend what had happened, and his body clothed only in undershirt and long drawers was collapsing before he could turn completely to face his men.

Selkirk ran across the high grass and found Rawley lying belly down, face turned to one side, eyes wide open but lifeless. When Selkirk rose up he saw that Tharp was still standing by the stacked arms, his rifle balanced loosely in one hand. The other eight men in various stages of undress appeared frozen in the attitudes they were in when the shot was fired.

"You crazed son of a bitch!" Selkirk shouted at Tharp. "You shot him in the back!"

"He killed Noah Burkett without mercy," Tharp retorted. "I owed him that for Noah. Eye for eye, tooth for tooth, the Good Book says."

Slowly Selkirk walked closer to Tharp. "Now what the hell do we do? We can't go on to —"

"We'll head for the Montana gold fields same as them who went with that Gen'l La Prade." Tharp looked around at the others, showing his cramped teeth and gums in a wild grin. "Only we don't have to tolerate Yankee trash like Rawley anymore. We're free men now. When the war's over we'll go back to Kentucky rich!"

Selkirk shook his head in disgust. "The Montana gold fields are five or six hundred miles west. Without horses or supplies, and with hostile Indians between here and there, what chance do you think we'd have?"

"You figure it out, captain. You can get us horses. You found plenty horses and *almost* sneaked us out of Ohio after Gen'l Morgan run off and left us at Buffington Island." He grinned again, at the surprise on Selkirk's face. "Yeah, I was there, in the big raid. I seen you more'n once with that crazy Englishman, Grenfell. You was a captain. You can find horses for us."

Selkirk felt his rage grow. He'd had his own plans for escape, and now this imbecilic killer had endangered everything. Selkirk's gaze was directed at the faces of the eight others; they all looked as if they'd been abandoned by both God and man. "The only horses within a thousand miles are in the army's forts or in the Indian tribes' herds," he said flatly.

Tharp grimaced mockingly, and then looked around at the others, who were mechanically fastening buttons and tightening straps on their uniforms and gear. "We can go on to the fort and steal horses there," he said in a tone of bravado.

Selkirk had already decided that the only sensible course of action was to try to reach Fort Standish, report what had happened, and hope the commandant would believe the story fully. He did not trust Tharp, however. The little reprobate was too cunning to walk right into the fort without some kind of scheme to protect himself. *He could just as easily shoot me in the back,* Selkirk thought, *if he thinks I might betray him. Nor do I trust those other eight men who're thinking hard about the Montana gold fields.*

"If we go on to Fort Standish," he asked Tharp "how do we explain what happened to Major Rawley?"

"You'll think of a good explanation, Mr. Acting Sergeant Captain. And we better get started now."

Selkirk shook his head. "We bury him first. We can't leave him out here, for the wolves."

"Wolves would not touch Rawley's carcass. Only worms." Tharp cocked his head back so that his popeyes bulged more than usual. "You don't have a gun. Maybe I ought to be acting sergeant." Motioning to the other men to come and take their rifles from the stack, he slung Selkirk's weapon over his back and kept his own at the ready. "Let's go, unless you want to stay here and do the burying by yourself."

Selkirk decided to humor Tharp; he could come back and bury Rawley later, with help from the fort. "I'll get the map and compass from the major's pocket," he said. When he returned, Tharp darted past him to where Rawley lay and reached down to jerk a Remington .44 from the dead man's belt. "You won't need this to find the way to the fort." He pointed the weapon at Selkirk, turning it from side to side, pretending to sight with one eye along the heavy barrel, laughing crazily.

With Rawley's map and compass, Selkirk set a course toward the northeast. For about a quarter of a mile they followed the creek until it made a sharp turn westward. "We'll have to cross here," he called back to the men. "Take your boots off and wade if you like." A moment later he saw hoofprints of horses. Dozens of them had crossed not long before; the sand was still damp where the passing animals had splashed water from the creek.

"Here's your horses, Tharp," one of the men said, looking at the tracks.

"Soldiers or redskins?" Tharp asked.

"Unshod," Selkirk answered. "Indians heading southeast."

"Let's track the devils," Tharp said. "Tonight we can steal their horses."

Selkirk thought he heard a distant sound, a throbbing of some kind, and then he was sure of it, for down the slope of a low ridge off to the southwest a line of mounted warriors was approaching at an easy gallop.

"They must've heard Tharp fire that rifle," Selkirk said. "We'd better load weapons and look like soldiers. They should give us plenty of room when they see our uniforms."

"Let's ambush the bastards," Tharp insisted.

"Take their damned horses."

Selkirk ignored Tharp's remark, but one of the others answered: "Hell, they've already seen us."

Clumps of small willows grew a few feet back from the creek, and the Galvanized Yankees used them for what little cover they offered. The Indians came on, nine of them on small fast horses, slowing their pace as they approached the shallow ford, finally halting about fifty yards away. None wore a war bonnet, but some had feathers in their hair and two or three carried lances with plumes spiraled down their shafts. One of them rode a white pony with a black slash across its forehead. He seemed to be spokesman for the party. He held his arms out, clasping his hands together and bowing his head slightly to the Galvanized Yankees. Then he held one hand half closed in front of his body, and with the other made motions as if filling and tamping a pipe.

"What the hell does he want?" Tharp asked. "Look, they're moving in closer." His voice turned high and excited. "All you fellows got cartridges in your guns? Enough horses out there to carry us to Montana. Selkirk, give us the firing commands, right down the line!"

"No. They mean to pass us peaceably."

"Hell, they got nothing but bows and pole

spears to fight us with."

The Indians turned leftward, evidently skirting the ford to avoid the position of the Galvanized Yankees, walking their mounts at a steady pace.

"Bastards!" Tharp raised his rifle and fired. Two or three of the men followed his example and also fired, wild shots. A wounded horse screamed in sudden agony, whirled, and dashed off with its rider toward the low ridge. All the Indians fled in that same direction, shouting, quirting their mounts fiercely. A wounded warrior, grasping at his pony's mane, lost his grip and fell hard on the ground. One of his companions made a quick circle back, pulled the other up behind him, and resumed the gallop flight.

Tharp cried out in disgust, a stream of profanity. "They got away with every damn horse." He turned toward Selkirk. "Next time I tell you to give us firing commands, Mr. Captain, you better do it or I'll put my bullet between your eyes."

Selkirk was still watching the Indians. They had stopped just out of range of accurate rifle fire, and seemed to be waiting for something, their eyes turned more often toward the ridge than toward the Galvanized Yankees at the creek.

"Christ!" Tharp yelled. "Look at 'em coming down that slope."

At that distance the uneven line of horsemen appearing on the ridge resembled a brown snake tumbling lengthwise. Their dust, caught in the slanting rays of the late afternoon sun, was a rolling golden cloud.

"We better move!" one of the men cried.

"No place to go," Selkirk answered. "Pass me one of the rifles, Tharp. This time I'll give the firing commands. Everybody spread out as best you can." As soon as Tharp handed him the slung rifle, Selkirk moved a few yards away from the others, taking a kneeling position in thick grass beside a willow sapling. No one said anything. All were watching the Indians sweeping down upon the flat. The small party waiting there had their ponies in motion when the fifty or more joined them. They were whooping now, readying lances and bows. One fired off an old trade gun with a loud echoing crack. Flying hooves drummed against the dry earth. Warrior faces came sharply into focus. Selkirk shouted firing commands. Four riders, separating from the massive charge, swept toward him, their horses crowding close as they splashed across the shallows of the ford. One on a gray pony carried a lance. For an instant Selkirk had the Indian's naked chest in his rifle sights. He heard the chatter of fire on his right, smelled powder smoke, heard the yelping of the Indians, the thwick-thwick of their streaking arrows. The rider on the gray horse was glaring at him with angry pitiless eyes, lance shaft braced under armpit, the stone point a magnet for Selkirk's own eyes. Selkirk pulled the trigger, but he never knew if his bullet found its mark. The stone point of the speeding lance seemed to fill the sky, which exploded into millions of brilliant fragments and then turned black.

Afterward he vaguely remembered awakening painfully, shivering in cold darkness, and looking up at a starfilled sky with only the sound of a stream flowing quietly nearby. For a moment he thought he was back on the *Effie Deans*, but he knew he was not. He could see from only one eye; the other was closed by an enormous swelling that throbbed when he touched it. Blood had run down his cheek and neck, but when he tried to follow its dried course with his fingers he found that his uniform had been stripped from him. He forced himself upon his feet and stood trembling from shock. Between him and the creek were three naked bodies, pale in the starlight, and when he turned he saw others, shadow-marked, back in the willows.

He stumbled toward the creek, wading a few steps and then sinking down to try to wash his face. The cold water revived his senses but also intensified the pain where the lance had struck its glancing blow, tearing flesh and skin away from the temporal bone. He smothered a cry of pain by lowering his mouth into the water, wondering if in his weakness he would drown, was overcome by lassitude, and began floating with the current. He never knew how long he was in the stream; sometimes he was aware of fish nibbling at his flesh and realized they were attracted by drops of blood oozing from his wound. The sky was gray in the east before he had the strength to stand in a shallow place. A few yards down the bank was a line of white against black grass. He wondered at the strangeness of it for a long time before he knew that the white object was Major Rawley in his undershirt and drawers. As soon as he crawled out, the air chilled his already cold flesh and he was shaking violently when he reached the body. The light was bright enough now for him to see insects crawling on the dead man's face. He turned away in a spasm of tremors, almost stepping upon the uniform that still lay where Rawley had left it — trousers and jacket carefully folded, boots, and that wide-brimmed black hat the major had fancied. There was also a watch, barely visible in the starlight.

He seized upon the clothing more for warmth than anything else, wrapping the jacket around his shivering upper body, and then sat down in the grass to laboriously pull on the trousers. The boots were very tight, and he had to place the hat far back on his head to keep the band from touching his raw forehead. The watch had stopped. He rewound it with the key on its chain and then stood up, swaying from vertigo, steeling himself for what he had to do, determined somehow to reach Fort Standish. Every step was an effort of will. He began counting his steps – ten, twenty, thirty – and then he would lie down again, fighting to keep from losing consciousness, seeing repeatedly against the bright light of morning upon the screen of his one good eyelid a vision of insects moving in and out of the nostrils and mouth of Major Charles Rawley.

Before that night in my stateroom on the *Roanoke*, Selkirk admitted, he had never told this story to anyone. He half reclined there in the top bunk, spelling the details out to me graphically. I was physically weary after my long day in the wagon, the rain, the talk and listening, the constant surprises. Yet I stood, or leaned against the wall, most of the time while he recounted the events on the Malpais, his voice sometimes only a hollow whisper. At the end, although there was no longer warmth in the stateroom, his forehead and his naked chest and arms were beaded with sweat.

"When I fully regained consciousness," he said, "I was on a litter of some kind, a drag travois such as the Indians use, a bandage over half my face, bumping across a perfectly flat prairie, grasshoppers flying about everywhere. When I moved my head, this blue-eyed sergeant riding alongside told me with Irish in his voice to take it easy, he'd have me into the hands of a surgeon at Fort Standish in another hour. 'Just lay there, major,' he said. I wondered why he'd called me by that rank until I looked out of my uncovered eye at the leaf insignia on the shoulder strap of that coat of Rawley's I was wearing. I knew I was in a dilemma."

"They thought you were Rawley," I said.

"Sure, they thought I was the major. Should I have told them the truth? All I wanted was to get clear of Dakota and find my way home to Kentucky. I was thinking pretty hard through the pain in my head, and I thought to myself, well, I'd just ride along with it, look out for a chance to escape at first opportunity. Maybe escape would be easier if they thought I was Major Rawley. Just so long as there was nobody who knew him at the fort, and it seemed unlikely there would be. But hell, I'd be a sight better off now if I'd just told the truth then, and maybe a lot more people would've been better off."

He raised up and slid his legs over the side of the bunk, wrapping the blanket tight around him and staring down at the biscuit tins against the wall. "I could do with some of those dry biscuits there. No food since late yesterday."

I offered to try to rustle some hot food from the galley. "It's late," I said, "but somebody may be about the kitchen."

He smiled very faintly. "I'd be appreciative, sir."

5

The central lounge appeared to be deserted, the musicians and the dancers gone for the night. Only one poker game was still in progress in the gentlemen's cabin. Two gray-bearded fur-company representatives lingered over drinks at one end of the bar. At the opposite end, the bartender's head rested on the polished wood. I woke him out of a drowse and asked if it was possible to find a decent bite of food at so late an hour. He directed me to the pantry, where a night cook was already assembling provisions for the next morning's breakfast. A bowl of warmed-over beef stew could be ready in half an hour, he assured me, in exchange for a two-bit piece. I gave him a silver quarter and went back to the bar to buy a pair of cigars for the same price. The stogie I lit was no fresher than the Havanas I'd been carrying in my bag since leaving Saint Louis, but I needed something to do while waiting for the stew to heat. I started pacing back and forth along the polished dance floor behind one of the red plush couches, leaving streamers of blue smoke in my wake.

All at once I was aware of a human head slowly rising above the rim of the couch's back, a mass of dark hair carelessly arranged, a few strands falling over the forehead, the wide open brown eyes of Nettie Steever staring at me. "God, Mr. Morrison," she said hoarsely, "that stogie smells good. You would not have another, would you?"

"I do indeed, ma'am." I handed her the other one I'd just bought. "Not of quality leaf, but the best the gentlemen's cabin offers."

She bit off the closed end and angled the cigar in one corner of her mouth. Turning to rest on her knees, she leaned forward for me to light it with the glowing end of mine. After expelling a circle of smoke, she said in a sarcastic tone: "Speaking of the gentlemen's cabin, that place is forbidden to gentle ladies such as I who enjoy a bit of whiskey with our smokes. If you would buy me half a pint, I'd be in your debt." From a pocket in her heavy skirt she withdrew a few coins, offering them to me.

"Allow me the privilege of playing host," I replied, and went and brought her a mug of bourbon and a glass of water on a tray, which I placed between us on the couch. She never touched the water, but sipped appreciatively from the mug after each puff on the cigar.

There was a certain coarseness about Nettie Steever, but hers was the coarseness of fresh-plowed earth or roughhewn wood or rawhide — something elemental. Perhaps I'm being a bit fanciful; what I mean to say is that I did not find her earthiness objectionable. I learned later that she had emigrated from England while a young girl, lived in Philadelphia until she married, and soon after that started for the West with her husband. Her British origin accounted for her mode of speech. To my ear it bore approximately the lilt of the Irish track-layers I'd recently met out on the Plains where they were building the Union Pacific Railroad.

Despite the cigar and the whiskey, she did not strike me as being masculine. The word that suited her, I thought, was *self-sufficient,* a condition that might have been galling to many of my male contemporaries, but was not to me, at least at that late hour of the night. When I'd met her earlier that evening I'd thought of her as being hard, a bitch, like so many independent women. But as we talked of trivialities — the weather, the dancing, the steamboat — she sipping at the bourbon, I trying to lead her into some revelation of her involvement with Major Rawley, smiles began to appear fleetingly on her face for the first time since I'd met her. The smiles that replaced the expression of weary despair revealed a different Nettie Steever, a younger, more animated woman.

I wondered how deep the relationship had been between her and Rawley, or Selkirk or whoever he was. Dr. Lieber had told me that the two became acquainted during the army's march to Killdeer Mountain and then months later Rawley had rescued her from Indian captivity in Canada. I wanted her to tell me about that, and although she had rebuffed me at the first try, I was determined to ask her again. I could hear Selkirk's hollow voice, not an hour ago, in my stateroom: *I've told no one, not even Nettie, of what happened out there.* The implication was that Nettie meant a great deal to him, was perhaps his most intimate confidante, the person most likely to be told his secrets.

Why then were they not traveling together on the *Roanoke?* I was almost on the point of asking her that question, just barely remembering before I spoke that his presence in my stateroom was unknown to her. But of course he could not go to the commemoration for the late Major Charles Rawley! He was Charles Rawley to some of the people who would be there, and they believed him to be dead. But who was he to Nettie Steever? Did she know he was alive?

At that moment she was smiling at me, somewhat intimately I thought. "Tell me about Major Rawley," I said quietly.

She drew her shoulders up, her smile vanishing as she lengthened the distance between us on the couch. Then she cocked her head back, lifted a leg and rested the ankle on her knee, as a man would. The curve of her ankle and calf above the grotesque brogue shoe struck me as being crazily incongruous. "Rawley was a beautiful son of a bitch," she finally answered. "Always treated me like a lady."

"Tell me how he died." As I spoke the words I watched her eyes closely for some sign of dissemblance or bewilderment. They blinked once; there was tobacco smoke in the air, but I saw no pain of memory in the brown irises. Did she know of Selkirk's compulsion to go to the commemoration at Fort Rawley? *I must see their faces,* he had said. *After all, what I tried to do was done for them.*

"He died in the fire, the explosion at old Fort Standish," she said quietly.

"Were you there with him?"

The look she gave me was not friendly. "No. I was at the woodyard."

"Where is the woodyard?"

"Above Dutchman's Landing. Look here, to hell with you, Morrison." She pushed the tray toward me and stood up, smoothing her woolen skirt. She stretched herself. "On rainy nights it's good to be in bed."

"Alone?"

She tried to pretend anger but could not keep a grin from her full lips. "Go to the devil, Morrison."

"The rain has stopped anyway," I told her.

The night cook came out of the pantry with a small cast-iron pot. He called my name. I could smell the aroma of beef and vegetables steaming from the edges of the lid.

She watched me take the pot, made some comment under her breath, and then turned toward the ladies' staterooms.

"Goodnight, Nettie," I called after her, but she did not respond, did not even glance back at me.

6

When Alex Selkirk was first brought into Fort Standish after the massacre on the Malpais, he was placed in a small barracks that served as post hospital. Only four or five of the dozen beds were occupied, the patients being enlisted men suffering from the usual dysentery or from lingering complications of venereal disease.

Although recovery was fairly rapid, he began feigning dizziness and symptoms of confusion for the benefit of the attendants and Dr. Lieber. He needed time to develop a plan for escape, and he thought a long convalescence might be the best shield for this purpose. Through the surgeon he managed to obtain a military map of the Department of Dakota, and to his dismay discovered that Saint Paul was almost as far to the east as the Montana gold fields were to the west. He'd had a half-formed plan in mind of making his way back across country to the Mississippi River and then returning to Kentucky, perhaps by raft or in a stolen rowboat. Although the map showed but few trails to Canada, the distance there was little more than a hundred miles, and just across the border was Fort Manitou, under a British flag that was more sympathetic to the Confederacy than to the Union. On a good horse he believed it might be possible to reach the fort in three or four days.

From the beginning of his medical care he was on good terms with Dr. Lieber, and their growing friendship helped him lose some of his uneasiness over taking the identity of Major Rawley. However after Colonel Herrick, the commandant, visited the hospital one day to pay him deference as the son of the great Senator Rawley, Selkirk realized that discovery of his real identity not only would be fatal to his plan of escape but probably to his life.

Major Rawley's Galvanized Yankee battalion was stationed only a few days' journey down-river at Fort Rice, and every steamboat bound upstream that stopped at the Fort Standish landing brought a danger of exposure from a transferred officer or by a military order in the official mail perhaps summoning him to rejoin them. Deciding to show more signs of recovery, he asked Dr. Lieber if he might obtain the use of a horse for short rides outside the fort. After making inquiries, Lieber informed Selkirk that he could use one of the fort's horses for exercise within the stockade, but that only military patrols in strength could take horses outside the gate. Fort Standish had lost so many animals to the clever Sioux that there were barely enough remaining to mount a defensible patrol, and Colonel Herrick was adamant against personal use of them by officers or noncommissioned officers outside the fort. Selkirk began riding up and down the cramped parade ground every day, and at the same time he deliberately set about developing a camaraderie between himself and the enlisted men who guarded the stockade's single gate. Every innocent-appearing scheme that he devised for riding a horse through the gate failed, however, and at last he decided that he would try for Canada on foot.

To relieve the monotony of living within the cottonwood-log stockade, Colonel Herrick permitted his officers to take short walks outside the gate during their off-duty hours anytime between sunrise and sunset. For their own safety they were forbidden, however, to walk farther than the three-hundred-yard target posts that Herrick had placed in a ring outside the north bastion and that were sometimes used for marksmanship exercises.

On his first walk outside Selkirk violated this rule slightly, without challenge, and then on the second day he strolled a considerable distance beyond the posts only to have Sergeant O'Hara come jogging out to remind him of the danger and ask permission to accompany him back to the gate. Then one day he delayed his outside walk until almost sundown, hoping to avoid notice until dusk concealed his presence, but like a faithful and watchful nursemaid, O'Hara ordered out a dozen riders to gallop after him with a spare horse. This time the sergeant remanded Selkirk to Dr. Lieber, who gave him a gentle scolding and informed him that Colonel Herrick had issued orders forbidding the major, for his own safety, to leave the post until he had more fully recovered from his head wound.

The arrival of a company of mounted Minnesota Volunteers and Colonel Herrick's offer of command reopened opportunities to Selkirk, and he entered into the training of his inexperienced charges with enthusiasm. He was on the verge of requesting permission from Herrick to take the troopers on a short patrol when the colonel unexpectedly sprang the news of the rendezvous with General La Prade at Burdache Creek.

Selkirk knew that if his Galvanized Yankees

were with General La Prade their presence would end his impersonation of Major Rawley. He tried in vain to persuade Herrick to leave him in command at Fort Standish, and then after the march to Burdache Creek he made up his mind to start for Canada that night. But he reckoned without the alert Sergeant O'Hara. When O'Hara hailed him as he rode out of the bivouac, Selkirk replied curtly that he was going to look for signs of a buffalo herd.

After riding two or three miles, with a purple dusk enveloping the monotonous landscape, he was certain that he had at last made his escape. But again the persistent O'Hara overtook him with a search party, and he was forced to pretend that he had lost his sense of direction in the darkness.

During the following days, Colonel Herrick's troops were assigned to the rear of the column to guard the immigrant train, and Selkirk began riding far out on the flanks with the cavalry. He became resigned to the fact that he must await a more propitious opportunity to escape. By day the land was like an enormous flat stage spotlighted under the glare of the sun, with all privacy voided. By night pickets were posted at very close intervals outside the circles of wagons. But each day the column moved closer to the Canadian border, and there were constant rumors of an impending battle with the Indians that might create enough confusion for him to ride swiftly away.

And then he met Nettie Steever. Selkirk had never known a woman who was in any way like Nettie. He had grown up in the Kentucky bluegrass, in a society where women were esteemed merely because they were women. To see one treated the way Steever treated Nettie offended his sensibilities, brought out all the anger and pity in him. Virtually a prisoner of her brutish husband, Nettie yet maintained an air of self-determination. Like Selkirk she was seeking an opportunity to escape; she did not know how or where. In their first tentative efforts at communication they must have sensed their common fate, their mutual objective. He never told her he was someone other than Major Rawley; he spoke only of going to Canada to start a new life. After that, every time they met, gathering buffalo chips or bits of dead wood together, or kneeling beside the cooking fires, she whispered to him of that new life in Canada. On one occasion her husband must have overheard the whispering between them. Without warning he stormed out at her in the vilest of language, and when she defied him, he struck her in the face, raising a dark welt on her cheek. Selkirk wanted to kill him, but restrained himself with the silent promise that he would take Nettie with him when he fled to Canada.

The last night before the immigrants' wagons were left at Heart River so that La Prade could make his forced march to Killdeer Mountain, Nettie slipped out of her wagon and came to Selkirk's blankets. Clouds screened the stars; the darkness was thick as black mud; the only sounds were occasional soft snufflings of horses and faraway howls of wolves. She had bathed herself from a washbowl in the wagon and smelled of soap. She wanted to start for Canada then, at that moment, but he knew they would be challenged before they rode twenty yards past the wagons. He told her a better opportunity would come; he swore to her that he would not leave without her. They made love in the darkness. She had not known before, she told him, that men could be as tender as women. Her husband was a rutting animal, she said.

The next morning Colonel Herrick started his troops forward at daybreak, ordering Selkirk to lead out with the cavalry company. Selkirk was not expecting so sudden a departure; there was no way he could say good-bye to Nettie Steever. He was not even certain that she saw his gesture of farewell as he led the troopers quickly past her wagon.

Colonel Herrick's troops, including Selkirk's cavalry, were among the last to reach Killdeer Mountain. General La Prade already had his attack force fairly well in position. Being a student of European tactics, the general had formed his soldiers into a hollow square, with his reduced train of supply wagons and the batteries of cannon inside the square.

Shortly after Colonel Herrick arrived, an orderly from La Prade's headquarters came galloping with written orders to lengthen the rear of the hollow square. Because of the sharp ravines slashing down the slope of the mountain, cavalry charges were obviously impossible, and so Herrick ordered Selkirk to dismount his company and deploy the men in a skirmish line along the right side of the extended hollow square. One of each set of four troopers served as a horseholder, and they were told to keep the mounts close by within the square. During his months with General John Morgan of the Confederacy, Selkirk had never seen a hollow square, but he soon realized that his Minnesota cavalrymen were being held in reserve, ready to ride to any part of the field where they might be summoned.

While the troops were being aligned, Dr. Lieber's ambulance rolled up only a few yards behind Selkirk. Before he could greet the surgeon, a half-dozen or so men in frontier garb rode in to an adjoining supply wagon and began exchanging their fringed buckskins for blue uniform blouses. They were Herrick's scouts and were taking precautions against being mistaken for Indians if the fighting turned fast and furious. One of them asked Lieber if he could spare a swallow of whiskey. The surgeon got a bottle from the ambulance and the scouts quickly passed it around. The last one tossed the empty bottle to Selkirk with a hoot of laughter. "Not a drop left for you, Major Rawley. Y'll have to trust in y'r native courage, sir, instead of whiskey bravado."

Selkirk shrugged and turned to watch the Indian warriors who were beginning to ride out from their big tipi camp on the bench of the mountain. *Why am I here?* he asked himself, *a man who calls himself Selkirk although that is not my name, a man who allows others to call him Major Rawley, although neither is that my name. What purpose brought me to this place?* He could not answer, no more than he had been able to tell himself why he had ridden with John Morgan's cavalry out of the bluegrass of Kentucky across the Ohio River to pillage towns and farms. Oh, they had enjoyed a high old time, playing foxes to the pursuing Yankee boys in blue, a testing time for all of them across Indiana and Ohio, but meaningless when one comes right down to it. Especially being captured and locked in that stinking prison in Illinois.

He looked up the sloping prairie where rank after rank of dust-streaked blue-uniformed men waited in the pitiless July heat, all watching that giant anthill of swarming Indians they called Killdeer Mountain. Why were they here, those Minnesotans and Iowans, most of whom had come from somewhere else far away at the beginning of America's sunrise or from across the waters of the Atlantic. He'd heard Herrick's scouts say that a few of the Minnesotans were seeking revenge for the uprising of the Santee Sioux some two years past. But the scouts also said there was only a scattering of Santees on Killdeer. Most of the woodland Sioux that escaped Minnesota had fled to Canada. The Indians up there in the smoke-stained tipis were Plains Sioux, not woodlanders. They'd had nothing to do with the Minnesota uprising. So why had the soldiers come here?

A small movement of wind surrounded him with a strong odor of horses, horse dung, and horse urine. He could smell his own salt-mottled sweat-soaked jacket, then a whiff of fragrance from wild tobacco.

Why had the Indians up there on Killdeer Mountain waited for the long columns of blue-clad enemy to come to them? Why did they not flee to the west? Their scouts surely had seen the twelve artillery pieces. Did they not know what thundering cannon could do to buffalo-skin tipis? Right then he noticed that some of the distant tipis were going down, dropping like skirts, vanishing against their background of gray rocks and green trees. Was it the women and children pulling back or were they all preparing to run, late as it was for them?

Riding with Morgan he had learned to read the landscape. Grand, dismal, majestic, a poet might say of that which lay before him. A cavalryman would avoid it. No surprise, no slashing charge was possible here. The tipi village was high on the bench, with ravine-split hills behind. The Indians could charge down the slope on horseback or pour out on foot from the gullies at either end. A withdrawal to the rear would be difficult for them, up those bare and rocky heights. If that was a camp of Union soldiers, John Morgan would bring up artillery to smite them. He guessed General La

Prade would do the same, except it would not be the same because the Indians had no artillery with which to retaliate.

He could see a few warriors on foot now. They had worked their way down through the woody ravines so that they flanked the upper end of La Prade's hollow square. Springing up then, as though by magic, on the rolling prairie below the tipi village was a line-front of horsed warriors. They cantered forward at an easy pace, almost leisurely, but they were stripped for battle and were waving their weapons in the air. He was surprised by the number armed only with bows and arrows.

Sergeant O'Hara was shouting Major Rawley's name. He started at the sudden recognition of it; he'd enjoyed being himself during the reverie. Colonel Herrick wanted his officers to gather at the supply wagons for a hasty council. They were to come mounted, the sergeant explained, as he handed over the reins of the horse. "Are you feeling all right, sir?" O'Hara inquired politely.

Why have they come here, these soldiers? he asked himself, and partially answered the question when he rode up to salute Colonel Herrick, who sat arrogantly erect in his saddle, a gross man, his abundant flesh pouring with sweat, brown curls like wet tendrils growing from under his hat over ears and forehead, a huge sun-blistered nose, his face dark-red from alcohol in the blood, eyes cunning and expectant. Herrick wanted to be a man of importance — a governor, a territorial judge, a senator — anything that would give him more power. He needed glory, renown, his name in large black letters in the pages of the Saint Paul newspapers.

"Gentlemen," he was saying to his officers as he held a tight rein on his nervous stallion, "I've just returned from a hasty meeting with General La Prade. We estimate near to two thousand Indian lodges up there on Killdeer, maybe six thousand warriors. Although we are outnumbered by three to one —"

General La Prade. Why did he bring us all to Killdeer Mountain? Two thousand and two hundred officers and enlisted men, against six thousand warriors. A lie. The scouts this very morning estimated the number of warriors at sixteen hundred. But six thousand defeated Indians would look better, sound better in the official dispatches. Sixteen hundred Indians bearing old trade guns and arrows against twenty-two hundred soldiers armed with the best Civil War rifles and twelve pieces of artillery. General La Prade. The rumors said he'd lost a whole brigade in the Shenandoah, trying for glory. The high command sent him out here to reshape himself. La Prade ached for a chance to sign a battle report that would shake the desk generals out of their chairs in the War Department back in Washington.

"Major Rawley, you will keep your men beside their mounts," Colonel Herrick's voice droned on, "in readiness to drive any Indians off our right flank. Should I give the order, charge them until you reach rough ground, then dismount and fight on foot. General La Prade will use the cannon to dislodge them from the heights, scatter them, draw them down here where we can finish them. Any questions?"

No one had any questions. They were all watching a single mounted warrior who had advanced some paces ahead of the rank of Indians that had cantered down from the tipi village. He wore a bright-colored war bonnet; his body was painted in streaks of orange, yellow, and black. Raising a rifle above his head, he called out a challenge in Lakota, and then began racing along the front of the dismounted Iowa cavalrymen facing him.

"Who is that crazy savage?" Colonel Herrick asked his chief of scouts. "Is that Spotted Horse, the Santee murderer?"

"Nah," the scout replied. "He's a Teton

Sioux. Long Dog, maybe. Or that new leader, Sitting Bull." The man spat tobacco juice on the ground. "Don't matter much who 'tis, colonel. They mean to fight us."

"If I could take Spotted Horse's scalp back to Saint Paul, they'd —" He shook his head impatiently. "Why don't the Iowa boys kill that goddamned show-off?"

Almost as Herrick spoke, a volley sounded from the rifles of the forward rank of Iowa cavalrymen. The challenging Teton stretched himself out flat along his horse's back, digging one heel violently into the animal's flank to send it into a gallop, and with a gesture of defiance disappeared from view over a fold in the prairie. The advancing line of warriors returned the cavalry fire with guns and arrows and then wheeled their mounts to the rear to reload and be joined by others racing down at full speed from the village.

"The ball is starting, colonel," the chief of scouts said quietly.

"Yes!" In his excitement, Herrick sawed hard on his reins, setting the stallion to prancing. "To your commands, gentlemen!"

Now, if ever, will come my chance to escape this madness, he thought, *to leave the names Selkirk and Rawley forever behind me and become myself again. The map shows less than a hundred miles to the border. Three days steady riding should do it.* He checked his canteen, refilling it quickly from one of the kegs on the water wagon. His saddlepack held enough hard crackers and dried meat to see him through.

From somewhere up the slope, sharp commands rose above the irregular rifle fire. The hollow square that had been lengthened to an oblong by late arrivals began moving slowly toward Killdeer Mountain. He rode forward to take a position at the head of his untried cavalrymen, who stood beside their mounts awaiting orders, watching the developing action ahead.

Within the last few minutes a crowd of Indians had gathered on a rocky ledge above the tipi village. Through his field glass he saw they were mostly old men, women, and a few children, standing so they could look down upon the battle. Most stood behind a low rim of rock so that only the upper parts of their bodies were visible, giving them the surreal appearance of truncated spectators floating in the atmosphere. *They look too confident,* he thought, *almost overweening in their sureness.*

Shrill commands from an artillery officer cut across the staccato of small arms and the war cries of the mounted Indians. The cannon's firing was like a distant cough overlaid by the scream of a projectile. It burst in the sky before reaching its target. Another cannon came quickly into action. The second ball exploded on target, hurling shrapnel among the noncombatants along the ledge.

John Morgan, he thought, *would have shot any artilleryman in his command for such an act against the enemy.* Morgan would have gone for the tipis, which were now being rapidly dismantled.

Concentrated rifle fire ripped suddenly along the left side of the hollow square, just opposite his position. To his surprise he saw a hundred or more warriors racing far out on the flat. Some had cuts of meat — antelope or deer — fastened to their ponies, a hunting party attempting to return to Killdeer Mountain.

A twelve-pounder cannon drawn by six horses came bouncing down the slope, men scurrying out of its path. The gunners quickly swung it into position and fired, the shell exploding among the galloping ponies of the Indians. When the dust and smoke cleared, five ponies were on the ground, mutilated, legs thrashing. Another galloped back the way it had come, snorting in terror, trailing its entrails in the dust. Five or six Indians were scattered among the downed ponies; one rose up, dragging a leg, trying desperately to reach cover.

Familiar cavalry commands resounded then above the rattle of rifles. *Prepare to mount! Mount!* The Iowans were going to charge the fleeing Indians. *Draw sabers! Charge!* In fours, the mounted platoons sprang out of the hollow square, horses' hooves drumming on the hard dry earth.

Some members of the Indian hunting party meanwhile had wheeled to recover their dead and wounded. It was done with such expert horsemanship, the riders dashing at full speed while hanging from their ponies, that Selkirk could not help but admire their skill and courage. With the Iowa cavalrymen pounding down upon him, one Sioux warrior coolly slipped a lariat over the leg of an unconscious comrade and dragged him roughly across the prairie to the safety of a timbered ravine.

Most of the Sioux hunters escaped in this same manner, the pursuing cavalry pausing only long enough to discharge their carbines into the thick brush and then returning to their positions in the hollow square. For a few minutes the artillery shelled the timbered hollow, and then General La Prade evidently ordered them to shift their batteries into positions for new targets. Selkirk guessed that one of the targets would be the tipi village, although many of the lodges were now skeletons of poles, and some of these were being brought down with the skins to be transformed into travois for transportation.

He was suddenly aware of how low the sun was in the cloudless sky. Black shadows were beginning to form across the face of the mountain, but the dry heat persisted, drawing moisture from the flesh of men and horses. *At first dusk,* he told himself, *no matter what is happening on the field of battle, I will leave it, ride east away from Killdeer Mountain and then turn straight north for the border.*

Eight cannons fired simultaneously with a tremendous rocking roar that shook the ground and made his mount plunge forward, almost unhorsing him. As he steadied the jumpy animal, he saw Colonel Herrick and another officer approaching at a rapid trot. The officer wore light blue broadcloth, dusty and dark with sweat. A brigadier's star was mounted on the front of his wide-brimmed black hat. General La Prade.

He's in too big a hurry. He won't stop. Who am I? Captain Selkirk or Major Rawley? God, it's Rawley. How can I guess if he knew Rawley, and if he'll know I'm not Rawley? He let the horse turn so that he would be facing away from them as they passed, but Herrick yelled out: "Major! Boots into stirrups and get ready to move!"

Reacting automatically, Selkirk shouted to the sergeants, and the cavalry company was already mounted when he turned his profile to the colonel. General La Prade pushed his horse in between them. The general's face was flushed, his eyes bloodshot as he gave Selkirk a quick glance. "Major Rawley, is it?" Then he was staring, not at Selkirk but rather toward the east side of the mountain, pointing with a long forefinger that was just to the left of Selkirk's nose. "I want your cavalry to act as the stopper in a bunghole, major. Right there, that brushy ravine. Leads up to something my scouts called Dead Man's Gulch. Only way the red devils can get away without fighting us. We're going to pound all hell out of their village up there, put down a barrage behind them and make them come down here and fight us." La Prade's voice was hoarse and he talked so rapidly that tiny drops of spittle sprayed the side of Selkirk's face. "Your job is to work your way up that ravine to the gulch. Kill everything that comes down that trail. Your men have full cartridge boxes?"

"Yes, sir."

"Two of Colonel Herrick's scouts will guide you in. We can give you artillery support for getting in, if needed. Is that clear?"

"Yes, sir. Quite clear." The general was

already in motion, glancing back at him only once, frowning as though puzzled, and then spurred his horse on toward the artillery batteries.

The cannons were firing again. The tipi village was a tangled clutter of mangled poles and skins, with smoke rising from the ruins. He could hear the artillery officer shouting new commands. The bombardment to drive the Sioux down the slope would soon begin. Infantrymen and dismounted cavalrymen were already moving cautiously forward from the front of the hollow square.

Two of Colonel Herrick's veteran scouts came up quickly from the rear. One of them was the chief of scouts, a man named Ward. Long strands of grizzled hair hung over his ears. His wiry chin-beard thrust out belligerently when he spoke. "Ready when you are, major."

As the men were already mounted, he gave the march command and as soon as the column was clear of the square he increased the gait to a trot. When they were about a hundred yards from the mouth of the timbered ravine, twenty or more warriors came rushing out on foot, some firing rifles, others holding bows in readiness for the approaching cavalrymen.

Selkirk felt a wave of exultation flow through

his body, the first such sensation since that summer day a year ago when he'd raced across the Ohio hills with John Morgan, the day before the Union boys surrounded and captured the remnants of his company.

"Form fours! Draw sabers! Charge!" As he shouted the last command he remembered the green Minnesotans had no sabers, but he knew it made no difference. The Sioux were already vanishing into the ravine, and he ordered a quick countermarch as a signal to Colonel Herrick to clear the entrance with artillery. A few moments later the batteries began raking the ravine with case shot.

After the smoke lifted, Ward suggested they dismount and lead the horses in. "Not much underbrush," he explained. "We can get out in a hurry if need be."

Selkirk gave the commands to halt and dismount. "March by file," he added, and began following the two scouts through the battered scrub. In some places it would have been possible to remain in the saddle, but too many narrow passages and low tangles interrupted the trail. They passed one dead Sioux, his blood-soaked hair already covered with biting flies.

After no more than ten minutes the scouts signaled a halt. They picketed their horses and then motioned to Selkirk to follow them up a steep knoll. The narrow top was almost flat, covered with rabbit brush and small shrubs. Just below was a wider trail pocked with hoofprints and furrowed with travois markings. From above, the trail snaked down the mountain, turned sharply at the base of the knoll, and then dropped off toward the north. Far below they could see the dust of several ponies dragging travois.

"They've already started," Ward said. "This is their best way out. Blind cannon fire won't stop the buggers, but if they try to break through, sixty rifles concealed along the sides of this knob can pile 'em up like a jackrabbit kill."

Selkirk sent the horseholders back several yards with the mounts and deployed the dismounted men in the brush along both sides of the rise. The second scout volunteered to go forward about a hundred yards to the first bend in the trail so that he could signal the approach of any fleeing Indians. Ward took a position on a ledge directly across from Selkirk's left.

While they were preparing the ambush they could hear the roar and thump of concentrated cannon fire against the heights above them. Between the artillery explosions, the rattle of rifles was more intense than it had been at any time during the afternoon. Although he could no longer see the battlefield, Selkirk heard the cries of La Prade's infantrymen surging up the steepening slope of the mountain. He lay on his belly in the rabbit brush, his field glass fixed on the upper trail.

Ward turned on the ledge, jerking a thumb toward Selkirk, who rose up on one knee. "Make ready!" Selkirk called to the sergeants. "Fire only at my command."

Up the trail a dozen warriors on foot showed themselves at the first turn. They were moving cautiously, the ones in the lead darting in and out of the brush. Selkirk could feel the tension of his men concealed in the undergrowth. He glanced across at Ward. The scout had flattened himself against the rock, his pointed chin-beard thrust upward, waiting.

At the bend behind the warriors appeared a confused clutter of travois, loose ponies, dogs, women and children, all hastening down the slope, setting stones to rolling and swirls of dust to rising. The scarlet blankets and bright-colored clothing of the women formed irregular spots of color against the drabness of the oncoming mass.

He thought he heard a low birdcall, then caught the frantic motion of Ward's arm signaling him to some action. The forward guard of warriors was in easy range. He gave the command to fire, and the responding crackle of rifles was startling in its loudness, reverberating among the surfaces of upthrust rock.

Excitement, inexperience, he'd seen the same wretched rifle fire in the early days with Morgan's men. And the targets, the warriors, they moved like dancers. He saw only two down in the trail, both riddled, but the others had vanished. They were loose somewhere in the brush. His unseasoned men knew that as well as he. They'd be skittery now, even less accurate in their next shots.

He'd expected the Indian women to slow the forward movement of the travois when their warriors were fired upon, but instead they seemed to be coming down faster than before. The scraping of travois poles, the barking of dogs, the cries of children all combined to create a weird windlike roar. An arrow streaked across the emptiness between him and Ward, but Ward was no longer there. He thought he could hear the scout moving somewhere below.

Already the onrushing women and children were approaching the turn in the trail, perfect targets. Several of the ponies they were driving before them bore recent wounds, their blood caked in dark maroon streaks or still oozing carmine from haunches or withers or necks.

If he was going to order his men to fire on the human components to this frenzied flight he must act now. *Kill everything that comes down that trail,* General La Prade had ordered. But these were not warriors. "Humanity," he whispered to himself. "No matter how savage. Humanity."

The face of the first Indian woman in the throng suddenly was there below him, only a few yards distant, head lifted, dark eyes searching the landscape. She was as tall as most men, and walked in long rapid strides. Her confident air gave her a certain wild beauty. She was carrying a child in a cradle on her back, and held the rope bridle of a pony that was dragging a travois. Just as she passed in profile, a single rifle shot cracked from his right. "Hold your fire!" he yelled.

The bullet had hit the tall woman's pony. It leaped in pain and terror, overturning the travois it was dragging, spilling buffalo robes, dried meat, brass kettles, and a blanketed old woman into the trail. The pony galloped madly down the slope, dragging a broken pole. All the women now began running, some bending quickly to catch up whatever loose pouches or parfleches or pans that tumbled in their paths.

Another shot was fired from the same place.

A curl of gray smoke lifted from the brush. "God dammit, hold fire!" he cried out angrily. "Let their children and women pass."

"Squaws carry weapons," a voice retorted. He recognized the accent of one of the sergeants.

He ignored the warning. A hundred women and children, maybe more, moved swiftly past him, a stream of humanity that was alien to his world. *Kill everything that comes down that trail.* He heard the horses then like a rumble of thunder, some of them neighing, their flailing hooves knocking stones loose on the slope. They were a flood of duns and bays and roans and piebalds and sorrels and pintos. As the dust whirled and lifted he saw naked warriors astride some of them, quirting the backs of the riderless animals, and behind the horse herd was a number of additional men on foot, how many he could not tell.

They were coming with such velocity that he was certain they would overrun the women and children he had allowed to pass, but when he glanced to the right he saw no women and children, only their ponies hitched to bouncing travois far down the trail. The women and children had vanished into the woods cover, no doubt joining the advance guard of warriors, or decoys as he now realized they were.

Reacting to a slight crunch of gravel, he spun quickly around, rifle at the ready. Ward was crouched on the edge of the rocks behind him. "If you'd stopped them travois, major," he said, "the trail would be so jammed that horse herd would panic back on its haunches. Now all hell couldn't stop 'em."

The animals were sweeping by already, saffron dust rising in a cloud, dust so thick he could catch only glimpses of running warriors among and behind the horse herd. As the din died, he heard scattered firing close at hand, then farther away.

"The humanity," he said, rising to his knees. "Women and children —"

"Was it that white woman made you hold fire?" Ward asked bluntly.

He raised his head. "I saw no white woman."

"They had one. A captive, I reckon. I think I seen her before — that Steever woman. With the immigrant wagons. I thought maybe you —"

The more distant firing off to the right resumed, and another arrow hissed through the air above the now empty trail. A sergeant called out: "Indians on our right, major."

"Them raw Minnesota boys of yours," Ward observed casually, "won't stand a chance, woods-fighting."

"Yes, we're outflanked," Selkirk said. He

shouted to the sergeants to withdraw the men toward the company's horseholders.

The cavalrymen came out of the brush quickly, turning to fire their weapons without aiming as they retreated into the narrow ravine. A few were helping to carry the casualties, a dozen at least. They fell back quickly to the horse herd. The second scout, the man who had concealed himself up the gulch to signal, was waiting for them there.

"What in hell happened, Ward?" he asked, forcing a false laugh.

Ward shook his head, saying nothing. Three horsemen were coming up the ravine from the prairie. The one in front was Colonel Herrick.

Leading his mount, Ward hurried forward to meet the colonel. Herrick dismounted quickly, tossing his reins to one of the aides. They were too far away for Selkirk to hear what was being said, although Herrick gestured wildly as he spoke. Once Ward turned and pointed either toward Selkirk or the knoll. Then both men mounted and started back toward the prairie.

For Selkirk everything held a dreamy quality; even the sepia light of the dying day was trancelike. He was walking, fairly rapidly he supposed, following the others out of the ravine, but he felt as if he were floating slowly through the shell-torn brush. He had to lead his mount to one side when a team of draft horses came charging into the ravine with a six-pounder gun. The artillery officer shouted a command to halt. "Drop the trail, drop the trail!" he cried. "Right there on that hump of ground. It'll give you enough elevation."

The cannon was already shotted, and before Selkirk had gone a dozen paces a gunner was standing beside it, lanyard in hand, preparing to fire the first shell. They were still firing blindly toward the gulch when he led his horse out of the brush and got into his saddle.

His cavalrymen were scattered along the open slope, some mounted, some dismounted. The casualties lay in the dry grass, two or three of the men moaning, most of them quite still. Dr. Lieber and his hospital steward were hastily cleaning and bandaging the worst wounds. Colonel Herrick and General La Prade were just beyond the casualties, their knees touching when their horses jostled together. Both were looking at him as they talked rapidly, snatches of their words being borne to his ears on a rush of air flowing down the shadowy face of Killdeer Mountain. "Unfit . . . seven dead! . . . white woman . . . inquiry . . . his father the senator . . . under garrison arrest . . . convalescent . . . us off . . . Surgeon Lieber . . . hush . . . inquiry."

Some of the words stung; others made no sense to him. He was about to shout an order to the sergeants to form the company when General La Prade abruptly slapped his horse into motion and came slowly toward him, his face turning grim when he glanced at the casualties.

Selkirk stared calmly into La Prade's angry eyes as the general pulled his horse up sharply in front of him. "You failed," La Prade said accusingly.

"I know, sir."

"You are relieved of command and charged with conduct unbecoming an officer. Until your return to Fort Standish I'm placing you under the medical care of Surgeon Lieber."

"Yes, sir."

La Prade looked toward the dead and wounded on the grass. "There must be an official inquiry, of course. Because of the casualties." He sighed. "To spare your father we'll try to keep the incident within the Dakota command."

"Yes, sir."

La Prade turned his horse and rode rapidly away, leaving Herrick there in his place, facing Selkirk.

"Damn you," Herrick said in a hissing under-tone. "If you were a nobody I'd have you court-martialed and shot. La Prade blames me for letting Spotted Horse and his braves out of the trap. His commander will blame him. God knows who Senator Rawley will blame if he finds out he has a coward for a son."

The colonel jerked at his reins and bellowed at the sergeants: "Form your ranks and prepare to mount!"

Without glancing at Selkirk he added quietly: "Give Lieber a hand. Until we reach Fort Standish, you're under garrison arrest to the surgeon's ambulance wagon. I assume you are a gentleman and will confine yourself to that area."

"Yes, sir."

For the first time he felt a sense of disloyalty, not disloyalty to the U.S. Volunteers but a betrayal of the man they all believed him to be, Charles Rawley. He had never really liked Rawley. The man had always been arrogant, vain, self-seeking, a braggart, a poor loser with a streak of viciousness in him that repelled Selkirk.

Yet he owed Rawley something; the Rawley family had a good name. After all, that name had protected him for weeks. If he fled to Canada now, the action would be viewed as cowardly, a betrayal of the Rawley name. He let the thought of flight recede in his mind. He had failed the ghost of Major Rawley, and somehow he felt he must atone for that failure.

7

It was morning and the *Roanoke* was moving. I could feel sunlight on my eyelids and knew the hour was very late before I opened them and blinked into the beam slanting through the narrow window of the stateroom. Lying on my back in the lower bunk, I believe I had not moved a muscle since falling asleep late in the night. I'd fallen asleep after my guest on the bunk above had finished his tale of Killdeer Mountain. Or had I? How much of it was mixed in my own dreams, how much was colored by fantasies of his disordered imagination, how much was reality? At least *he* was real, breathing like a softly purring cat, just above my head.

The *Roanoke* chattered and shuddered, using the full power of its engines to stem the Missouri current. While I was dressing, I peered through the dingy windowpane. The river flow was swift after the night's rainstorm. Dead limbs, logs, and occasional small trees raced past. I was suddenly very hungry, and wondered if I'd awakened too late for breakfast.

"I'll bring you something," I said to the man in the upper bunk, but he did not reply. He was curled into a bearlike hibernation when I left him.

Only two people were still at breakfast, Nettie Steever and the Indian girl, Towanjila. As the other tables had been cleared and pushed back against the walls, I asked permission to join them.

"Late sleepers can't be choosy of their company," Nettie replied. Her voice was not very friendly, but her eyes were bright and I could see no hostility in them. Her face was younger than when I'd last seen her in the night, and I recalled one of Dr. Lieber's sayings — that a good night's sleep will do more for a woman's face than all the beauty creams in Araby.

Late though it was, a good supply of baked ham, poached eggs, and corn muffins were left on the table platters. The food was no warmer than the tepid coffee, but as Nettie remarked, late risers can't be choosers on Captain Adams's *Roanoke*.

"Your cabin mate is still asleep, I suppose," Nettie said, her words startling me into spilling a large splash of coffee. "Don't look so sheep-faced," she added. "I shan't peach on you to the captain." She was buttering a muffin as calmly as though she had merely made an insignificant observation on the state of the weather.

"I thought that was *my* secret," I finally replied.

"Towanjila saw you last night when you brought him up from the main deck." She exchanged conspiratorial looks with the Indian girl. Each seemed to be having difficulty in controlling a strong inclination to laugh at me. I remembered how last night I'd thought I saw a wraith on the outer promenade, and how my strange guest had gripped my shoulders and stopped me in my tracks. So Towanjila had been there. But why? At that moment a repressed smile showed faintly at the corners of the girl's lips.

"What does it matter to you two?" I asked somewhat huffily. They reminded me of mischievous schoolgirls, quite unlike the somber pair I'd met the evening before.

Nettie gave me a broad teasing smile (she had remarkably white and even teeth for a woman who had endured so many hardships) and although I was provoked I could not help but admire her utter frankness. "Oh, we know this buckeen you've taken in, or maybe has taken you in, to put it proper." She laughed, showing those fine white teeth. "He's off his head. Pay him no mind, he's never who he says he is."

"Who do you think he is?" I demanded.

"A sly-tongued miserable person of no importance," she answered evenly. He had said that of himself, I remembered, *I am no one of importance.*

I poured another cup of the lukewarm coffee. "I think he is of importance to both of you," I said. "Otherwise you'd not concern yourselves with his presence in my stateroom."

To my surprise Towanjila pressed one of her small hands gently against the back of my hand that was resting on the table. Her voice in English was metallic, forced out like the sounds of those hollow Indian-rubber dolls that little girls squeeze to make whistling noises. "He is father of child," I thought she said. She tapped her breast with one finger. "My child." She was wearing earrings with tiny blue-and-red stone pendants that moved like fluttering butterflies when she spoke.

"Yes," Nettie said. "For that reason he must be looked after."

Towanjila held the fingers of one hand together, and pointing them upward in front of her forehead, she began spinning her hand gracefully at the wrist. "Foolish," she said in that mechanical tone of hers. "Foolish in head."

Nettie was pushing her chair back from the table. "He'll go back to Bell's Landing on the first downriver steamboat," she promised. She and the Indian girl excused themselves and went off toward the ladies' cabin.

After they'd gone I took one of the unused napkins from the end of the table, unfolded it, placed some muffins and a generous slice of ham upon it, and tied the ends together. Thrusting the napkined packet into my side pocket, I turned and started toward the exit to the outer promenade. Smiling at me from a chair beside the melodeon was Kathleen Hardesty, her red hair neatly coiffed, her green eyes looking into mine. She was holding some music sheets in her lap. I had no idea how long she'd been there; I'd thought the central lounge was empty.

"A pleasant morning to you, Mr. Morrison," she greeted me. I mumbled a reply.

"Don't tell me you're a secret gormandizer," she went on gaily, her eyes fixed upon the bulge in my side pocket. "Or do you have a pet that must be fed, hidden away in your state-room, a dog perhaps?"

I wanted to tell her it was none of her damned business, but I did not. Fortunately the exit door was flung open before I found words to reply, and Captain Adams stepped in, bringing with him a gust of fresh Dakota air. "Ah, Sam Morrison. And Mrs. Hardesty." He rubbed a finger over his drooping mustache. "Mrs. Hardesty and I missed you at breakfast, Sam."

"Yes, I'm as slow as the *Roanoke* this morning."

"Current's strong and winds contrary," he replied in a defensive tone. "But Mr. Allford assures me we'll make it to Fort Standish — Fort Rawley, that is — by tomorrow afternoon."

Mrs. Hardesty put the music sheets aside and stood between us, her eyes shining as she kept her gaze on me. "Captain Adams has invited me to visit the pilothouse," she said in the manner of a young girl boasting about a special favor.

The captain bowed, his face flushing slightly. "Ah — Sam," he said to cover his embarrassment, "Doc Lieber and Emilie have been looking about for you. They're both up by the texas."

"I'll join them after a moment."

"Yes. Advise you to wear a heavier jacket. Wind's brisk and rather chilly up there."

With his usual exaggerated air of courtliness, Captain Adams ushered Mrs. Hardesty out upon the promenade. I followed them as far as the door of my stateroom.

Everything seemed to be as I'd left it except I could no longer hear the soft snoring of my guest. He was not in the upper bunk. The pillow and blanket had been neatly smoothed and folded. "Selkirk," I called quietly. The closet door was ajar and no one was in there.

"The damn fool," I said aloud, and pulled the tied napkin from my pocket and placed it on top of one of the biscuit tins beside the wall. My sympathies for that strange hollow-eyed man began to ebb. He would not stay put either in my stateroom or in my mind. Yet again I had an odd feeling that if I did not keep close track on him, he would become no more than vapor, an illusion of my own imagining.

Before going up to the hurricane deck, I made a quick circuit of the *Roanoke*, peering into nooks and crannies, searching around the boilers and engines, and opening the doors of unlocked closets, but I found no sign of my missing guest. I left the hurricane deck for the last. As I came up the front companionway, Kathleen Hardesty shouted a greeting to me from the pilothouse. All I could see of her was her smiling face above the twelve-foot wheel, one edge of which she held with both hands. Captain Adams and Henry Allford stood at her sides, both wearing tomcat grins from ear to ear.

On the deck below the open window of the pilothouse, Dr. Lieber and his wife Emilie were seated in one of the double chairs. Emilie was bundled into a white blanket coat with a red scarf over her head and ears.

"Quite a change in the weather," I said.

"It'll warm up soon enough," she replied. "We're enjoying the invigorating air while we can."

Lieber nodded. "Delightful. If only our female pilot" — he rolled his eyes upward to indicate Mrs. Hardesty at the wheel — "keeps us afloat."

Emilie laughed. "Konrad is saying that only for my benefit, Mr. Morrison. He's as silly about that woman as are Captain Adams and Mr. Allford. Not to mention that jaunty young lieutenant colonel."

"Sam has paid her far more attention than I," Lieber protested. "Put him on the list."

"Mr. Morrison is too worldly-wise to be taken in by specious coinage —" She stopped, her head turned to listen. The object of our gossip, escorted by Captain Adams, had descended from the rear of the pilothouse and in a moment she rounded the corner of the texas, her musical voice never ceasing. "Time for charades," she cried enthusiastically. "Come along, you three."

"I do enjoy charades," Emilie responded. "Konrad? And you, Mr. Morrison?"

Lieber glanced at me. "I believe I promised to give our journalist a bit of information he is seeking."

"Can't it wait?" Mrs. Hardesty asked.

"Shan't take long," I said. "We'll join you later."

She shook her head impatiently. "Oh, well, we have the captain. And Lieutenant Colonel Harris promised to gather a few of his acquaintances. We need men, you know." She tried to lock her green eyes into mine, but I turned deliberately to gaze at a distant herd of antelope running far out on the plain.

After they'd gone down the companionway, Lieber smiled. "I must be getting old," he said. "When I was courting Emilie back in Saint Louis, I loved charades. Now they tend to bore me." He rubbed his hands together. "I suppose you want me to tell you about Killdeer Mountain."

"No, I'd rather you told me about Major Rawley, after he was put under arrest and confined to the area of your ambulance."

"Ah. Did I mention that? Well, he was in a state of black dejection the first few hours. My young hospital steward and I had more than we could do — you see, General La Prade left all his wounded with us when he dashed off in pursuit of the fleeing Indians. Not too many serious wounds, but they all had to be looked after. I soon realized that what Major Rawley needed was to be kept busy, to force his mind off his despondency. I put him to helping me with two nasty arrow penetrations. The arrowheads were in his cavalrymen so he had a personal interest in seeing that I removed them with as little flesh damage as possible. One was a hip wound to the bone, the other deep into a shoulder. As beautiful a pair of arrowheads as I ever saw, splendid workmanship, tooled and attached to the shafts in such a way to cause the victims to slowly bleed to death if not removed. I have both in my collection. Be pleased to show them to you sometime in Saint Louis."

At dawn of the day following the battle, Lieber told me, Colonel Herrick assigned a small detail to bury the nine soldiers who had died in the fighting and during the night. He ordered Major Rawley (or Selkirk) to take charge of the burial party. More than half the dead were from the major's cavalry company, and Herrick made that point, quite cruelly, Lieber thought. The major stood by while the graves were dug deep, the bodies carefully covered, the surfaces leveled, and horses marched across the ground to conceal their presence. He tried to find a drum and bugle to formalize the final rites, but all the musicians had gone with General La Prade's pursuit column.

During the morning, Colonel Herrick ordered his troops to move up to the site of the Indian village and destroy what was left of it. There they found several dead Sioux, a few wounded ponies, and a large number of dogs that had been left behind in the precipitate retreat of the Indians. Herrick ordered the dogs and ponies shot and the Sioux buried under stones. Although Lieber's ambulance and wagon followed the column up the slope, both he and the major were occupied in keeping the wounded men as comfortable as possible and they took no part in the final action at Killdeer Mountain. Instead, during the last hour or so they were quiet spectators of the total destruction of what remained of the tipi village. Everything that would burn — poles, skins, buffalo robes — were heaped into piles and set to blazing. Large quantities of dried meat and berries that had been collected by the Indians for use during the coming winter, and hundreds of buffalo bladders filled with marrow and other fats and oils were added to the fires. Kettles and pots were smashed or punched full of holes. Occasionally a soldier or one of the scouts would keep a robe or a bladder, attaching it to his pack.

During this time, Dr. Lieber and the major relaxed in the shade of the ambulance, chewing on stale hardtack and trying to swallow coffee made from exceedingly unsavory water.

"They had a white woman captive," the major said suddenly, turning to look directly at Lieber. "That's why I could not bring myself to give the command to fire."

Lieber said nothing for a few moments. He rummaged in an old leather bag that lay beside one of the ambulance wheels until he found a half-empty brandy bottle. He held the bottle up and when the major nodded he poured a few drops into his coffee cup. "The scouts told me about her," the surgeon said then.

"She was Nettie Steever," the major declared. "I caught only one glimpse of her. I keep seeing her in my mind's eye, like a brightly lighted magic-lantern picture, frozen there. She was bent forward, her hair hanging over her face, something on her back. It's not clear." He stared helplessly at Lieber. "I did not want to believe what I saw. I refused to accept it — until it was too late to fire on that mob — of humanity."

At the time Lieber did not know whether the major was imagining more than he had actually seen. But three days later the vision was given some substantiation when Colonel Herrick's troops arrived at Heart River to resume escort duties for the civilian wagon train bound for Montana. One of the Iowa mounted infantrymen informed Lieber and the major that the Steevers' wagon had slipped away from the corraled train soon after General La Prade left, and nothing had been heard from them since. "So far as old man Steever's concerned, I'd say good riddance," the infantryman added. "But I do feel sorry for the woman. If the redskins took her."

"Did you see any Indians about?" the major asked anxiously.

"They harassed us in the mornings the first two days," the man replied. "Then they went off."

Lieber and I were bathed in full sunlight now in our chairs below the *Roanoke*'s pilothouse, and the pleasant coolness of the morning was rapidly being displaced by warm humidity. "Colonel Herrick's orders were to escort the wagon train west to Flat Top Butte on the Little Missouri," he said, "and await a rendezvous there with General La Prade. We spent a week getting to the Little Missouri, and then had to wait another week before La Prade came back down from the north."

"How did the major behave during this time?" I asked.

"Very well, although he had little to do. He was deliberately shunned by his fellow officers and had no one to talk with except the hospital steward and me, and oh, yes, Sergeant O'Hara came around frequently. The major could not keep his mind off his failure to order his men to fire that afternoon at Killdeer Mountain. At least once a day he would tell me of seeing the woman, Nettie Steever, in the midst of the fleeing Indians, a bright magic-lantern picture in his mind, he would say. He described everything about her in the most minute details.

"He was quite nervous the day General La Prade rejoined us, spending much of his time in the ambulance or the canvased wagon. La Prade had chased Spotted Horse's Sioux to the Canada line, but there the general was forced to halt. He was forbidden to cross into the British possessions where the Indians found refuge. La Prade was in a foul mood because he had been unable to overtake the Sioux, and I was relieved to learn from Colonel Herrick that at next daylight we should be prepared to start the long march back to Fort Standish. It was a pleasure to escape the presence of such a martinet as La Prade, as well as being rid of responsibility for the civilian wagoners. A greedy, inconsiderate, impatient lot, most of those gold-seeking low-lifers were. As for La Prade he soon afterward was recalled to the East, for some sort of supererogatory assignment to General Grant's rear headquarters. He was replaced by General Sully, a far more effective commander, and events gradually settled down out here. The departure of La Prade from Dakota probably saved Major Rawley from dismissal by the army, or worse, but there is no way of knowing that for certain.

"The march back to Fort Standish was an unpleasant business. We had so slender a stock of hard bread that we were on one-third rations the last few days. Water was also in short supply, and what we could find was unpalatable. We had no grain for the horses, and grasshoppers had consumed all vegetation except for the very coarsest bottomland grass and leaves of willow trees along drying stream beds."

A crosscurrent of wind caught the blue-gray woodsmoke pouring from the steamboat's stacks above our heads, sending swirls of it down upon us. "I suppose we'd better make an appearance for Mrs. Hardesty's charades,"

Lieber said without enthusiasm. He held a handkerchief over his face against the smoke, and we started for the companionway.

"The hearings on the major's conduct at Killdeer Mountain?" I asked as I fell into step beside him. "What was the outcome?"

"Nothing really happened in the end. To keep himself in the clear Colonel Herrick questioned and crossquestioned everyone who was in any way remotely connected with Major Rawley at Killdeer Mountain. Herrick ran the hearings in rigid military fashion. They went on well into the month of November. On the last day, when he announced solemnly that in his opinion no further proceedings were necessary in the case, he informed young Rawley that he must remain under garrison arrest at Fort Standish until the record of proceedings could be transmitted to the judge advocate general in Washington for a decision on further action.

"At Herrick's request I read the final record that he carefully composed. There was nothing in it that could possibly bring the major a reprimand from higher command. Herrick was quite aware that the powerful Senator Rawley sat on important congressional committees relating to the War Department, that he was a self-appointed adviser to high government officials, possibly even to the judge advocate general. The colonel was not a man to drop hot irons into anybody's lap. So there was no reason for Major Rawley to remain at Fort Standish. He not only had been removed from command of the Minnesota cavalry company, he had been replaced as commander of the Galvanized Yankee battalion which remained through the autumn and winter down at Fort Rice."

We turned into the promenade that would lead us to the central lounge. "What did he do with himself all those days of waiting?" I asked.

"I brought him books to read. He was allowed to ride within the stockade. We talked for hours in the late evenings."

"What did you talk about?" I persisted.

"Damn you newspaper scribblers. I remember he was especially interested in Colonel Herrick's obsession, which I told him about."

"What was —"

"The obsession?" Lieber smiled, somewhat derisively, I thought. "Herrick was determined to capture old Spotted Horse. Capture the chief and take him personally to Saint Paul for a public hanging. He went so far as to send a cavalry patrol far up near the Canada border. For a while he was convinced that Spotted Horse would bring his people back across the line before winter. I have no proof of it, but I sincerely believe that Herrick employed a fur trader to go to Fort Manitou, the British outpost near where Spotted Horse was said to be camped. At any rate the trader reported to Herrick — along in November as I recollect — that Spotted Horse and his followers were in tipis a few miles west of Fort Manitou. From that day, Herrick spent all his time planning a raid into Canada to seize Spotted Horse and bring him back to Fort Standish. Much of what he was planning was done in secret. He and the trader — Fromboise his name was — were always talking together in the colonel's office, their voices low and indistinct. Yet Herrick was so full of his scheme he had to tell some of it — mostly to me, I gather."

"And you passed the story on to the major?"

"To keep him alive."

We were nearing the door that led into the central lounge. I caught Lieber's arm and pulled him to a stop beside the guardrail. "Why didn't he run away?" I asked quietly. "Just leave the damned fort?"

The doctor's mouth opened in surprise. "He'd have sooner given up his own life. I'm surprised you'd ask that, Sam — the honor of the Rawleys — you must know as much about that as I."

I still held on to his arm. "Are you certain the major *was* Charles Rawley?"

His eyes stared into mine for a moment before he laughed. "Why in heaven would he not be?"

"Did he write to his family?"

"I'm certain of it. A letter or two came for him on almost every upriver steamboat. From a sister, from his mother, probably from the senator. Yes, I recall writing a brief letter for him to the senator, also one to the sister."

"Why you?"

"He'd sprained his writing hand badly. Stumbled while mounting a horse. Asked me to write a few words so that his sister would not worry about him."

"That was before he went to Canada?"

"Yes." He pulled slowly away from my grasp on his arm.

"What did he ask you to write his sister?"

Lieber swore a mild German oath. His accent was also beginning to thicken. "My God, Sam. What are you driving at?"

The door to the lounge opened and the green eyes of Kathleen Hardesty were fixed with mock severity upon us. "I thought I heard males voices out here," she said in a scolding tone. "We need you both for the next charade." She lowered her voice to a whisper: "Can you pantomime 'Pretty Betty Martin'?"

I must have blinked in surprise.

"You know the ballad?" she asked.

Only a few hours earlier, down beside the boat's boilers, I'd heard Selkirk singing the words softly. Only he'd sung "Pretty Kathy Martin."

"Nettie Steever suggested it," she added.

Early that afternoon we rounded a bend and stopped at Dutchman's Landing for wood. Captain Adams apologized for abandoning the checkers game we were playing, and I walked down to the boiler deck with him to watch the wood brought aboard. "Damnation!" he cried in a tone of disgust, after a measuring glance at the woodpile on the bank. "There's not enough wood there to take us to Fort Rawley. The *Roanoke* burns a cord an hour upstream." He began ordering the crew ashore with axes and saws to cut a few trees from a thinning grove that stood along high ground above the mouth of the little creek flowing into the Missouri. It was easy to perceive that this was a task that none of the crew cared for. They moved reluctantly along the gangplank as they left the boat.

Three Indians in white man's clothing were sitting on a log beside the low pile of cordwood. "I'll have to go and pay them," Captain Adams said plaintively, "or they'll never haul that wood aboard."

Instead of going ashore with him, I moved over to the guardrail and rested my arms on the rough planking, watching idly. A moment later I heard Nettie Steever's heavy brogans on the steps behind me. When I turned she nodded briefly, but her attention was on the captain and the three Indians as she joined me at the railing. After the captain left them and started toward the woodcutting crew, the Indians began bringing the billets aboard. To reach the woodrack beside the boilers they had to pass close beside Nettie and me. The man in the lead was wearing one of those knitted scarlet caps fancied by Canadian fur trappers, the color badly faded. He had pulled it low and in a slant over his forehead so that it gave him the air of a buccaneer. The Indian's piercing gaze shot beyond me to Nettie, and when I glanced at her I knew that some secret and silent communication passed between them. The faces of the other two Indians gave no hint of recognition.

As soon as they dropped their heavy loads of cordwood into the rack, they turned and started back toward the gangplank. Nettie stepped forward, raising a hand, her face as composed as the faces of the Indians, saying something quickly in Lakota to the man wearing the faded scarlet cap. His eyes shifted to me. His voice in reply to her was as deep as the bass tones of an organ. She spoke again, and then stepped back to the rail. He frowned, gave me what seemed to be a cold and measured look, and turned to follow his two companions.

"You know them," I said to Nettie.

"Yes."

I moved closer to her. "Last night you told me that when Charles Rawley was killed in the explosion and fire at Fort Standish that you were at a woodyard near Dutchman's Landing. These Indians came from that same woodyard?"

She shrugged, her face turning hard and indifferent.

"The stranger in my cabin last night —"

She turned and cried triumphantly: "He's no longer there!"

"He also is from the woodyard, is he not?"

"He's only a rover." After a quick glance at the three Indians loading themselves with billets, she moved toward the stairway.

"Do you know him as Selkirk?" I called after her.

She paused only momentarily before starting up the steps. "He's whoever he says he is." She tapped her forehead with her finger. "Daft as a henhussy."

Before dinner that evening I returned to my stateroom. The napkin I had left tied around the muffins and cold ham lay flat and empty atop one of the biscuit tins, a few crumbs left upon it. Selkirk, Rawley, or whatever his name, was still on board the *Roanoke*, yet for some reason he had abandoned my stateroom as a hiding place.

After dinner the dancing began as it had on the previous evening, with Kathleen Hardesty first playing the melodeon and then being succeeded by the noisier and less musical performers of the crew. Mrs. Hardesty was wearing a lowcut dark green dress that seemed to turn her eyes an even deeper green, and also revealed the bareness of her upper breasts. Every male on board, young and old, eagerly sought her as a partner. I was able to dance with her but once, and then was quickly replaced by Lieutenant Colonel Harris who soon lost her to someone else. I finally persuaded Nettie Steever to do me the honor, and was surprised at how easily she moved about the floor in those wretched brogans of hers. But she danced only a few measures before guiding me back to rejoin Towanjila.

The young Sioux refused even to try the dance floor, and when I endeavored to question her about the man who she said had fathered her child, she pretended not to understand a word I was saying. Nettie was of no help either. She only grinned at me, shaking her head along with Towanjila.

I suppose I was in a distraught mood that evening. What I most wanted was to find the stranger and get him to talking again. I was eager to know what had happened in Canada when he went there to find Spotted Horse. So I slipped away and prowled the boat, searching more thoroughly than I had done during the morning. When I finished, the hour was late but I was almost certain he was no longer aboard. If I could have ventured into the stateroom occupied by Nettie and Towanjila and found it empty, I might have been completely certain.

Next morning I was awakened by the sound of the *Roanoke*'s bell followed by a series of quick blasts from her hoarse whistle. The boat slowed at once, then backed with a loud splashing of the paddle wheel. It turned sharply in the river, but I could see nothing outside my stateroom window but the greening flatness of Dakota plain and the rippling waters of the Missouri, running much clearer than on the previous day. From somewhere on the starboard side came the sound of excited voices, but soon they died away and the boat resumed its motion upstream.

That morning I was an early arrival for breakfast. Only Kathleen Hardesty, Mr. Allford the pilot, and Enoch Adams were at the captain's table, and it was the captain who beckoned me to join them.

"What was all the ringing and tootling and commotion about?" I asked.

The captain glanced sidewise at me. "Henry saw a big fish just after going off midwatch," he said. "Thought it was a human."

"It was no fish," Allford retorted sharply. He split a hot biscuit with his knife and dropped a thick slice of butter between the halves.

"Barely daylight," the captain said mildly. "Could've been a barked log."

"Had hair on it," the pilot persisted. "You know I can read this river the way you read a newspaper, Enoch."

Captain Adams took a swallow of tea. "I saw a drowned Indian once, tumbling in that fast channel other side of Fort Pierre. Could as well have been a dark fish."

" 'Twarn't a fish. Had a man's coat fastened around it by the sleeves." Allford stared at me as if demanding my confirmation of his statement.

"The bell and whistle woke me up," Kathleen Hardesty said. She was wearing her peppermint-stick dress, and the peach-colored morning freshness of her skin made her unusually attractive. In spite of their continuing argument, neither the captain nor the pilot was able to keep his eyes off her.

"I beg forgiveness, ma'am," Allford said, "but it was necessary if —"

"You did try to rescue him, if it was a man?"

Allford threw his head back and downed the last of his coffee. "Oh, it was a man, leastways a human. There he was, flung up by the current but in that light I could not tell if he was struggling or if the force of the water made him seem to be. I signaled the engineer to stop the paddle wheel, so he was not cut to pieces when he was drawn astern. We saw no trace of him after that. He must've drowned for sure."

"Dreadful," she said, and for a second or two contorted her lovely face into images of horror and pity.

Allford arose reluctantly from his chair. "Must go look at my charts. We're coming up to Devil's Shoals, and from the looks of the flow none of that rain fell above here. May be shallower than I figgered."

"We will get to Fort Rawley today?" she asked anxiously.

"Most likely, ma'am, but 'twill depend on the sandbars. They could slow us some."

We reached the lower stretch of Devil's Shoals late in the morning. Sunlight gleamed from a series of slender rippled sandbars that resembled ribs along the right side of the river. The narrowed channel on the left appeared deep enough for the *Roanoke*, but Henry Allford declared it would be touch-and-go. "We're drawing all the water in the channel right now," he said, and turned to climb up to the pilothouse to assist his number two man. "Judging from the surface, I'd wager we'll need to use the capstan before we're around the big bend."

With Dr. Lieber I had been listening to some of Allford's tales on the forward hurricane deck. After the pilot left us, we sat silent for a few moments, enjoying the sun and scenery.

"Amazing man, that Allford," Lieber remarked. "The way he can judge the depth of the muddiest of waters solely by surface appearances. I doubt if there is a furlong of this two-thousand-mile river whose characteristics he does not know."

Except for the panting of the engine and the

splashing of the paddle wheel the scene was remarkably tranquil. The day was turning off quite warm, with a gentle wind bringing the perfume of fresh grass from the plain. Beyond the sandbars along the right bank, the leaves of the tall cottonwoods seemed to be bursting forth in explosions of pale green as we moved slowly past them.

Voices broke over the steamboat's sounds. Captain Adams and Kathleen Hardesty were coming up the companionway to join us. He began bustling about officiously, pushing chairs in closer to the forward rail.

"Are you certain this is the place, Captain Adams," she asked, almost querulously, "where the expedition across the Malpais began?" She held some sort of sketchbook in one hand, a large pencil in the other, and was looking first at one side of the river and then the other. Dr. Lieber and I arose, shifting our chairs to make room for them. She gave each of us a quick smile. "I must sketch this place," she said. "Not that I'm much good at drawing, but I want a picture for the folio I'm preparing in memory of my late husband."

I was too surprised to ask her the question that came instantly to my mind and she went on, the words flowing tremulously: "These endless specimens of little bluffs and flat plains and low hills, day after day, day after day. It is like watching a long line of brothers and sisters and cousins from one of those big families back in Kentucky where they all resemble one another. I'll never understand how Captain Adams and Mr. Allford ever know where they are on this repetitive river."

She took the chair next to mine, while the simpering and mildly embarrassed captain seated himself on her other side, with Dr. Lieber beyond him. She laid the sketch pad on her lap and held the oversized pencil horizontally before one eye in order to sight upstream along it. "The exact spot, Captain Adams. I must sketch the exact spot where they left the *Effie Deans* and went ashore."

The captain cleared his throat and pointed beyond the sandbars. "Right along there, Mrs. Hardesty, about where that big cottonwood leans out a bit. The channel was narrow in low water — just as it is now. Oh, we were nosed deep in the sand that day. But an hour after Major Rawley went off with his platoon, we got a freshet rise and were soon on our way again. We put in at the Fort Standish landing next day for an hour or so, and I passed the word that the major and his men were out on the Malpais. We had no notion of what had happened, of course, and did not hear of the massacre until months later."

She was beginning to sketch rapidly. Her representation of the trees, the sandbars, and the narrowing river took on an airy form quite similar to that of a child's drawing. Several times she bent forward to erase a line, muttering softly to herself. "The perspective," she cried petulantly, "is all wrong. If only the boat would stop still."

"It very nearly has stopped," Captain Adams said. "We're beginning to wallow in the sand." Far below us the engine was throbbing, the entire boat seeming to strain against the burden of mud and sand.

"Do you mind us watching you sketch?" I asked her. "Perhaps we should go away so that you can concentrate in solitude."

"No, no." She turned, her face very close to mine, and put her hand quickly on my forearm as if to stop me from going. "I know how amateurish I am, but I don't mind." She frowned at the river scene for a moment. "I'll bet any one of you gentlemen could do a better delineation than I."

In chorus we all protested that we could not approach her efforts. And then from the open window of the pilothouse behind us, a torrent of profanity sounded above the noise of the stalling steamboat. The *Roanoke* came to a complete stop, the paddle wheel continuing to turn slowly.

Captain Adams whistled as he sprang from his chair. Mumbling an apology to Mrs. Hardesty for Henry Allford's strong language, he started for the pilothouse. "We're in for a capstan pull," he explained hastily. "Henry will be calling for a charge of tar and resin to raise steam pressure in the boilers." He hesitated briefly on the steps. "Bits of fire may issue forth in the black smoke, Mrs. Hardesty. A wind change would make things unpleasant up here."

She answered him without slowing the quick movements of her hand: "I'll go down as soon as I've finished."

After a minute or so she sighed, added a few hasty smudges with the edge of her pencil, and abruptly closed the sketchbook. "It's so strange. To know that Drew walked up that very riverbank. Marched off to die."

I glanced at her profile, expecting to see grief on her face, a tear perhaps, but instead she was smiling. "I did not know," I said, "that he was with Major Rawley's platoon."

"Nor I." Lieber spoke louder than was usual for him, his words slightly accented. "I have not inquired, thinking it a painful subject for you, Mrs. Hardesty. I assumed he was one of those at Killdeer Mountain."

Below us two men in a hastily launched rowboat were hurrying upstream to take soundings in the channel. "You intend to recover his remains from out there on the Malpais?" I asked.

"Yes. I owe that to him. When he's buried in Kentucky the last chapter of our lives together will be ended." Her hands nervously closed and unclosed against the cover of the sketchbook.

Lieber moved into the empty chair vacated by Captain Adams. His voice was kind and sympathetic, his words very thickly accented: "I think it would be wiser if you did not try to do this thing, Mrs. Hardesty."

"Why not?" she demanded. Her tone was that of one who has been challenged and is contemptuous of the challenger.

"The dead were buried in a common grave. The condition of the —" His voice broke off. He was trying to be considerate of her feelings. "You could never be certain of identity." He went on, stumbling over his words: "The place would be most difficult to locate. I was present the day of burial, but I could never lead anyone back there."

Her attention seemed fixed entirely upon the roustabouts below. In preparation for lifting the *Roanoke* over the sandbars, they were connecting ropes and pulleys to the capstan on the main deck. "Because I am a woman you underestimate me, Dr. Lieber." She spoke quite slowly as though measuring her words. "Before I began this journey I made many inquiries, made certain that what I wanted to do for Drew could be done. The sergeant who was in charge of the burial, Sergeant Joseph O'Hara, has assured me that he can take me to the grave."

"O'Hara!" Lieber almost shouted the name. The doctor's face revealed a mixture of astonishment, admiration, and perhaps anxiety. "You found O'Hara?"

"The army found him for me. He is at Fort Rawley."

"So he reenlisted?"

"No, he is a trader, I believe, of sorts."

Lieber nodded his head slowly. "Yes, I suppose O'Hara could find the grave. But the identification —"

"It will be grievous for me, I know that." She was still watching the men at work below. "However, there will be no uncertainty of identification. When I left the *Belle Peoria* to stop at Fort Rice on my way up here, the commander was gracious enough to let me see the descriptive roll of the men in Major

Rawley's platoon. The records give the height of each recruit. My husband was a good four inches taller than any other man in that platoon, Dr. Lieber."

"Ach," he said with a long-drawn-out sigh. "You do amaze me, Mrs. Hardesty."

From a crane on the bow below us, roustabouts were lowering two vertical poles that would serve as crutches to lift us over the sandbars. Clouds of oily black smoke were beginning to boil from the stacks above us, trailing swift shadows across the hurricane deck.

"We must go," she said firmly, and Lieber and I arose to accompany her. As we descended the companionway, the surgeon suggested that she would need more than the support of a former sergeant for the ordeal ahead of her. "I was present at the burials," he said. "I might be of some help to O'Hara in locating the place."

I also offered my services, perhaps more out of curiosity than of compassion. "Mrs. Hardesty," I added as we turned into the saloon-deck promenade, "did your husband enlist in the Galvanized Yankee regiment under his real name?"

"Yes, of course." She seemed slightly angered by my question. "Why would he not?"

"I've been told that many Confederate

prisoners of war used false names when they enlisted under the Union banner."

"Drew had nothing to hide. He enlisted as Drew Hardesty."

The engine turning the capstan began snorting so furiously that further conversation was impossible until after we entered the central lounge. "Do you have a list of the names of the ten men?" I asked her then.

She replied that she had not made such a list.

"Do you remember any of the names? Did you see the name Alex Selkirk?"

She closed her eyes for a moment, then shook her head. "I don't think so. No, I would surely remember such a name. Who was he? Someone you knew?"

As I could not tell her the answer, I lamely passed off my inquiry as a newspaper scribbler's vagary, an aberration of my simple mind.

An hour or so later, after the steam-driven capstan had lifted the *Roanoke* into deeper waters, and we were well on our way again, I rejoined Dr. Lieber in the gentlemen's cabin. While we drank our afternoon toddies he told me of how Major Rawley was persuaded to undertake the secret and illegal mission into Canada to abduct Spotted Horse.

The compact was made on Thanksgiving Day, he said. Colonel Herrick, after avoiding the company of Major Rawley for days, decided to invite him to the post's festal board for Thanksgiving. Observing Herrick's friendly treatment of Rawley, the other officers also unbent to some extent. Although no mention was made of Killdeer Mountain during the dinner, the other officers evidently assumed that Rawley had been cleared of the charges against him.

After dinner Herrick invited Rawley and Dr. Lieber to join him in his quarters for a brandy. Within minutes Herrick brought up the subject of Chief Spotted Horse.

"As I've mentioned before, Morrison," Lieber said, "that wicked Indian had become an obsession for Colonel Herrick. He ranted for several minutes about the chief's vileness, his cruel tortures of women and children, his black guilt for starting a slaughter of Minnesota settlers without warning. A thousand innocent whites had died at the hands of Spotted Horse and his bloodthirsty savages, Herrick claimed. A gross exaggeration, no doubt, and I have heard since that Spotted Horse was forced into that war against his will. But that is neither here nor there. Spotted Horse was in Canada, a fit subject for hanging but protected by the British. As a patriotic Minnesotan, Herrick believed it his duty to make certain the villain was brought to justice."

"Why didn't Herrick go himself and bring Spotted Horse out?" I asked.

"He would've gone across the line into the British possessions, but he had been unable to obtain permission to leave his post. He could not send a uniformed force across the border without creating an international incident. President Lincoln was having enough trouble with the British, and if Herrick was blamed for causing a confrontation with them, his military career would be ended. No, the capture of Spotted Horse must be done clandestinely, by ordinary citizens, using guile rather than force. It was a mission for a bold young man eager to make a name for himself.

"Not once did Herrick mention the political advantage that would come to him if he could supervise at the hanging of the most hated name in Minnesota. Nor did he invite Rawley to become that bold and eager young man. He did not have to invite him. Rawley volunteered, not guardedly but with a shy sort of eagerness. I could see that he was surprised when Herrick accepted him — the poor chap had lived with a such a low opinion of himself since Killdeer Mountain.

"Unfortunately Charles Rawley did not know what I knew of Herrick's ambitions. If the venture succeeded, Herrick would be launched on his political career. If the attempt failed and created an uproar, Herrick would surely disclaim any connection with it. If need be, he would have no trouble placing the blame entirely upon Rawley. Don't you see, Morrison, the young man had a record of disastrous failures."

Dr. Lieber swallowed the last of his toddy. Lifting his gold watch by its chain from a vest pocket, he clucked his tongue. "Time does move on. I'd best go help Emilie with our baggage. If Mr. Allford's forecast proves correct, we should be arriving at Fort Rawley within the hour."

Following him out of the gentlemen's cabin, I turned and took the outer passage to my stateroom. Standing at the rail a few feet from my door was Nettie Steever, a black scarf wound round her head. Instead of the usual indifferent, self-sufficient Nettie, she appeared to be perturbed, although her face revealed relief and expectancy at her first sight of me.

"If you had not come soon, I would've forced my way into your cabin," she said flatly. "Have you seen him today?"

"No. Do you think he's come back to my sanctuary?"

Irritated by my flippant manner, she hesitated a moment before answering: "They say the pilot saw a man in the river this morning."

I pushed the door in, and motioned her to enter.

We found no trace of him. I had left another napkin filled with bits of food on one of the biscuit tins but it had not been touched.

"Is he a good swimmer?" I asked.

She did not reply. Before she turned and hurriedly left my stateroom I saw the muscles of her face tighten against some overpowering emotion. Whether it was anxiety or terror or bereavement, or a mixture of the three, I could not tell.

8

Late in the afternoon the *Roanoke* turned a narrow bend in the river, and there before us was the Fort Rawley landing, with the freshly painted *Deer Lodge* moored at one end and a shabby old craft, the *Octavia,* at the other. Several young men were engaged in the frustrating task of unloading mules from the *Octavia,* and herding the stubborn animals along the riverbank.

After sounding several long blasts of his resonant whistle, Mr. Allford brought us smoothly and gently in between the other two steamboats. A few moments later the deckhands ran the gangplank out, and those of us who intended to remain for the commemoration next day hurried ashore.

A reception committee of three or four splendidly uniformed officers was there to receive the invited guests, whisking them away in a procession of buggies and converted ambulances that moved rapidly up a slope toward the new fort atop a bluff on our right.

Like two abandoned immigrants, Kathleen Hardesty and I were left there on the split-log landing, I with my worn leather bag, she with a small brass-ribbed dome trunk. Lieutenant Colonel Harris had circled us twice, chattering about seeing Miss Kathleen as soon as his duties were completed at the fort, and then hurrying off with the pompous air of a very important emissary of President Andrew Johnson. Emilie Lieber had called to us to join them in one of the ambulances, and Dr. Lieber was equally optimistic that quarters could be found for us in the fort. Even Nettie Steever waved in a beckoning gesture as the vehicles wheeled smartly away. Mrs. Hardesty, however, was determined to waste no time in finding the former sergeant, Joseph O'Hara, who was reported to operate a tavern in connection with his other enterprises.

My recent experiences with Missouri River hostelries had left me rather skeptical of the quality of such establishments, but I was willing to give O'Hara's tavern a trial. If the place was impossible, we could return for one night to our staterooms on the *Roanoke*. Captain Adams was delaying departure of the steamboat for twenty-four hours so that he and his upriver passengers might attend the next day's ceremonies at Fort Rawley.

I lifted Kathleen Hardesty's brass-ribbed trunk upon one shoulder and we set off up the dusty road. She volunteered to carry my bag and I offered no objection; Mrs. Hardesty was a healthy young woman, and her heavy trunk pressed upon my back like a hod of bricks. At the top of the first rise, the trail split, one road leading up to the fort, the other turning sharply to the left and forming a street of log, adobe, and plank structures. It was a duplicate of dozens of such streets that I'd seen on recent travels in the West. The buildings' high false fronts of planking made them appear to be much larger than they were. Strung across the street from the roof of one saloon to another was a brilliant-hued banner that read WELCOME TO FORT RAWLEY. The place-name was another characteristic of the American frontier. Towns that grow up around forts often take on the name of the military establishment they serve, so that long after the soldiers are gone and the stockades have rotted away the names on the maps will surely cause those who come after us to wonder at the reasons for such ubiquitous evidence of the martial spirit of the people who settled this Republic.

The names painted on the false fronts also revealed the variegated nationalities and races that came to the frontier – German, French, Spanish, Scandinavian, British, Asian, and others. Saloons predominated but the signs also included clothing stores, restaurants, bakeries, laundries, blacksmiths, gunsmiths, wheelwrights, saddlers. Everything was still in a state of creation, and the smells of paint and sawed wood drifted in the dusty air.

HOTEL COMO, J. O'HARA & G. MARTINI, PROPRIETORS. The sign above the wooden sidewalk was so new the letters glittered in a reflection of the setting sun. An Irishman and an Italian had formed a propitious alliance in one of the most improbable boomtowns on the Missouri, and within minutes all my doubts as to the quality of lodging accommodations had vanished. The rooms were very small but amazingly clean; the mattresses were stuffed with excelsior but they had not been pressed flat by use, and the inevitable cottonwood beetles and bedbugs had not yet invaded the premises. And as I was soon to discover, the Como's dining room supervised by Signora Martini offered the finest dishes served anywhere on the Missouri above Saint Louis. (But like many other transient communities of our movable frontier, it was all too good to last. When I stopped there on a later journey up the river I found the military post closed and the buildings of the once busy town of Fort Rawley occupied only by ghosts. A railroad had destroyed its bond with the lifegiving river.)

After Mrs. Hardesty and I were settled as guests in the hotel, she had no difficulty in persuading me to escort her in a search for Joseph O'Hara. Although she was not aware of it, I was as eager as she to meet the former sergeant. I wanted to hear his story of the journey to Canada with Major Rawley, or the *late* Alex Selkirk, if he had indeed drowned that morning in the backwash of the *Roanoke*.

When we went out into the dusty street the sun was already behind a streamer of flame-colored clouds facing us on the western horizon. From the open door of a saloon came the wailing of a sad and drunken troubadour. My musically inclined companion picked up the lost melody, humming softly, but her voice was soon overridden by the rhythmic shouts of an itinerant preacher. He stood upon an empty whiskey barrel, waving his bony arms and stamping his boots to emphasize his condemnation of the sins that flourished around him. A few yards farther along two men were arguing over the merits of a horse that one was desperately attempting to sell to the other. They seemed very close to blows, but backed quickly apart, stopping their flow of profanity in surprise at the presence of a well-dressed female on that gamy thoroughfare.

J. O'HARA, LIVERY AND OUTFITTER. The white letters almost filled the side of the last building on the street, a long low structure of brown-cemented adobe supported in cottonwood frames on a stone foundation. The dozen or so openings for windows were boarded up, awaiting the availability of glass panes. A corral beyond the building was crowded with mules. We entered the solitary door which stood ajar, and in the gloom of the unpartitioned interior gradually discerned the figures of a man and woman. They were counting buffalo hides, the man tying them into bundles, the woman marking the counts in a tally book.

"Are you Mr. O'Hara?" I asked.

"Yes." He cocked his head back, almost belligerently, waiting for us to explain our presence.

"This is Mrs. Hardesty," I said. "I'm Sam Morrison."

He smiled quickly and then introduced the woman with him, his French-Assiniboin wife.

Both seemed pleased by our interruption, probably because it gave them an excuse to cease temporarily their tedious work. O'Hara had a makeshift sort of office at the door end of the building, with pine boards for a floor, and log benches built into the walls. A desk had been improvised from a wooden packing case, which from its shape must have once housed a piano. His wife brought coals to life in the fireplace, and hung a coffee pot over them.

Joseph O'Hara, former sergeant, looked to be in his middle thirties. Because he was shorter in height than most men he had a habit of tilting his head back whenever he conversed. His skin was ruddy above a close-trimmed blond beard. He was stocky of build but was not swag-bellied in the way so many soldiers become after leaving military service. Energy was compressed within him like a spring, and a smile often flickered at the corners of his mouth. At first meeting he talked slowly and cautiously, but when he'd warmed to a subject he became garrulous, his words flowing in a graceful rhythm.

O'Hara informed Mrs. Hardesty that he had obtained permission from a Captain Lowe, the fort's acting commander, to disinter her husband's remains, and that a detail of cavalrymen would accompany her and O'Hara to the burial place on the Malpais. This could be done the day following the Fort Rawley commemoration. "Day after tomorrow, if it pleases you, ma'am," he added in that lilting manner of his.

"Day after tomorrow will be satisfactory," she replied.

He glanced at me and then looked sympathetically to her. "If you feel the task to be a trial for you, ma'am, I think we can manage it without you. After all, he was by far the tallest —"

"No, no," she insisted, and arose from the bench. "We will go early in the day, I suppose."

"At daylight. If we hope to be back before sundown."

"I shall be ready at sunrise, day after tomorrow."

Before we left I broached the possibility of a conversation with O'Hara later that evening, explaining that I was a correspondent for a Saint Louis newspaper and would like to ask him several questions about Major Rawley. He seemed surprised that I would single him out for that purpose, but did not object. "I will be late, sir," he said apologetically. "My boys and I must load buffler hides on the *Octavia*. After eight o'clock, maybe."

"Will I find you here?" I asked.

"Oh, no, sir. My wife and I have rooms in the Como."

I complimented him on the quality of his partnership hotel, and it was agreed that we would find each other later in the evening.

He found me on the hotel porch — I call it a porch, although it was really only a raised setback of the wooden sidewalk. From its hand-hewn benches it afforded an excellent close-up view of the picturesque throng passing back and forth along the short but bustling street. Out of the mauve light of dusk O'Hara appeared suddenly, like a migrating bird separating from a flock of its kind. He had recognized me, and his lips were curling in a smile. For the first time I noticed that his legs were bowed. He walked like a proud sailor, rocking with confidence, obviously a man well satisfied with his lot in life. "Give me a few minutes to wash up, sir," he said, cocking his head back. "Why don't you come on along to my quarters?"

The Como was two stories high, the rows of tiny rooms on each side divided by hallways. The building was narrow, but it ran all the way back to the edge of the low bluff that over-looked the Missouri. From a window of the O'Haras' cramped living room, the landing was in clear view, and I sat watching darkness fall over the three steamboats moored there. I could hear the muffled voices of O'Hara and his half-blood wife in a room overhead.

I marveled at their prosperity. How could he, on the meager pay of an army sergeant, have accumulated enough to start up these flourishing enterprises of his? Did his wife have money? Most unlikely. For that matter how had Nettie Steever acquired her establishment at Bell's Landing, the Steever House? O'Hara and Nettie. Both had been with Major Rawley on the return journey from Canada. Between them they could not have possessed enough funds to purchase a shanty. Now they both owned hotels.

He was coming down the slanted steps from the room above, his small booted feet almost dancing on the boards, his whole being filled with the hubris of the ancient Greeks, pride and arrogance. I had the impression that he was always struggling to keep his vanity from showing. He was no braggadocio, but it was there in his manner, almost a swagger when he moved.

Instead of lighting a candle, he put a match to the wick of an ornate oil lamp, and that act, the possession in itself, was a form of flaunting in that time and place on the frontier. His blue eyes, their color accentuated by the light, looked at me with unconcealed delight, the way a child's will when showing off some prize object. He had scrubbed his face and hands so that they glowed, and the starched white shirt he had donned for my benefit was a symbol, like the lamp, of his new civilian rank.

"You must be a natural man of commerce, Mr. O'Hara," I said, "to have built these prosperous businesses so soon after the war."

He made a little bow of thanks. "Luck," he insisted. "With some hard digging. I started right after my discharge from the army. Bought some worn-out wagons that'd been condemned by the quartermaster at Fort Standish."

He'd repaired the vehicles and filled them with excess rations left over at the end of the Civil War and hauled the stuff overland to the Montana gold fields. After that he became a trader to would-be miners coming upriver, greenhorns in need of tools and dried foodstuffs and mules — especially mules. For a miner a mule was a necessity, but none of the newcomers realized this until they stopped at Fort Rawley where J. O'Hara, Livery and Outfitter, sold mules at four times their cost in Saint Louis plus steamboat freight charges.

Very profitable, mules were, he declared with a cherubic smile, and went on to tell of how the miners who were lucky in their gold strikes had got into the custom of floating downriver on flat Mackinaw boats to spend their winters at Fort Rawley. They arrived well-stocked with pouches of gold dust, but with their threadbare clothing and cracked boots in need of replacement, and with unkempt hair and beards in need of trimming. They also had mighty hungers for whiskey and women. After they'd had their flings in the saloons and dance halls, those who still possessed any gold wanted comfortable lodgings and good meals. O'Hara had recognized the demand the year before, and when he found Giovanni Martini and his wife trying to make a living peddling pies from a tent, he saw them as the proper partners for his Hotel Como. The name, by the way, was Martini's suggestion.

A frontier success story, but a bit suspect, like a perfect hand in poker that one stares at in disbelief. I wanted to reserve judgment on the rapid postwar rise of ex-Sergeant Joseph O'Hara.

He poured whiskey from an unlabeled bottle into two wine glasses that bore a steamboat's name pained in gold on their sides. After presenting me with one of the drinks, he was ready to talk about Major Rawley.

"A strange sort of officer," he said. "Kept

things inside himself, if you know what I mean, sir. Acted odd at times. I laid it to that wound he'd got on the side of his cranium. At first I did. But later on, I wondered if perhaps he'd always been peculiar in his ways."

The party going to Canada consisted of four men – Major Rawley, Sergeant O'Hara, Antoine Fromboise the French trader, and a man named Ben Shanks. Shanks appeared suddenly at Fort Standish one day, and O'Hara readily discovered that he had been summoned from Saint Paul by Colonel Herrick. "A fidgety sort of man," was the way O'Hara described him. "Skin and bones." O'Hara was clever at finding out things about people. He soon knew that Shanks and Colonel Herrick had been partners in Saint Paul. Before the Sioux uprising in Minnesota, Shanks was an Indian agent. He had once been accused of cheating the Indians, but Herrick used his influence to get the charges dropped. Undoubtedly the two were bound up in various unsavory political schemes, and it was Shanks not Rawley who was Herrick's trusted agent in the plan to abduct Spotted Horse from Canada. Shanks carried the gold for bribery, and if gold failed and force failed, Rawley was there as a shield, a scapegoat.

"Snow came late in Dakota that winter,"

O'Hara said. "It was very cold as usual, but we'd had only flurries up to the time we left the fort. I wondered if we could get in and out of the British possessions and back to Fort Standish before a big January blizzard hit us. We prepared as best we could for it. As neither the major nor I would be wearing our uniforms I arranged with a trader for buffalo coats and muskrat caps and gauntlets. The buffalo robes were splendid, with quilted linings and soft buffalo-calf collars for covering our faces. The major was quite gratified."

"I've been told," I interrupted, "that Major Rawley sometimes resented the way you watched over him, guarded him like a helpless child."

He looked hurt. "And who would have told you that, sir?" he asked defensively, but without waiting for a reply continued: "The Assiniboins have a saying that if you save a man's life he becomes your burden. It was I who found him on the Malpais. While he was recovering I kept an eye on him, yes, and I was loyal to him after that business at Killdeer Mountain. If he resented me, he never showed it. In fact, in spite of our differences in rank, we were like brothers during that hard march in and out of the British possessions."

"Was he really eager to go?" I asked.

"I remember at first he wanted to know all about Spotted Horse, if he truly was a murderer, and if he would get a fair trial should he be brought back to Dakota Territory. Colonel Herrick swore the old chief would be properly tried, but allowed that evidence was mighty heavy against him. The colonel hated Indians. More'n once I heard him say the Sioux nation should be wiped out to the last man, woman, and child, the way the Israelites went after the Canaanites. Anyway, after Major Rawley was convinced that Spotted Horse should be captured, he was for it like a bear after honey, and once he'd started on the thing he put his whole soul into doing it right and proper."

O'Hara stopped to take a hearty swallow of his dark-tinted liquor, and I followed his example, almost choking on the stuff. It was not Irish whiskey, as I'd thought it might be, but was pure firewater, and from then on I only occasionally touched the tip of my tongue to that wild mare's milk.

"Of course there was another thing," he went on after wiping his lips on the sleeve of his starched white shirt. "The major felt disgraced by what happened at Killdeer Mountain. He wanted to prove that he was no coward. He thought if he went into the Sioux camp in

Canada and brought Spotted Horse back, nobody would ever look on him again as a coward. He talked to me about that later on. Redemption, he said it was.

"Well, one morning we left Fort Standish at sunrise. Ten below zero on the thermometer, with thin clouds of ice crystals overhead, but we had our buffalo robes and muskrat caps and gum-coated blankets. Also snowshoes for each of us in case of a storm. We took four spare horses, so we had a good supply of pickled pork and dried fish — and extra amounts of coffee and sugar for trading if need be. Ben Shanks was carrying the gold in a bag, how much I don't know, but he never let it out of his sight and you could tell by the way it sagged that it wasn't light."

On the second day's march they rendez-voused at Maison du Chien Butte with a Canadian named Amos Medlock. Antoine Fromboise had arranged the meeting some time before, and it was apparent to the shrewd O'Hara that the two men had been involved previously in various dealings across the border. Someone had built a solid shelter of rocks at the base of the butte, and it was there that they found Medlock with a retinue of several *métis* — half-bloods who worked for the trader. Medlock had some kind of license from the Hudson's Bay Company to trade with the native tribes.

After Fromboise finished with the introductions, Major Rawley ordered O'Hara to picket the horses on the lee side of the shelter, and the others went inside to escape a bitter wind blowing up from the north. When O'Hara finished his work and joined them, Medlock was explaining to Rawley the difficulties of dealing with the Hudson's Bay Company. "They rule everything in the western territories," he said. "They are the Queen's government."

"Every man has his price," Ben Shanks declared. He picked at his bony nose. "Who is head man at Fort Manitou?"

"Robert McDougall," Medlock replied. There was a tinge of bitterness in his tone. "Fancies hisself a lord. You'd best go around him. I can do that for you." He stared at Shanks. "And you know my modest price."

Shanks nodded. "I just want to be sure it's done right. No foofaraw. Quiet and peaceful like."

"Do you trade with Spotted Horse's people, Mr. Medlock?" Rawley asked.

"No, I do not," the trader answered flatly. "My license is for the native tribes. Assiniboin and Chippewa mostly. McDougall and Hudson's Bay look upon Spotted Horse's people as refugees under their protection for the duration of your Civil War." His humorless laugh was harsh. "Don't matter to me about the trading ban. The Sioux have little to trade except a few robes. Still trying to kill enough buffalo to piece out their tipis and dry enough meat for winter."

"How far is their camp from Fort Manitou?" Rawley asked. "And how large is it?"

Medlock closed one eye. "Three leagues maybe. I've seen it from a distance — about two hundred lodges."

"Antoine Fromboise tells me you have a plan for drawing Spotted Horse out of his camp without disturbance." Rawley's tone was questioning.

"I have a way."

Shanks spoke then. "No violence."

Medlock shook his head, his mouth twisting in a grin.

"We'd like to know the risks," Rawley said, turning toward Fromboise. "Do you know, Antoine?"

Fromboise shrugged. "Oui," He winked at Medlock. "You can put confidance in these Americains, Amos. They not rob you."

Medlock leaned closer to Fromboise and said

something softly in French.

"Au contraire," Fromboise replied, shaking his head vigorously. "C'est vrai." His shaggy white eyebrows lifted, and his naturally bulging eyes turned toward Ben Shanks. "Tell him the monnair is in gold and he will tell you how he brings Spotted Horse to you."

Shanks looked startled. He touched the waterproofed canvas bag beside his boot, his fingers trembling slightly. "You'll be paid in gold," he said in his high whine.

Medlock nodded. "All right. That old Sioux has a taste for strong water. His squaws make a few first-rate buffalo robes. So we trade, on the sly. All I need do is drive a wagon out to the trail crossing of Spruce Woods Creek and post a pennon. Spotted Horse and some of his trusted braves will soon show. Strictly illegal, of course. If Master McDougall got proof of it he would flail my ass, but he's got better things to do than watch over his Sioux refugees with a Spruce Woods patrol."

"So." Rawley's tone was dubious. "We capture Spotted Horse when he comes to your wagon for whiskey?"

"Oh, no, not then or there," Medlock answered hastily. "I'll not risk trapping the chief and whatever other redskins may be with him out there in the open. No, I'll have no liquors with me, but I'll invite the chief, or him and whoever may be with him, to toddies after dark at my trading post. There and then, you'll take over, Major Rawley — after Ben Shanks has paid me in full." His eyes had a yellow sheen in the light of the low fire in the center of the shelter. "My terms are half now and half after I bring Spotted Horse to you."

"One-quarter now, and three-quarters on delivery," Shanks said, his voice turning higher.

Medlock shrugged. "All right. But all in gold, none of your Uncle Sam's greenbacks."

Rawley bent down to warm his hands over the fire. "Suppose Spotted Horse doesn't come forth when you take your wagon out there? Can you go into the tipi camp to invite him?"

"He'll most likely show because he's been two weeks between drinks. If not, we'll wait a day. He'll show. No, it's too risky to go into their camp. Out of bounds by McDougall's orders. He's touchy about the reports of two white captives being held by the Sioux — a woman and a young boy. He don't want it pressed or talked about."

Rawley stood quickly upright. "White captives?" he repeated in a loud tone. "A woman?"

"They deny it, the Sioux, I mean. But my Assiniboins who've visited the camp say they saw her and the boy."

Rawley stepped around the fire so that he towered over the squatting trader. "What is she like?" he demanded. "Her hair color, her size, her age?"

Medlock slid backward a few inches. "Damn it, major, I have not seen the woman. Wait a minute." He turned to peer at the *métis* who were sitting or lying along the rock wall in the shadows cast by the firelight. "Hanska," he called, and spoke rapidly in French. A round-faced large-paunched man wrapped in a dark blanket stepped closer to the fire. He knew only a few words of English, but with Rawley prompting and Medlock and Fromboise interpreting, the half-blood's description of the woman he had seen in the Sioux camp matched Nettie Steever's appearance.

"I know that woman," the major declared. He strode back and forth in the cramped shelter, his voice edgy with excitement: "We must get her out of that camp. The boy, too, though I know nothing of him."

Medlock frowned. "Such an enterprise would take some doing, major. Dangerous, very dangerous. Not even McDougall and the Hudson's Bay Company could handle it without great risk of a brawl. The company shuns such. Uprising might spread, you know. Whatever Sioux brave claims that woman, or the boy, would have to be dealt with. If the Sioux are willing to surrender the captives, they'd still want ransom of some kind — goods, horses, maybe money."

"It's a case of abduction pure and simple," Rawley said. "From U.S. territory into British territory. By international law the British authorities must return the captives to us."

Ben Shanks laughed. "Ain't we about to do the same thing to old Spotted Horse, major? Abduct him across a national line? You'd better leave that woman be till we've got Spotted Horse back in Dakota Territory."

"If Medlock can't help us," Rawley said, "I'm going to the Hudson's Bay people, to your man McDougall, and demand that she be released to our custody."

Shanks shook his head firmly. "Better sleep on it, major. We're without any official power here. We ain't even supposed to come into the British possessions without their permission. If you start making official demands —"

Medlock yawned and turned to reach for his blanket roll. "I'm for some rest, gentlemen. We've got a long day's journey ahead of us at daybreak, and the weather don't look good."

Next morning there was no sunrise because

of clouds, and the travelers started north from the shelter in a dismal gray light that was nearer to darkness than dawn. The land they were crossing was vast, yet also intimate and secret. "High, lonesome country," was the way O'Hara described it. "Cold, barren, and bleak. To be avoided by man during the winter months." Before noon tiny snow pellets were spinning out of the sky, rattling against the frozen earth. A buffalo herd rumbling southward swerved to the east to avoid the horsemen. Snow and ice on the animals' coats warned of the paralyzing harshness of the advancing weather.

Medlock and Fromboise, riding just ahead of O'Hara and Rawley, fell into an argument over the probability of a blizzard. "May catch us before dark," Medlock said dourly. "Not this day," Fromboise retorted. "Wind turning to west. And look at clouds. Too thin. Take time to make big blizzard. It come. But not this day."

Fromboise was the better forecaster. Just before dusk, at their first sight of Fort Manitou across a scattering of frozen swales, thin strips of pale blue showed in the sky. When they rode past the graveled approach to the main building, there still light enough to see British and Hudson's Bay Company flags flying from twin staffs and read the neat lettering above the entrance: HEADQUARTERS HUDSON'S BAY COMPANY.

Medlock did not slow the pace until Major Rawley forced his mount up alongside the trader's. "Is it there I'll find McDougall?" he asked.

"Yes, likely you will, major, but I warn you to stay clear of him until your other business is completed." Behind them the other riders slowed to avoid crowding the leaders, some of the *métis* turning aside and wheeling so that the movements of the little column in the street began attracting attention from the few passersby.

"Let it wait till later, major!" Shanks demanded, his voice almost a wheeze in his effort to keep it from carrying too loud on the heavy air.

"No." Rawley turned his horse toward the entrance of the headquarters building. "Sergeant O'Hara, fall out and accompany me." He turned in his saddle, calling back to Medlock: "We'll find your place later. There may have to be a change in plans."

O'Hara stood up, stretched his thick arms, and walked to the window overlooking the river. He rested his hands on the wide sill and looked down at the lights of the steamboats. "God, that seems a long time past," he said quietly. "But I remember like it might've happened an hour ago — the way I felt when we hitched our horses to that polished rail in front of Hudson's Bay Company headquarters. The dying daylight was a kind of brownish color, all the buildings were painted brown, everything neat, not a mess of untidiness the way it usually is around most of our posts.

"The major walked right up the whitewashed steps and knocked hard on the heavy door. A deep voice bid us to enter. The air inside seemed too warm after that bitter cold we'd been breathing all day.

"McDougall was alone in the main room, reading a book. He had one leg cocked up on a rough table, and he was smoking a long-stemmed pipe. Logs were burning in fireplaces at both ends of the room, big roaring fires with leaping flames.

"Major Rawley wasted no time on what you would call the civilities. Maybe he was bluffing a little, but he came right to the point. Claimed he had crossed the line in search of Mrs. Nettie Steever, believed to be a captive of the Sioux who had fled to the protection of Fort Manitou."

Robert McDougall, according to O'Hara, was a man of about forty, black hair sprinkled with gray, forehead skin weathered into deep lines, cheeks fiery red. His long-flowing side whiskers were of the fashion known as dundrearies, and his waxed mustache was enormous.

After greeting Rawley and O'Hara, he stood with his back to the fireplace nearer the table, facing his unexpected callers. He tried to put on a fierce and pompous mien, but was not too successful at it. He admitted having heard rumors of white captives among the refugees, a woman and a boy, had made inquiries in fact, but the Sioux he communicated with denied any knowledge of captives in the Spruce Woods camp.

"I have reliable firsthand information that they were seen in that camp," Rawley insisted. "Not more than ten days ago."

McDougall rocked back and forth on his heels in front of the fire, hands locked behind his back, blinking his eyes at Rawley. "For God's sake, Mr. Rawley," he lashed out suddenly, "why do not you and your man remove those beastly-smelling buffalo robes? You must be sweltering."

Rawley smiled for the first time. He and O'Hara laid their robes on a chair, and moved closer to the fireplace. "Could you help us, Mr. McDougall? We may need to search every tipi in Spotted Horse's camp."

"I suppose you came across the boundary without papers of any kind. Like all the others." McDougall reached for a large box on the table, removing two form sheets and handing them to Rawley. "Fill these out, Mr. Rawley. Where it says 'purpose of entry,' write 'to purchase furs and skins,' or something of the sort. Record nothing about white captives."

Noting the quizzical expression on Rawley's face he added quickly: "Oh, for God's sake, don't you understand my delicate position here? A handful of whites in a country of thousands of red Indians. To survive we must keep the peace. You Americans drive your hostiles over on us and we don't have the power to drive them back. If we could do so we would not, out of fear of stirring up our own natives. And then your outrageously mad Civil War. Out here in this wilderness we must maintain the chilly attitude of Britain's government toward your government while at the same time we depend upon your cooperation in shipping our furs and hides, even our mail, by way of Saint Paul and Chicago. There is no all-weather trail through the Canadian shield, you know." He stopped with an imploring gesture, showing his teeth in an ironic smile.

"The look of the world depends upon one's viewpoint, I suppose," Rawley said.

"Yes. It does, doesn't it?" McDougall took a deep breath. "Well now, we must think of something to do about your white captives, eh, Mr. Rawley. Let me put it this way. Hudson's Bay Company will neither support nor oppose any attempt made by you to recover the white captives. Yet if there are repercussions of any kind, if you place yourself in such peril that your life is at stake, expect no help from us. I shall deny that I ever saw or heard of a Mr. Rawley." He clasped his hands over his belly, staring at the ceiling. Then he reached for the unfilled forms still lying on the table and dropped them back into the box from which he had taken them. "I meant to invite you and your man to share my quarters for the night, but that will be quite impossible since you are here unlawfully."

"We'll find shelter," Rawley said.

"At Medlock's lodging house?"

"Yes."

"How many others came with you, Mr. Rawley?"

"Two."

"Their names?"

"Ben Shanks and Antoine Fromboise."

McDougall grunted. "I know Fromboise. An untrustworthy rascal. Your guide, I suppose. Who is Shanks?"

"He has an interest in the case," Rawley replied.

McDougall reached his enormous hand across the table and shook Rawley's. "Luck, sir. Oh, I say, does one of your men understand and speak Lakota?"

Rawley glanced at O'Hara. "Sergeant O'Hara can manage a few words."

"Ah, so you *are* military." McDougall's eyes brightened. "I'd hoped as much. You go in there with your sergeant, you may come out alive, sir. Leave your other two men out of it. If you secure the captives, beat a retreat from Canada as fast as you can, will you?"

Amos Medlock's lodging house was barely tolerable, eight wooden frame beds to a room, the sleeping supports of animal hides, fusty bearskins for covering. The breakfast prepared by one of Medlock's *métis* was even worse — chunks of gamy meat in a greasy gruel, fried mush, and very bitter tea. During the meal, Ben Shanks continued to argue against any action to rescue the white captives until after Spotted Horse was in their hands and well across the border. When Rawley declared that he was going to attempt a rescue by visiting the Sioux camp that morning, Shanks showed sudden anger, threatening to make a full report of the major's actions to Colonel Herrick. "If you cause us to bungle the capture of Spotted Horse, if there is a failure of duty," Shanks said, "all blame shall fall on you, major, and I have witnesses to support me."

Rawley made no reply, and after a few moments of silence Medlock expressed surprise that McDougall had offered no interference. "He's a sly one, Master McDougall is. You'd best mind your step, major. I'll go along to assist you. Perhaps we can kill two birds." He winked at Shanks, whose thin face was still dark with anger.

"I have permission to take only Sergeant O'Hara," Rawley said as he arose from the table.

The trail to Spruce Woods Creek was a rough wagon track winding around rises and swales. Instead of facing a cold north wind as on the previous day, they found the still air to be almost warm by contrast. The sky was milky with rows of small fleecy clouds stretching from horizon to horizon.

In less than three hours they reached the creek, where a morning mist still lingered after depositing a thick film of frost over the ever-greens. The creek ford was a fusion of frozen mud and shards of dirty ice that had melted and refrozen in several successions. As soon as they crossed, the Sioux camp came into full view, a circle of tipis along a bench of grassy ground fronting a highbanked narrow stream, and then beyond were other lodges on a higher level that reached to a growth of tall trees blocking the skyline.

What struck O'Hara at first glimpse was the condition of the tipis. Almost all were new, with very little blacking around the smoke holes. Some were half covered, others were as yet only pole frames. The usual colorful designs and stripes that he had seen on the lodges at Killdeer Mountain and elsewhere had been painted here on only a few of the outer surfaces. British flags, mounted above two or three of the larger tipis offered the most color although they hung motionless in the dead air. At a widening of the stream, a dozen scrawny ponies stood in broken ice trying to drink from the shallow flow. Beyond them, women and children were lifting water up the sharp bank in wooden pails.

After pausing for only an instant, Rawley started his horse along a path that led across an eroded wash toward the lower circle of tipis.

The Sioux had sighted them now. Dogs began barking, some rushing out to snarl and then retreat. Shy children ran to their family shelters. Old men peered out from tipi flaps, and the nearer women stopped what they were doing to watch the intruders warily.

"I see no young men," O'Hara said in an undertone.

"No." Rawley's attention was fixed upon a tall woman who was placing small sticks of wood under a camp kettle. She kneeled to blow coals to life and not until the wood began blazing did she stand to stare at the approaching white men.

"Look at her," Rawley said. "Cooler than the ice in that stream. If her skin were lighter she'd be a Grecian goddess, tall, well formed, a Diana. I've seen her before, O'Hara. At Killdeer Mountain. Spared her life, you might say. She owes me a favor, eh, although she knows nothing of it." He pulled his mount to a stop only a few paces from her. Defiance showed on her face. "Ask her where the captive white woman is, O'Hara."

"I'll try, sir, but as I told you I know only a few of their words." O'Hara made the peace sign, clasping his hands in front of his body. Not knowing the Lakota word for white woman, he used the word for white man.

"Wasicun," he said, and quickly made the sign for female.

She frowned, her eyes full of puzzlement; then her full lips parted to reveal her amusement. She made two or three quick signs with her hands. O'Hara nodded. "I know the meaning of that. She says if we come in peace we ought to dismount."

"Well, dismount, sergeant." They both dropped to the ground, the woman backing away to the opposite side of the fire, which was beginning to blaze.

"White woman?" Rawley's tone was demanding. "White woman?"

She shook her head.

"She don't know our talk," O'Hara said, "but I think she got my sign meaning." He repeated wasicun, and ran his fingers up and down each side of his body as though combing long hair. She was amused again, speaking rapidly in Lakota. "Itokiyopaya," she repeated several times.

"I think she wants to know if we've come to trade for the white woman," O'Hara said.

Rawley spoke quickly: "Tell her yes." He nodded frantically to the woman.

She turned then and gestured gracefully upstream. "Sunkawakan," she said, and added the English word: "horses."

A hundred yards up the winding stream bank were several unfinished tipis, with women, old men, and children occupied at various tasks around them. "I see no horses up there," O'Hara said.

"Maybe she means we can trade horses for the captives," Rawley said, and after a bow of thanks to the tall woman and a signal to O'Hara to follow, he started upstream, leading his mount by the bridle rope. Around them a pack of dogs and children had quickly collected, swirling, barking and chattering, announcing their approach to the old men warming themselves by outdoor fires while they fashioned or repaired arrows, and to the women who were scraping, fleshing or smoking hides. Rawley searched the face of every woman they passed, and was wondering aloud whether he should risk stopping to enter closed tipis when he halted abruptly, his eyes fixed on the backs of two women. One was folding a scraped hide into a cone shape over a small pit that contained a smoldering fire. The other was on her knees scraping a green buffalo hide that had been staked with its hairy side to the ground. Both wore faded blanket scarves over their heads. Their hide dresses were so recently made they had not yet been beaded.

At the sound of Rawley's approach, the

woman at the fire pit was the first to turn. Her face was wrinkled, her eyes rheumy and squinting to see; she evidently saw only a blur of strange men and horses. She called in Lakota to the other woman who swung around on hands and knees, then stood quickly erect, flinging her arms up in astonishment.

"God's mercy!" Nettie Steever cried. Both hands were covered with blood and fat and flesh from the buffalo hide. "Major Rawley! How —"

"Who is she?" he interrupted, with a motion of his hand toward the old woman.

"My captor's mother," Nettie explained. "She will do you no harm."

The dogs and children had caught up with them and began to circle the horses. O'Hara strained at both bridles to hold the animals steady. Rawley walked a few steps closer to Nettie but still had to shout to make himself heard above the noise. The old woman picked up a dried hide, flourishing it and scolding the dogs and children until they scurried off a few at a time to the stream bank where they stopped to watch silently from the safer distance.

"I'll be direct," Rawley said. "Where is your captor, the Sioux who claims you?"

"Gone with the other young men and the

chiefs to hunt," she replied without emotion.

"When will they return?"

She shrugged. "Tonight perhaps, or tomorrow if they must ride far for buffalo or antelope."

"What will happen if you leave this place right now? Riding pillion on my horse?"

"Leave to go where?" she asked.

"To Dakota of course."

She stooped to clean her hands on the dead prairie grass. Looking up at him, she said: "The last time we talked you promised we would flee to Canada. Why should I, or you, or both of us, go back now to Dakota?"

For a moment his face revealed his discomposure. He glanced sidewise at O'Hara, who took the gesture as a signal to move out of earshot and started to lead the horses away. "Stay by me, sergeant!" Rawley ordered in a sharp tone.

When he stepped closer to Nettie, the old woman beside the fire pit arose to a crouching position, reminding O'Hara of a wild canine preparing to defend its young. "I can't tell you why I must return," the major said quietly. "It's something I must do. After that, we can go wherever we choose, you and I."

"Why should I trust you?" she asked. "All

my life I have been betrayed by promises for the future."

He shook his head. "You *must* trust me. What choice do you have? This life must be terrible for you."

She smiled. "I am not mistreated here, Major Rawley. Life is no harder with these people than what I lived with Steever. Given the choice of returning to what I had, or living like this, I would not go back."

"You will not be going back to Steever," he said.

"It could be worse than Steever," she replied. "I know what people back there think of white women captives who return. Soiled goods, diseased, tainted like fish too long from the water."

He threw out his hands in a gesture of impatience, then seized her by the arm and turned her toward the stream bank. The old woman followed them slowly, keeping her distance like a distrustful guard dog. O'Hara heard Rawley say: "We can go where no one knows who we are. To California, perhaps." And then their voices were too indistinct for him to hear. They stood facing each other on the stream bank, sometimes gesturing and talking slowly and earnestly, sometimes saying nothing.

At last they turned and started back, the old woman scurrying awkwardly aside into a clump of brush to be out of their way. Without a word to O'Hara, the major climbed into his saddle. "Let's go," he said then, and they rode back through the camp, the dogs and children resuming their noisy attendance, their numbers increased by a few curious old men. The tall woman, still working beside the camp kettle, stopped what she was doing to watch the procession pass. Rawley lifted his cap to her, but she made no acknowledgment of the salute other than to stand straight as a soldier at attention, her eyes fixed on the two horsemen until they turned toward Spruce Woods Creek.

Before they reached the ford, the last of the dogs and children abandoned them, and after they crossed, leaving the camp screened by the evergreens along the creek, the land seemed suddenly silent and empty.

"The white boy captive," Rawley said then to O'Hara, "went with the hunters. Nettie Steever says he is a foundling raised by the Sioux and would resist any effort to remove him from the tribe. More Indian than Indian is the way she put it."

"I've heard of others like him, sir," the sergeant commented. "Most usually mixed blood though."

They rode on, Rawley keeping silent until O'Hara asked: "Mrs. Steever, sir, she can't mean to stay there, like the boy?"

Rawley's answer was blunt, almost hostile: "We'll know tonight, sergeant." He slapped his reins, urging his horse into an easy canter.

On the trail back to Fort Manitou they met no one, and when they turned into the single wide street only two or three human beings were in sight. At Medlock's lodging house they found only a few *métis* lounging in the rear. None of them knew where their employer or Fromboise and Shanks had gone. As it was late afternoon, O'Hara and Rawley were both half famished, hungry enough to endure the greasy food offered by the *métis* in the kitchen.

Before they'd finished the acrid tea, a rosy-cheeked boy enshrouded in silvery furs from head to foot entered the dining room and asked for *Meestaire* Rawley. *Meestaire* Rawley was wanted at the headquarters of the Hudson's Bay Company by *Capitaine* McDougall.

Rawley went alone to see McDougall, and when he returned an hour later in the dying light of the short winter day he seemed bemused, and sat staring into the dining-room fireplace for several minutes before speaking to O'Hara. "That man McDougall," he said at last, "is an Argus with a hundred eyes in his head. He knows Shanks and Medlock and Fromboise rode north about noon, but he does not know why or where, and I could see he did not believe me when I told him I did not know either. He knew everything about our visit to Spotted Horse's camp. When we arrived there, how long we stayed, and that a trade is possible for Nettie Steever. He is curious as to our next move, what course the Sioux will take. I told him I did not know their minds, that we would wait only two or three more days, at most. He seemed anxious to be rid of the responsibility for Nettie Steever's presence here, but you can be certain he will do nothing to aggravate the Sioux." Rawley laughed, as though privately to himself. "I did not tell McDougall, of course, that you and I will be returning to the camp as soon as it's well dark. We'll see if his spies inform him of that."

O'Hara, sitting across from me in the pride of his living room in the Hotel Como, under the yellow light of his prized oil lamp, gave an imitation of that self-laughter of Charles Rawley. "He was a secretive man at times, the major. He had not bothered to tell me until then that we would be riding back to the Sioux camp in the ball-freezing cold of night. We would be taking with us the four spare mounts

224

we'd brought up from Fort Standish, one of them to be saddled. I guessed that three of them were a trade for Mrs. Steever. He had just finished looking at his watch and telling me it was time to go out to the stables to saddle our mounts and prepare a hitch for the four spares when we heard a slight commotion from the kitchen, the back entrance of the lodging house as it were.

"They came in then, overly quiet about it, I thought. Ben Shanks was coughing in the dry heat of the dining room, Medlock throwing off his heavy furs and wiping melting frost from his mustache, and then old Fromboise and two Indians came in, big men they were, not fat but tall and strong-looking. As you may have guessed, one of them, the older and handsomer Indian, was introduced as Spotted Horse. He had a solemn old face, but I would not have taken him for a chief. I had not known many chiefs at that time, however, and had no way to judge. The other Indian had a strange habit of grimacing, not a smile or a frown, just a funny way of twisting his lower face when something struck his fancy, and sometimes he'd add on a crazy-sounding snicker. Neither knew more than a dozen or so English words, and most of them profane oaths.

"Medlock treated them like visiting kings,

taking their heavy outer robes and hanging them on pegs, and serving them mugs of rum. He told them to drink up, making the sign to be certain they understood him, and assured them they'd talk about a trade later."

"And what of the Major all this time?"

"Of course he was itching to be on his way back to the camp. But he knew he had to go through the formality of being polite to Spotted Horse. He took Shanks aside to whisper their plans."

O'Hara learned that early that day Medlock had got wind of the big Sioux hunting party from some of the Assiniboins and had immediately gone out with Shanks and Fromboise in hopes of crossing paths with Spotted Horse. It was more or less a piece of luck that they had sighted the Sioux returning to camp, traveling slow with butchered antelopes lashed to their ponies. The rest had been fairly easy, getting Spotted Horse and his companion – Whirlwind his name was – to come in under cover of darkness for some friendly grog.

"At first chance, the major signaled me to slip out and ready the horses. A few minutes later he was in the stables and we started off as quiet as possible. The night was dark as sin, and colder than that. We'd struggled along over that rutted trail for about a mile when bits of stinging ice mixed with small snowflakes showered suddenly down upon us. Enough soon fell to lighten the way, and we were able to move as fast as by daylight except for occasional slowdowns caused by the led horses.

"We made it to Spruce Woods Creek well before midnight, and I was wondering what our reception would be in that dark village of tipis. Instead of crossing the frozen stream, however, the major turned us aside and we dismounted, taking shelter under a wide-limbed evergreen where we waited with only the soft sound of ice particles brushing the needles above us. After a while we heard dogs barking in the camp, and not long after that we sighted two shadows moving along the opposite creek bank. The major ordered me to mount up, and bring the spare horses."

"Could you make out who they were?"

"There was enough reflected light so that I could recognize the white-skinned face of Mrs. Steever. The other was Sioux Indian, the head blanketed. I'd expected a man — knowing the hunting party was back — but when the head turned in the half-light I was surprised to see the face of the old woman, that crouching guardian of Mrs. Steever we'd observed earlier by daylight."

O'Hara described how the major and Mrs.

Steever talked in undertones while the old Sioux went quickly from one of the spare horses to another, examining their feet, forcing their mouths open to feel the teeth, running her hands over the withers and shoulders. While the woman was doing all that, Mrs. Steever mounted the saddled horse they had brought for her. "The old woman, however, wasn't going to let us off easy. She caught hold of the bridle of Mrs. Steever's horse and began a quarrelsome harangue. As best I could make out, she wanted that horse as well as the other three, and the saddle to boot. Her noble son, who owned Mrs. Steever, would be satisfied with no less of a trade.

"Out there in the cold dark of that wilderness, with dogs beginning to wake and bark again in the encampment, the major wanted no fuss. 'Take the horse and saddle, damn you,' he said, and lifted Mrs. Steever over onto his horse, behind the saddle. He mounted quickly, she holding tight to his buffalo robe as the horse wheeled toward the trail."

They wasted no time getting back to Fort Manitou. The frozen ground was well covered when they rode up to Medlock's stables in the dead silence of a windless snowfall. It was well after midnight.

"The major helped me unsaddle and blanket

the horses. Mrs. Steever was shivering, her teeth chattering when she tried to talk. 'There's no purpose in it, major,' she kept saying. I promised her she'd be warm soon enough with a rum toddy to do the trick.

"We could see candlelight through the frosted windows as we walked across to the kitchen entrance, but there was no sound of voices. When I opened the door for the major and Mrs. Steever, the warm humid air that flowed out was laden with the odors of rum and tobacco smoke and unbathed men.

"They were all there, after five or six hours of drinking and eating, about as we'd left them. Two or three *métis* lay asleep on the floor near the fireplace, one of them snoring loudly. Medlock lolled in a chair. He opened one bloodshot eye to signify that he was aware of our arrival. When he saw Mrs. Steever, he opened both eyes and sat up straight in his chair."

"And the others?"

"As best I could tell, Spotted Horse and Fromboise were asleep in their chairs. The chief's friend, Whirlwind, sat on the floor with his back to the fire, blinking his heavy eyelids and chortling to himself now and then. Only Shanks appeared to be in full command of himself, very wide awake he was.

"When Major Rawley sought a draft of rum for Mrs. Steever, but could find only empty bottles, Shanks said there might be a full bottle left in the kitchen cabinet. I told the major I'd go have a look, and Shanks followed me into the kitchen. He was carrying that canvas bag he'd brought from Fort Standish. It didn't look to be much lighter, and I wondered if he'd given Medlock his final payment in gold. He found a bottle in one of the cabinets and laid out a row of pewter mugs. While I was pouring the liquor, Shanks slipped a small dark bottle from inside his coat and shook several drops into one of the mugs. 'That's for the Indian setting on the floor,' he said. 'The one they call Whirlwind. He's a hard case to put under.' I asked if it was a poison. 'It's only laudanum,' he said to me. 'Rock him to sleep for several hours is all.'

"He had had some already. Spotted Horse, the one we wanted, was well under. We could take him now, but Whirlwind had to go with him. We couldn't leave him behind to start his bloody-minded people swarming after us.

"I took two of the mugs into the dining room, and a few moments later Shanks followed with two more. He set one down on the table beside Medlock's chair and carefully placed the other into one of Whirlwind's hands.

"Mrs. Steever was standing by the fireplace, her blanket piled in a heap on the floor, her face already rosy from the fire. She swigged the rum I gave her like it was water. The major sipped at his until Shanks motioned for him to join him back in the shadows of the room. They whispered together for several minutes.

"Whirlwind tried two or three times to stand up, but he could not. Each time he tried he would slip back down again, snickering crazy-like and grinning from ear to ear. He blinked his eyes at me as if he was signaling some meaning or other.

"Pretty soon Shanks came to me and said very quietly that I should put on my robe and follow him out to the stables. He led the way to the far end where five or six dogsleds were leaning against the log wall. He pointed out that we'd need two. I was surprised at how light the sleds were. They were made of willow and rawhide, and I had no trouble in dragging them around to the kitchen entrance where Shanks hurriedly inspected the ties while I held his lantern. 'Get the horses ready,' he said then, 'and bring them around here. The four we rode, and pick two of Medlock's best. Saddle one of 'em for that woman the major burdened us with.' His voice had a sneer in it. 'No woman's worth four good horses, and certainly not that frump who's lain with redskins.'

"When I'd saddled the horses and led them to the backdoor of the lodging house, Shanks and the major were strapping Spotted Horse to one of the dogsleds. They had wrapped the chief in his buffalo robe, pulling the headpiece over his face and belting a few extra skins over his body so that the sled gave the appearance of being loaded with furs instead of a stupefied Indian. From where I stood I caught a whiff of chloroform. They were taking no chances of a sudden awakening.

"We had less trouble putting Whirlwind to slumbering than in waking Fromboise. Shanks just swashed some reeking chloroform onto a handkerchief and held it tight over Whirlwind's face. For a few seconds Shanks pressed one of his knees into the struggling Indian's chest; then Whirlwind started breathing peaceful as a papoose. As for Fromboise, we shook him, slapped his face, and finally the major and I lifted him out of his chair and walked him to the backdoor where the frosty air soon revived him."

"What did you expect to do about Medlock?" I had to ask.

"Shanks said we should leave him be. I glanced at the major. He shrugged. The last I saw of Amos Medlock he was half in and half out of his chair, fingers gripped around the empty rum glass that Shanks had brought him. I say it was the last *I* saw of him. Shanks was to see Medlock once more, and then again in hell probably.

"Mrs. Steever appeared to be a bit unsettled, but whether it was from drinking too many toddies too fast, or from what was being done to the Indians, I could not tell. When Major Rawley informed her it was time to go, she began wrapping herself in blankets, muttering something about 'those poor bastard Indians.'

"Fromboise was wide-awake by the time we'd finished hitching the dogsleds to the horses that would be ridden by the major and Shanks. The Frenchman took the lead, a hundred paces or so ahead of Mrs. Steever, and then the major followed her, dragging Spotted Horse's sled, and after him rode Shanks with Whirlwind's sled. I was last in the file.

"When we passed the Hudson's Bay Company headquarters I fully expected Captain McDougall to come charging out, his mustaches aquiver, demanding us to halt for inspection. But it was that time of night when honest men sleep soundest, and the headquarters was only a blur of shadows through the falling snow, no light showing in any window.

"We didn't stop moving until Fromboise halloaed back that we had crossed the line into Dakota Territory, and then Major Rawley ordered a halt to rest mounts. We all drew closer together and dismounted, the major and Shanks stamping through the snow to examine their prisoners. Spotted Horse was groaning, his muscles straining against the rawhide bonds, but I don't believe he was yet aware of what had happened to him. Whirlwind still breathed deep and easy — he'd got a mighty dose of chloroform.

"When the major rose up and saw me standing there, he slapped me on the shoulder. 'By God, sergeant,' he shouted, 'we've done it!' He was happier than I'd seen him since the days when he was training that company of Saint Paul cavalry recruits at Fort Standish, a big smile on his face, his laugh a genuine laugh. Then he lowered his voice as though he was speaking to me in private: 'I reckon this vindicates the name of Charles Rawley, eh? Wipes out Killdeer Mountain. That's why I'm here, sergeant, to redeem Killdeer Mountain. Once we've delivered this villainous Sioux to Colonel Herrick the name of Charles Rawley will be cleansed of Killdeer Mountain. Then I can depart this abominable Dakota Territory.'

"Mrs. Steever's moccasins crunched on the snow behind us. The major whirled around in surprise, almost as though he'd forgotten she was traveling with us. She asked us what we had been palavering about, and in a tone that I thought was rather overfamiliar. Then without waiting for him to reply she demanded a swig of liquor to warm her blood against the cold. He told her that a small amount of brandy was packed on the led horse with our other supplies, that we had not time to unpack, and she should wait until we reached the rock shelter at Maison du Chien Butte where everyone in the party would receive a ration. If she was cold, he added, he would remove some of the furs from Spotted Horse's sled and give them to her."

"And how did that sit with Mrs. Steever?"

"Not too well. I don't suppose she thought she was somebody of special importance in the company, she was just thirsty for a drink, that's it. We've all been that way at times, I'd wager, haven't you, Mr. Morrison?"

O'Hara weaved his way across the floor of his Hotel Como living room, waving the unlabeled bottle of snakehead whiskey. I'd noticed his tongue had been thickening during the last part of his narration, and I wondered what the effect was going to be on his memory. He clucked his tongue in disappointment that the steamboat wineglass he'd given me earlier in the evening was still more than ·half filled. Nevertheless he poured it full again, right to the brim.

He went back to his chair and sat down heavily. "Well," he said, "what more can I tell you for your newspaper piece about Major Rawley?"

I wanted to hear more about the journey through the snowstorm to Fort Standish, but to put him at ease I asked: "What was Rawley's physical condition at the time? Did his old wound —"

O'Hara interrupted: "He felt so fine about bringing out Spotted Horse he could have endured anything, I think."

"But the journey through the blizzard must have been hard on all of you."

"It was an ordeal, sir. Times I thought we'd not survive, yet we did. I give the credit to the major. He would not abandon hope and would not allow us to abandon hope."

"You said something just now about Shanks and Medlock."

"What about them?" he asked with sudden suspicion in his voice, the way a man too far gone in drink sometimes turns distrustful of those around him.

"You said that you never saw Medlock again after you left Fort Manitou, but that Shanks probably saw him in hell."

O'Hara brushed his fingers across his eyes, his brow wrinkling as though trying to remember. "Shanks killed Medlock," he blurted out. "I thought you knew that."

"No. When did he kill him?"

"On the way back from Fort Manitou. Medlock followed us to Maison du Chien Butte."

"Why?"

O'Hara's mood turned resentful. "Look here, Mr. Morrison, none of that had anything to do with Major Rawley. Hellfire, Shanks put laudanum in Medlock's last toddies the same as he did for the Indians'. Then he went off without paying him the gold."

"So Shanks killed Medlock when he came after him. But how did he see him in hell?"

O'Hara took a long swallow of his fiery liquor, almost gagged on it, but turned the reaction into a forced yawn. "Shanks was wounded in the fight, that's it," he said haltingly. "He died in the blizzard soon after. If you believe in hell, sir, they saw each other there."

It was plain that O'Hara was finished for the

evening. He was having trouble forming his words when he spoke.

I stood up and thanked him. "Tomorrow is Major Rawley's day," I added. "The commemoration."

"Yeah, yeah, sir," he stammered. "We must be there at the proper time." He managed to get to his feet as if to follow me to the door like a proper host.

"Whatever happened to the bag of gold that Shanks was carrying?" I asked casually. He stopped in the middle of the room, rocking unsteadily on his small feet. His face revealed his sudden confusion. Cunning quickly replaced the confusion, or was it evasiveness? He seemed to be reaching for control of himself through the alcoholic haze. "It was the major's responsibility, sir," he said, standing stiff and straight as if ready to offer a military salute.

"Goodnight, Mr. O'Hara," I said, and closed the door behind me.

9

The Hotel Como's upstairs hallway had no lights of any sort. It was like a dark cave except for a tiny glow of yellow candlelight seeping from beneath one of the badly fitting doors. What I had in mind after leaving Joseph O'Hara's living quarters was to return to my room and get to work on some neglected dispatches to the *Saint Louis Herald* and let them know where I was. All pay above expenses that I received from that ungenerous newspaper came from measured inches of what the editor chose to print, and if I did not compose some letters describing my travels and file them on one of the downriver boats, my employer might soon discontinue even the expense allowance.

I was guided to my numbered room by that pale beam of light on the hall floor, and not until I'd let myself in with the door key did I remember that the room with the light was the one assigned to Kathleen Hardesty. Through the outer walls of my room the sounds of saloons and dance halls along the street easily penetrated — a tinkling piano, raucous voices, a female singer, an occasional shout. The evening was not yet waning in the newly-wrought boomtown of Fort Rawley.

Groping in the darkness of the room I found a tallow candle atop the crude washstand. Not a match could I find, however, neither loose in my pockets nor in the tin box in my bag. Needing a light to work by, I crossed the hall and knocked on Mrs. Hardesty's door. Her interrogating voice sounded frightened, but when she recognized mine she opened the door quickly.

"Sam Morrison," she cried, "I'm so relieved to see you."

Her welcome was like that for someone who has been absent over a long period of time, and I must have shown my surprise. "Something strange has been happening," she added. "I've had the oddest feeling all evening, and except for you I know no one in this hotel to tell of it." She was talking too fast, and realizing this, she brought herself up short. "I'm sorry, Sam. Come in and I'll explain." She stood aside until I'd entered; then closed the door and dropped a wooden bar into a latch. Her red hair was done up in some kind of nightcap, and she was wearing a green silken robe. She offered me the single straight chair and sat on the edge of the narrow bed. There was not much room for visitors in the Hotel Como's cubbyholes.

"Have you had the feeling, Sam, that someone was following you, watching you?" Under the candlelight her green eyes were very intense, with dancing pinpoints of brightness in them.

"Often, during the war," I said.

"In the dining room this evening I felt eyes watching me. When I looked around very casually several times, I could catch no one at it, saw no one in fact who might *want* to stare at me. But then when I went for a walk along the wooden sidewalk I had the same sensation. I knew you were meeting Mr. O'Hara so I came right up here to my room. No sooner had I latched the door than I heard footsteps coming slowly along the hall. Whoever it was stood for a long time outside my door. I could hear him breathing, Sam. I was frightened out of my wits."

"Probably a smitten admirer," I said to reassure her. "The town of Fort Rawley doesn't often see unattached women as lovely as you, Kathleen."

She shook her head. "No, it was more than that. Being admired pleases me. But from this

— all I get is a creepy feeling." She sighed and leaned forward, resting her head in one hand. "I don't know. Perhaps I should not have come here — to the place where Drew died. Ever since I arrived I've felt myself in the presence of ghosts."

"Nonsense," I said.

One corner of her mouth twisted in a half-smile. "No, I don't believe in ghosts. But I'm glad you're in reach — just in case."

"I came to borrow a match," I said, starting to rise from the chair, "or a light from your candle."

"Wait. I want to show you something." She slid off the bed and kneeled to lift the lid of her dome trunk, rummaging about in a miscellaneous collection of women's geegaws. "Would you mind opening the window, Sam? It's close in here." She turned and grinned at me. "Even up here on the second floor, I didn't want ghosts floating through my window."

The window was hinged, with a hook fastener. When I opened it, fog drifted in heavy with river odors. Sounds were muffled yet seemed closer. The piano no longer played; laughter and shouts were less frequent. A male singer, his voice hollow-toned, began a ballad, ended it, started another, and was silent.

"Look," Kathleen said. She held out an

opened locket, heart-shaped, with a faded portrait of a young woman fitted inside. "This was sent to me with Drew's personal belongings when the War Department notified me of his death."

I studied the photograph a moment and asked her who it was. "I don't know," she replied. "For a time I thought it was perhaps someone he'd loved before he married me. But recently I've come to believe that the locket belonged to one of the other soldiers. If it had been Drew's, surely he would have shown it to me sometime or other. I never saw the locket before."

"What do you propose doing with it?" I asked.

"I'd like to return it to the War Department. That portrait haunts me, Sam. I want to be rid of it, see that it reaches whoever —"

Kathleen stopped in midsentence, her eyes widening in surprise. Or was it fear? The words of the deep-voiced singer sounded clearly from below the window. He hesitated over the harmonizing of a chord, seeming to reach for some long-forgotten lyric. "Ghosts," she said, shivering slightly. "The voice of a ghost."

"You could return the locket to the commander at Fort Rawley," I suggested, "and ask that an attempt be made to find an owner."

The voice below us, carried by the fog, seemed to flow right through the window into the tiny hotel room:

> *Pretty Kathy Martin*
> *Tiptoe fine,*
> *She could not get a man*
> *To suit her mind.*

I thought Kathleen was going to faint and fall to the floor. She did drop the locket, and I reached out and caught her shoulders to steady her. She leaned her head against my chest. "It is a ghost," she whispered. "It is a ghost."

"It's only a half-drunken boatman or miner," I said.

"No. The song is 'Pretty *Betty* Martin.' Only Drew Hardesty sang 'Pretty *Kathy* Martin,' and he sang it only to me."

The reverberating voice continued below:

> *Some were too coarse*
> *And some too fine,*
> *She could not get a man*
> *To suit her kind.*

Kathleen sat on the edge of the bed, holding her hands over her ears. I walked to the window and looked down through the fog. The lights of the three steamboats appeared to radiate from the depths of the river, overlapping into a weird glow.

"I've heard the song sung as 'Pretty Kathy Martin,' " I said.

When she looked up at me her eyes revealed doubt and fear. "Then you heard Drew Hardesty sing it," she whispered.

"No, the singer was a man named Selkirk," I said. "I'm going down there to look for him. When I find him, I'll bring him up here to prove it."

She held on to my arms like a bewildered child. "No, stay here with me, Sam. I feel safe with you." She forced a quick smile. "Maybe it's because you remind me of Drew Hardesty, the way he was before the war, easygoing, so absolutely sure of himself." She drew a handkerchief from a pocket of her robe and pressed it against her face. "You resemble him in other ways. Tall, strong, even your eyes, those dark brown eyes that see everything at once."

She did not want to release me. I wondered if she dreaded what I might discover for her down there in the fog. Hardly any sounds came from the street or the river landing. "Lock and latch the door after me," I said quietly. "I'm going to expunge that ghost for you."

With a sigh of resignation she let me go. I stood outside the closed door until I heard the wooden latch fall into place, and then hurried along the dark and empty hallway. The dining room and foyer downstairs were also deserted. Only a few passersby, some staggering or weaving from too much drink, were moving on the wooden sidewalk. Between the hotel and the nearest saloon was an alleyway that led toward the river. It was gray with fog that smelled of horses and hay and manure. At the end I found a livery stable fronting the slope to the river. Through a wide door that was open to the spring night, I saw a lantern suspended from a low rafter. A blacksmith's forge barely glowed beneath it, giving off a pungent odor of coal smoke. A man was there under the circle of light, seated on a heap of horse blankets, his back against a burlap bag of oats. One hand held an empty whiskey bottle, the other moved in the air as if he were directing a choir. He was humming "Brinon on the Moor" with considerable force.

Ah, my Good Samaritan," he cried mockingly when I came within the ring of lantern light. He waved the empty bottle at me. "Sorry, I can't offer you a welcoming drink."

"We thought you had drowned," I said.

"No such luck." Under the lantern his eyes seemed sunk deeper than ever into their cavernous sockets, and the long ugly scar that was like a burned brand from ear to chin was distended by the shadows. He was not a man easy to be congenial with, this spectral being who called himself Alex Selkirk.

"I met one of your former associates today," I said. "The ex-sergeant, Joseph O'Hara."

"Yes, I know." He lifted his head so that I could see the gleam in his eyes for a moment, and I wondered if the irises were dark brown like mine. "You and the Iron Maiden," he added, flicking his tongue across his lips. "You went with her to see him."

"You followed her tonight, didn't you?" I said accusingly. "What is she to you?"

He was silent for a time, then reached out to grasp the handle of the bellows, turning it to blow the coal in the forge into brilliant flame. "We will speak not of the maiden," he said in a stagy intonation. "Only of the bobtailed little centaur, O'Hara. How he relishes his sudden prosperity!" He stopped turning the bellows handle and the flames fell back upon the orange-red coals. "O'Hara has no past, you know. He must've been born the bobtailed size he is now and was immediately swaddled into a blue army uniform. He had some learning somewhere, though, learning that was more than most officers out here had got. Maybe he'd killed a man, or impregnated a respectable girl, something like that somewhere back east. He was more than your profane, guzzling, brawling Irish noncom from the bogs. Somewhere he'd known what having the upper hand is, mastery, control of the reins, sir. He wanted to control *me*, his major, pull on my bridle."

"He gave you the credit for his survival and the survival of the others on that blizzard march back from Canada," I said. "O'Hara praised you for never abandoning hope nor allowing any of the others to abandon hope."

I could not determine from Selkirk's face whether he was surprised or not, but his tone softened a bit. "So O'Hara said that, did he? Well, he was wrong. Our deliverer was Blue Sky Woman. Towanjila. Without her we'd all be skeletons somewhere between here and Maison du Chien Butte. Let me tell you about it."

10

Snow fell only intermittently after they left the Canadian border, Selkirk said, but dawnlight came slowly. At midday when they reached the rock shelter at Maison du Chien Butte, the sky was still gray and forbidding.

While O'Hara and Nettie Steever got a small fire going inside, the others removed the thongs that held Spotted Horse and Whirlwind to the sleds. After the two Sioux were allowed to relieve themselves they were taken inside the shelter, where Fromboise and Shanks carefully retied their wrists and ankles. Both Indians were still groggy, but were now well aware of what had happened to them. Whirlwind's face showed fright and humiliation, but Spotted Horse appeared to be more puzzled than anything else.

For some reason Selkirk decided that the two captives deserved an explanation of their condition. He asked Fromboise and O'Hara to inform Whirlwind that he would soon be released to return to his people. As soon as Whirlwind understood, he responded with smiles and nods of his head.

"Tell Spotted Horse that he will be given a fair trial," Selkirk said. "If he is innocent of crimes against American citizens he also will be set free."

Both Fromboise and O'Hara made an attempt to impart this abstract promise to the Sioux chief in his own language. The trader spluttered aimlessly in a mixture of Lakota and French, then threw up his hands in a gesture of hopelessness. "I can't get it across to him, either, sir," O'Hara finally protested. "With signs or words."

Spotted Horse looked from one to another of the white men, finally fixing his gaze upon Selkirk as the one with most authority. In a deep voice he spoke a few words of Lakota, slowly.

"What did he say?" Selkirk asked.

"He say he want nothin' to do with Americains," Fromboise interpreted. "They not treat him well."

Selkirk admitted to himself that Spotted Horse certainly did not have the appearance of a savage murderer. The chief was rather handsome in the way old men can be, with iron-gray hair parted in the middle and falling shaggily over his ears. His nose was too broad, his mouth wide and heavy-lipped, but his eyes — that seemed intent upon staring down Selkirk — gleamed with an alert intelligence. Selkirk found himself admiring the man's calm acceptance of his captivity, and he regretted that he could not exchange thoughts with him.

After a few moments of silence the Sioux spoke again, and Fromboise interpreted: "You have driven me from my country, white man. You own my country now, yet you come over into the Grandmother's Land to bring me back to Dakota."

"What does he mean by Grandmother's Land?"

"Queen Victoria's Canada," Fromboise explained.

"Why do you seek me out?" Spotted Horse continued. "I seek nobody. Least of all do I seek Americans."

Selkirk started to have Fromboise tell Spotted Horse that he was a murderer of white settlers, but he stopped in midsentence. Conversation with the Sioux chief was fruitless. After all, he thought, if he were Spotted Horse he would feel the same way.

That night the four white men stood successive guard watches, both inside and outside the shelter, but the dark hours passed uneventfully. By first dawn the snow had stopped falling, but the skies were still heavy and gray, and the wind was rising. It made a weird keening at the corners of the rock shelter.

After a hasty breakfast they began preparations to resume the journey. Fromboise saddled his horse first and then stood beside the animal, sniffing the weather. "I tell you somet'ing, commandant," he said to Selkirk. "I don't like what I feel in my bones. I think we see much snow this day."

They had decided to release Whirlwind when they were ready to leave the shelter, but the Sioux seemed unwilling to be separated from Spotted Horse. His faint-hearted manner of the previous evening was replaced by a fierceness in his speech. Spotted Horse on the other hand submitted with resignation when Shanks and O'Hara carried him out to the sled and fastened him tightly upon it with the rawhide thongs.

Before O'Hara finished loading the pack horse, Fromboise started his mount forward to take the lead across the unmarked expanse of powdery snow. The wind had already whipped it into rolling drifts so that the land resembled a stormy white sea. Nettie Steever waited a minute, then climbed into her saddle and followed Fromboise. She had spoken only a few words that morning, and seemed lost in a melancholy reverie.

"Look to the north!" Shanks cried suddenly. "Horseman heading our way."

The horse and rider formed a tiny black triangle quivering against the line where gray sky met the white land.

"He's coming fast," O'Hara said.

Shanks made a circle of his gloved hands and squinted through them across the snow. He studied the rider for two or three minutes and then said quietly: "It's Medlock."

"Why Medlock?" Selkirk asked.

"He wanted more than we agreed to pay." Shanks walked to his horse, pulled his rifle from its boot, and checked the load; then he replaced the weapon loosely.

"What are you going to do?" Selkirk demanded sharply.

Shanks was already in his saddle. "Go and deal with the bastard, major. That's my duty, not yours." He patted the saddlebag where he carried the canvas sack of gold.

Selkirk turned and was surprised to see how far Fromboise and Mrs. Steever had gone. "Shall we call Nettie and Fromboise back?"

"No. Go on." Shanks lifted his bridle reins. "I'll catch up to you."

"What of the Indian tied up in the shelter? You don't want him free between you and us."

"Leave him there," Shanks cried impatiently. "I'll turn him loose when I come back by here." He started his horse off at a fast walk. The hoofbeats were muffled almost into soundlessness.

"Watch yourself," Selkirk called after him. "Medlock could turn mean."

The wind swept Shanks's reply away, but it sounded to Selkirk as if he'd said: "I can handle him."

After ordering O'Hara to move slowly with the pack horse so as to keep within Shanks's view, Selkirk mounted and started with the sled. He could see Nettie a short distance ahead, but Fromboise was obscured by the fine windblown snow that was also rapidly filling in the hoof marks made by the forward horses.

About an hour later Selkirk noticed that the snow lifted by the wind was growing denser, screening out the riders ahead of him. When he looked back he could barely see O'Hara's two horses. It was then that he realized the flakes were falling from the sky. The storm had renewed itself, this time with a wind force that drove the snow horizontally and in blinding sheets. He raised himself in his stirrups, calling out Nettie's name, and a few minutes later he saw the black shapes of two standing horses. Nettie and Fromboise had stopped and dismounted.

"We stay together now," the French trader said. His bushy white eyebrows were enlarged by snowflakes that clung to the hairs until he brushed them away. "I think we better turn to east now, commandant. We find shelter in bottoms of La Petite Mauvais. Some brush, some wood for fires may-be."

In a few minutes O'Hara arrived and Selkirk noted that the pack horse was blowing badly. The sergeant followed Selkirk's gaze. "No, sir, that animal don't take to this weather. Too old, I'd say." He dropped easily from the saddle. "Did you hear anything like rifle shots, sir?" he asked, cocking his head back to look up at Selkirk.

"Rifle shots? No. When?"

"Half-hour past, I judge. Soon after I lost sight of Shanks. I dared not stop when the snow started up again for fear I'd lose sight of you. It might've been only ice cracking under the snow."

Selkirk nodded. "The wind does funny things with sounds out here. Perhaps it was cracking ice."

The wait for Shanks seemed endless. For a time they stood on the lee side of their horses, frequently stamping their feet and waving their arms to fight off the invading cold. A fire was impossible; not a scrap of fuel of any kind existed on that plain of icy whiteness.

Fromboise alternately warned and complained of the delay. They needed all the daylight that remained to reach the wooded bottomland, he said. "No," Selkirk insisted. "We wait for Shanks. If he does not come, we'll go back for him when the storm lets up."

Shaking his head, the trader muttered to himself in French, then added soberly: "Storm will not stop this day."

At last a gale-driven sheet of falling snow lifted suddenly like a curtain to reveal a horse and rider. They might have been blown there by the wind, disembodied phantoms dusted by white powder. Selkirk and O'Hara strode together toward Shanks, saw at the same instant the dark streaks of frozen blood on his trouser leg when he tried to dismount and stumbled in the snow. O'Hara caught the bridle of the frightened walleyed horse while Selkirk tried to lift Shanks to his feet.

"What happened?" Selkirk demanded.

"Damn." Shanks's voice was a gurgling rasp. "God damn!" He fought to gain control of himself, holding desperately to Selkirk's offered arm, then collapsed on his back in the snow. Selkirk opened Shanks's buffalo coat; blood still oozed unfrozen from his shirt over his belt.

"He's gut shot," Nettie Steever said as

though pronouncing a sentence of death without emotion. When Selkirk turned at the sound of her voice, her eyes were all that he could see of her. She had twisted a blanket shawl around her head, leaving only a slit above her nose.

"If we can get him back to Fort Standish," Selkirk responded sharply, "Surgeon Lieber can save him."

They put Shanks on the sled, after removing Spotted Horse from it and transferring him to Shanks's saddle, lashing his legs together with a girth tie. Then they started, slanting away from the wind, still in single file, keeping close together, with Spotted Horse between Selkirk and Nettie Steever. Instead of slackening, the snowfall thickened, and after they passed the first low ridge in a series of undulations, Fromboise called for frequent stops while he tried to match his compass with obscured landmarks.

All afternoon they were either ascending or descending, the horses struggling through great drifts or stumbling into gullies leveled by snow. Late in the day they came to the first wooded slope, but the drifts were so deep that only the tops of trees were visible. As Fromboise turned them toward a flat-faced bluff, Selkirk heard O'Hara's voice calling shrilly from the rear. He ordered a halt, summoned

Fromboise to guard Spotted Horse, and then dismounted and walked back over the beaten trail to find the sergeant.

The pack horse had stumbled and rolled into a snowfilled swale. Selkirk found O'Hara on the rim of the hollow, trying to retrieve some of the packs from the prostrate animal.

"Front leg's broke," O'Hara said. He lifted one pack. It was darkened with water that was beginning to freeze. O'Hara had slipped into the half-frozen marsh and his boots and trousers were also filming with ice. The horse stopped floundering but was breathing in quick rasping gasps.

"Shoot the animal," Selkirk ordered.

"I saved only this one pack," O'Hara replied. "Most our dried meat's under the damned horse."

"Shoot the suffering beast," Selkirk repeated impatiently. "You'll be solid ice yourself if you don't get dried out. Come on, we'll try to find wood for a fire. Or you'll be a gangrenous corpse before we reach Fort Standish."

It was Fromboise's opinion that they should stop on a ledge at the base of the bluff ahead. The frozen creek that ran between them and the ledge was buried beneath several feet of powdery snow, but after Fromboise's horse fought its way across, the others followed easily. During the crossing Selkirk noted clusters of driftwood that had been caught in the crotches of trees during past floods. As soon as Fromboise brought the little column to a halt, Selkirk asked O'Hara and Nettie to get a fire going as quickly as possible and gather all the dry wood they could find before darkness fell.

When Selkirk lifted the fur covering from Shanks's head and saw bloody mucus oozing from a corner of the man's mouth, he knew there was little hope for the gaunt keeper of Colonel Herrick's gold. Later, when he and O'Hara eased Shanks off the sled and placed him on a bed of willow tops, with his feet toward the fire, the wounded man opened his eyes and spoke imploringly: "My bag, my bag. Where is my bag, major?" He kept repeating the question until Selkirk went to Shanks's horse and brought the canvas bag, still heavy with gold, and let him touch it with his fingers. Shanks tried to sit up and lift the bag; he would not stop muttering and struggling until Selkirk placed it between his legs where he could feel the pressure of coins against his blood-soaked flesh.

By nightfall they had a crude shelter of poles and brush erected, with its opening to the fire. The single pack roll that O'Hara had retrieved from the fallen horse contained only a few boxes of hard biscuits and a bottle of brandy. Selkirk rationed these carefully; no one could guess how long the scanty resources would have to sustain them. If the blizzard continued, they would have to try digging other packs out of the ice below the dead horse.

With the snow continuing to fall, in fine stinging particles now, he saw no reason to post guard except for keeping the fire going. Shanks remained unconscious, whether sleeping or dying, Selkirk could not tell. They all lay or sat under the shelter, warming one another, Shanks and Spotted Horse flanked by Selkirk and O'Hara on one side, Nettie Steever and Fromboise on the other. They seemed hypnotized by the flakes spinning wildly above the fire, some falling into the flames, others being whirled away by erratic wind currents along the bluff.

"Humans are no more than snowflakes," Nettie said. "Blown about. No more control over our lives than a snowflake." She shivered under her layer of Hudson's Bay blankets. "I could be warmer," she added, "with another swallow of that brandy."

"Tomorrow we'll really need it," Selkirk replied.

"It's long hours till tomorrow," she protested.

"Talk passes time," he said. "Tell us about Nettie Steever."

"You tell us first about Major Rawley," she retorted.

"We'll each tell of our worst ordeal," he suggested. "You start, O'Hara."

The sergeant grunted in surprise. "I reckon my worst trial, sir, had nothing to do with fortunes of war." He stopped and stared dreamily into the fire, but his jaw clamped shut as if to stop any further revelations of his past life.

"What was it then?"

O'Hara shrugged. "Nothing uncommon, sir. A woman, it was."

"What about this woman? How did she put you through your fiercest ordeal?"

"She was another man's wife." The sergeant frowned and bit at his lower lip. "I'd rather not go into it, sir, if you don't mind."

After several moments of silence, Nettie spoke up sympathetically: "It does no good to look back, does it, O'Hara? That is what most of my life has been — ordeals, as Major Rawley calls them. Horrors brought by broken promises. Lies and deceptions." She leaned toward the fire, opening her blanket to let the heat warm her breasts. "You want talk, major. All right, I'll tell you a story. One of the Sioux women who knows our lingo told it. The Indians are no different from us. Deceitful like us, honest like us. But it is always of another people, is it not, when any of us tell wickedness? The Sioux say the beautiful wicked woman of this story was an Arikara instead of a Sioux. The beautiful woman was wicked, so she was of another people, yes. This beautiful Arikara gave birth to a boy baby. She and her man and this little boy lived happy together for five, maybe six years. Then one summer the man went off on a long hunt, several weeks he was gone. During this time a younger and handsomer man noticed the beautiful woman was alone and came to court her secretly at night. She liked the handsome young man and she did as he wanted her to do. After the husband returned, they continued to meet in secret and because each desired the other with such fire they decided they must live together, away from the husband. Neither the young man nor the beautiful woman could raise enough boldness to slay the husband. So they made another plan. The woman feigned sickness and then pretended to be dead. In the custom of the tribe, her grieving husband built a burial arbor and wrapped her in a fresh buffalo hide and placed her upon the scaffold. That night her young lover came with three dead dogs that he had killed and skinned. He helped her down from the scaffold and put the dead dogs in her place under the buffalo hide. The handsome young man had brought with him men's clothing — leggings, moccasins, and such, and in these the beautiful woman dressed as a man. She tied her breasts down tight with wide strips of cloth so that not much of them showed. Then they went off to another village where the woman passed herself as a young man.

"After they stayed a long time in the village, living happy with their secret, the woman grew eager to see her child, the little boy, so she and the young man painted themselves as for a hunt and went to the edge of their former village, seating themselves on a rock beside a spring where everyone came during the day for water. Among them the little boy came for water, and when the disguised mother saw him she wanted to take him up in her arms. 'No!' the handsome young man warned her, but she insisted, thinking her son would not know her dressed as a man. She went and stood beside a tree on the path, and when her son came by she said, 'Little boy, will you let me drink from your bucket?' While she drank the boy looked closely at her, and then went on to his tipi and told his father that he had seen his mother.

The father would not believe him, of course, but the boy said, 'There are two people dressed as men on the path to the spring, and one of them is my mother.'

"Again the father did not believe his son, but the boy was so persistent that he decided to test the two young men. He would put them through an ordeal without their knowing it, if such a thing is possible. First, he started some dried buffalo meat to boiling and then sent his son to invite the two young men to come and eat in the tipi. 'If it is true that one of the two is not a man,' he said to himself, 'but instead is my wife returned from the dead, I will find out. There are two things they must do when they enter my tipi. First, they must step over the ridge at the entrance. If they are both men they will step with their feet straight forward. If one is a woman she will step over the ridge with her foot sidewise. Second, after they have eaten and I offer them a pipe to smoke, I shall know that one is a woman if she refuses to smoke.'

"Soon the two persons dressed as men came to the tipi. The first one stepped over the ridge with his feet forward. The second one instead of stepping forward placed each foot sidewise. By this the husband knew that the second person was not a man. He gave them food and after they had eaten, he filled a pipe with kinnikinnick, lighted it, and gave it to them to smoke. When the woman took the pipe and put it up to her mouth, instead of drawing smoke the way a man would, she blew into the pipe.

"The husband at once took a sharp knife from his belt and said: 'I have found you out. You are my wife returned from the dead.'

"The woman screamed and asked forgiveness of him, saying she would live with him again and try to be a good wife. At the same time the handsome young man jumped up and ran out of the tipi, deserting her.

"Being very angry, the husband said, 'You are dead to me still. But I will save you from having your breasts tied down to make you look like a man. I will cut them off so that your breasts will always be smooth.' With his knife he then cut her breasts off.

"The woman ran and fell at the tipi entrance and died. The man went to the platform where he had placed her the day she pretended to die, and there he found the three dead dogs. He knew by this how she had tricked him."

Nettie Steever stopped abruptly, and bent forward with her hands to the fire.

"That is all of your story?" Fromboise asked, yawning over his question.

"Yes." She laughed. "It was putting you to

sleep, Antoine. The way it put the old Indian to sleep."

Spotted Horse was snoring quietly, oblivious to the laughter of his captors.

"I suppose the story has a moral," Selkirk said dryly. "What does it mean, really?"

"It means that people are not always who or what they seem to be."

"Yes." He looked away from her. "Most of us are not what we seem to be."

O'Hara took the first fire watch, but Selkirk could not sleep and regretted not taking it himself. He lay under his buffalo coat, with furs packed between him and Shanks, who lay as still as death, breathing in irregular gasps, occasionally moaning indistinguishable words, or calling Medlock's name. Beyond him Spotted Horse still snored quietly as though he was indifferent to what fate held for him and the others. Selkirk closed his eyes and longed for sleep to ease his weariness, but he could never reach closer than the edge of consciousness. His eyes would open and he could see the silhouette of O'Hara's muskrat cap against the glow of the fire. At last he heard O'Hara moving, felt the sergeant's hand touch his foot.

When Selkirk raised up, O'Hara whispered:

"Snow's stopped falling, sir."

Selkirk stood up outside the shelter, his teeth chattering as he got into his coat. "Here's your watch," O'Hara said, handing him the gold-cased timepiece, and then turning to crawl under the furs in the shelter. Selkirk heard him sigh. *He probably fell asleep instantly,* he thought with resentment as he sat down on the pile of dry wood facing the fire. He stared at the watch in his hand, at the initials *C.R.* engraved in the hunting case. Charles Rawley's watch, the one he'd found beside his body on the Malpais, a century ago it seemed. *Except for duty hours, of what use is a timepiece out here?* he thought. *Daylight and dark and survival — they're all that count.* He felt for the tiny key on the chain, inserted it in the winding slot, and turned it slowly until he felt a tightening of the spring. He then slipped the watch carefully into an inner pocket. He was drowsy now from the flickering warmth of the wood flames, but knew he had to fight against sleep until four o'clock when Fromboise's turn would come.

He did not have to awaken Fromboise. About an hour before his time, the trader crawled out of the shelter, muttering that he was unable to sleep. He talked in a mixture of French and English, in phrases instead of sentences, mumbling about the impossibility of sleep while lying beside une femme who kept him warm. Dormir sur les deux oreilles was not possible avec la parfum of this femme, the warmth of her body beside him.

Knowing that Fromboise was an early riser, anyhow, Selkirk saw no reason why the trader should not start his fire watch early. He stayed beside the older man for a few minutes, talking of the chances of reaching Fort Standish in one long day's journey. C'est possible if the storm has passed, the trader considered. Also the condition of the drifts, the direction and depth of the drifts. If the wind left enough open prairie so the horses could move swiftly, yes, il est possible de la faire by sunset.

"Speaking of the horses," Selkirk said, "they've been restless the last hour."

Fromboise squinted across the fire at the dark shapes of the animals picketed twenty or thirty yards down the sloping edge. "Hungaire!" He surmised. "We cut cottonwood bark for them soon."

"Wake me at first light," Selkirk said and turned into the shelter to burrow under the furs vacated by Fromboise. He could feel the warmth of Nettie Steever, and remembered the time when they had first been together with the wagon train. They had drawn close to each other then, like lovers, but everything had changed between them. He had no special feeling for her now and he wondered if it was something within him that was repelled by the knowledge of her life as a captive. Soiled goods, she had said, tainted like a fish too long from water. If that was it, he was ashamed of his feelings, yet he could not help himself.

Unlike Fromboise, he now found the warmth of Nettie more soporific than arousing. He never slept so soundly.

It was Nettie who awakened him, her cold hand slapping gently against his face, laughing at his confusion. "Antoine Fromboise is fast asleep out there and I fear the fire is gone," she said. He raised up quickly. Fromboise was bent forward, his head between his knees. Something was wrong, something was missing in the starkness of the winter landscape.

The horses, all of them, were gone from the slanted ledge. A wave of dismay, of defeat and culpability, flooded through him. He should have been more cautious, more military. Amos Medlock must have followed them through the blizzard and now he had their horses to trade for the gold that Shanks had kept from him. In an instant he shouted O'Hara awake, and at the same time aroused Shanks who tried to sit up but had not the strength for it. "Where — are we?" Shanks said weakly.

"Halfway to Fort Standish," Selkirk answered him. "Horses are gone. I think Medlock took them during the night."

Shanks shook his head, and a faint smile quivered across his dry lips. "Not Medlock. I shot him between the eyes — after — after he shot me in the belly."

Selkirk hurried past Fromboise who was kneeling to blow on the dead coals, trying to bring fire back to them. The Frenchman darted a sheepish glance at the major, but said nothing.

O'Hara, still half asleep, caught up with Selkirk at the place where the horses had been picketed. The snow, trampled by hooves and stained yellow with urine, had refrozen. Leading away from there was a broad trail that soon narrowed where the horses evidently had fallen into single file. It continued across the frozen creek.

"Maybe they broke loose, sir," O'Hara said, "and wandered off for forage."

Selkirk pointed at what was left of the picket ties; the ropes had been cleanly severed with a sharp knife.

By this time the sun was on the horizon, bleary, almost colorless, without warmth. To the north, across the creek, Selkirk caught a flash of movement on the low sharp-backed ridge that had been swept clean of snow. Seconds later two riders came into full view and halted facing the ledge where Selkirk and O'Hara stood. "That's Medlock's horse!" O'Hara cried.

"Yes, with an Indian in the saddle, and he's brought along a friend." Selkirk swore angrily. "Perhaps old Spotted Horse can tell us who they are. They'll probably want to trade for him."

Spotted Horse confirmed what Selkirk had already guessed. The Indian on Medlock's horse was Whirlwind. After a few minutes, the other rider started slowly toward them. The sun had broken through the clouds momentarily, and the refracted light from the snow created an illusion of horse and rider dancing down the slope. The horse was heavier than the usual Indian mustang, but the rider though wrapped in furs and blankets appeared to be no larger than a child.

"Towanjila!" Spotted Horse cried, adding a few Lakota words almost breathlessly.

"What did he say?" Selkirk asked O'Hara.

The sergeant shook his head. "Wiwasteka, wiwasteka," he repeated. "A woman, I think."

"Yes," Nettie Steever spoke from behind

271

them. "I've seen her before on that horse, in the tipi village. She lives back in the woods with Spotted Horse's people, but often comes down to the creek for water."

Towanjila rode slowly up the ledge. She dropped the silver-streaked collar of the fur coat from around her head, and Selkirk was surprised by the beauty of her young face. With no sign of uncertainty or fear she dismounted and walked across the hard-frozen corrugated snow in her boot moccasins to the captive Sioux. "Sun Pejuta," she said, her low voice the only sound in the silence of the winter morning. She stood straight and motionless while he put a hand on her shoulder and repeated her name: "Towanjila, Towanjila."

"Sun Pejuta!" Nettie Steever said, looking first at O'Hara and then at the Indian. "He's the old Sioux medicine man."

"Yeah. Sun Pejuta means Medicine Horse." O'Hara stepped closer to the Indian, pointing at him. "Sun Gleska. You Sun Gleska?"

The Sioux appeared to be startled by the question. He shook his head, tapping his chest with his clenched fist. And then he told them something that changed everything. "No, no. Sun Pejuta!"

"Good God, Major Rawley," O'Hara cried.

"We've brought out the wrong Indian! He's not Spotted Horse. He's Medicine Horse!"

The time was well past midnight in the town of Fort Rawley, and I was sitting on a stool in that dingy livery stable with its odors of horses and hay and manure mixed with blacksmith's smells of metal and coal sulphur, all relieved by the fainter aroma of a river in springtime. I was wondering if Selkirk's long silence meant that he had told me all he was going to tell of that harrowing blizzard journey from Canada. The glass chimney of the lantern hanging from the rafter above his head was beginning to darken from a smoking wick. Although seated only a few yards from me he was indistinct, a shadow among shadows, and I had the same feeling about him that I'd had before — that if I lost the flimsy link existing between us, he would cease to be anything more than an illusion. I knew that I must say something to him.

"I can imagine how shattering was the realization," I said, "that your captive was not Spotted Horse."

"No. No, you can't, Mr. Morrison." His voice was deep, and reverberated as if sounding from a well. "Not even with your fancy newspaper scribbler's tricks, you could not come closer than the other side of that river in conceiving what was in my brain and heart at that moment, what the effect was upon my soul — if there is such a thing — when I was told that I had Medicine Horse, not Spotted Horse. You forget Killdeer Mountain, you forget the Malpais, you forget the charade in which I'd entrapped myself, you forget the pressure of time which without warning might collapse the house of straw I'd created. All I could envision at that moment, when Nettie Steever and Sergeant O'Hara revealed the deception, was Fort Standish headquarters and the arrival there of the brave and persevering Major Charles Rawley, saluting Colonel Herrick and presenting him with the iniquitous Spotted Horse, erasing forever the cowardice of Killdeer Mountain with which I'd stained the family name of Rawley. And freeing me so that I could leave the damned Territory of Dakota forever unfettered and become myself again. You understand, Mr. Morrison?"

"Yes. You were faced with a dilemma."

"No, not a dilemma. There was an easy way out. Towanjila offered it while my head was still wheeling from the shock of realization. She and Whirlwind were willing to trade our horses back to us for her father. Her father,

Sun Pejuta. Medicine Horse. It might have been easy except for that image in my brain of my arrival at the Fort Standish headquarters of Colonel Herrick, with a fierce Sioux chief in my possession. And then the Frenchman, Antoine Fromboise, suddenly added a complicating factor to the equation. He'd sauntered down from the shelter, rifle cradled in one arm, an expression of suspicion on his face. 'So the little squaw stole our horses, eh?' he muttered, carelessly pointing his rifle at her.

" 'She's the daughter of that old Indian,' I told him, motioning toward our captive. 'And he's Medicine Horse. Not Spotted Horse.'

"For a moment Fromboise showed astonishment. 'Medicine Horse, not Spotted Horse?' His white eyebrows twitched up and down as he glanced back and forth from the old Indian to Towanjila. 'The little squaw told you this, commandant?' he asked quickly. I nodded and he pointed a finger at the girl, yelling, 'Dupery! Cakala! Trickster! Amos Medlock knows that old man is Spotted Horse.' He stared hard at me. 'You take her word against his, commandant?'

"Nettie was shaking her head. 'I've seen her with this old man,' she insisted. 'Several times, watering ponies at the creek.'

" 'Have you ever seen Spotted Horse?' I asked her.

" 'No, he stayed in his lodge back in the trees. I heard he was suffering from wounds.'

"Meanwhile Towanjila had been standing there beside her father, holding the rope halter, waiting for us to tell her if we'd trade Sun Pejuta for our stolen horses. So I asked Fromboise to inform her that her father was a prisoner, that he would be tried in a court of law for his participation in the Sioux War. If proved innocent he would be freed. I doubt if she comprehended much of that. She did understand my assertion that if our horses were not returned we would walk to the fort on the Missouri and that her father would walk with us.

"She replied with no show of disappointment or anger that she must tell Whirlwind of our refusal to trade. After a long look at her father she mounted and rode slowly across the frozen creek and up the slope to join Whirlwind. In a moment they both vanished down the farther side of that saddleback ridge.

"All this time Fromboise was telling me how crafty Indian chiefs could be, especially those who were hostiles. They changed their names to fool the white men, he said. Sun Pejuta and Sun Gleska could be the same chief. Le colonel

Herrick was a man of much savoir, he added, *clever enough if need be to make the world believe Medicine Horse was Spotted Horse."*

Selkirk's voice had lost its deep tones; he was feeling his fatigue, and I wondered if I'd be able to convince him to return with me to Kathleen Hardesty's room in the Hotel Como. But he wanted to finish the journey, and I wanted to know the ending of it.

His voice came stronger then, out of the shadows of the smithy: "I'll admit it to you now, Mr. Morrison, that transient remark of Fromboise's stuck in my mind. Oh, not consciously at first maybe. I never really believed it could be done, substitute an unknown Indian for an infamous Indian in a court of law."

"Was the man you'd captured Spotted Horse?" I asked.

He laughed, that wild way he'd laughed at me on the *Roanoke*. "He was condemned as Spotted Horse."

"Do you believe he was Spotted Horse?"

He made no reply. The silence of the sleeping town was broken by the howling of coyotes somewhere across the river.

"The five of you," I said then, "O'Hara, Mrs. Steever, Fromboise, Shanks, yourself — you did come out of the Bad Lands on foot — three days, wasn't it?"

"Four of us taking turns pulling Shanks on the dogsled until he died. He was better off dead, wounded like he was we could do nothing for him, suffering in his own filth on that sled, his skeleton limbs trembling, constantly whining to God in his madness. When he died we buried him under the ice with all his traps, except the gold which became my responsibility.

"Maybe the Lord did stretch out his arms to the rest of us. If he did, it was through Towanjila. For two nights and a day after we lost our horses, we had nothing to eat but hard crackers and brandy. We did not leave the bluff ledge until darkness fell because during the day Whirlwind kept hovering in our rear, sometimes firing a shot at us, but the bullets never came very close. He was using Medlock's long-range Spencer. I don't know whether his misses were caused by his unfamiliarity with the weapon or were deliberate because he feared he might hit Spotted Horse.

"At sunrise after our first night march, we made camp on the wind-cleared side of a rocky knoll. Buffalo chips were plentiful there, as the animals had used the place for shelter. We soon had a strong fire burning, and a good thing it was, too. We were all weak from hunger and the cold was intense. The glare of the morning sun on the icy landscape blinded us so that none of us noticed the approach of Towanjila until we heard the hooves of her big horse crunching through the snow crust.

"Both Sergeant O'Hara and Antoine Fromboise had their guns on her in an instant, but she showed no sign of fear, nor slowed her horse until she was a few steps from our fire. She clasped her hands in that peace sign the Sioux make, then dismounted, and in a few Lakota words — Fromboise interpreted them for me — she said that Whirlwind would no longer endanger us by shooting at us as long as she camped and traveled with her father. She had brought food for him, she said, and would share it with us.

"Fromboise feared treachery, and warned me in his parlez-vous lingo that I should order her to ride far ahead of us, but after she'd produced a sizable cut of frozen antelope meat the French trader was less hostile toward her. We all sat around the fire and shared the meat; it was burned but delicious. She told us that Whirlwind had killed the antelope the day before and that she had almost lost our trail trying to overtake us during the night. She also revealed something that Shanks had failed to mention before he died. Instead of releasing Whirlwind as he had promised, Shanks left him in the rock shelter at Maison du Chien Butte. Had Towanjila not found him and cut the rawhide ties, he surely would have died during the blizzard. He therefore owed his life to her.

"That afternoon we tested Towanjila's promise that Whirlwind would allow us to travel unmolested. We started straight for the Missouri River in broad daylight, and although I occasionally saw our pursuer silhouetted against the northern horizon, he never came close enough, nor showed any inclination, to fire at us.

"We camped that night with the frozen surface of the Missouri below us, and for the first time since leaving Maison du Chien Butte I felt confident that I would survive to see Fort Standish before another sunset. I took late sentry duty, and to my surprise Towanjila came to sit across the fire from me, and was soon shyly trying to convey her thoughts by signs and the few words of English she knew. As best I could tell, she wanted me to know that her father was a man of peace and that I should release him to return to his people. At that time I did not know whether to believe her or not, and I was so rude as to make little effort to respond to her overtures. As my watch had stopped, probably from the intense cold, I did not know when to awaken Fromboise, and I was gratified when he crawled out of his blankets, yawning and groaning and casting suspicious glances at Towanjila. When I told him that I had no idea how long it was until daylight, he searched out a flat pebble and hurled it toward the starry black sky. 'Old man's arm no good,' he said. 'You throw one, commandant, high as you can.' I flung the pebble he gave me as hard as I could and saw pale light flash upon it when it reached the apogee of the throw. 'So,' he said with a shrug. 'You don't need a watch, commandant. Gravelstone tell us sun will rise soon. Hour maybe. Catch some sleep fast, commandant.'

"We had no shelter that night other than the branches of cottonwoods above us. While I was wrapping myself in furs and a blanket, Towanjila rolled a stone she had placed beside the fire up to my feet, then brought another for her father.

"With warm feet I slept through sunrise, was awakened by a strange crackling sound and the smell of smoke. A strong wind had come up to beat at the ice clinging to the bare limbs of the trees which shivered and screeched as though in pain. When I walked across to the fire, the iced grass stems broke like brittle bones beneath my boots.

"Towanjila was a worker of miracles. From one of her buffalo-skin saddlebags she had taken some flour, mixed it with melted snow, and was baking the dough on the end of a green willow stick. She gave the first baked roll to her father, but later there was also one for each of the rest of us. I think it may have been that morning, standing above her kneeling figure, looking down at her small hands and the delicate nape of her neck that I became bound to Towanjila the Blue Sky Woman." He stopped, then laughed that wild laugh again. "Love, as you may know, Mr. Morrison, can be a corrupting force."

"Yes," I said, holding back a question, waiting for him to continue.

"But not as corrupting as gold. That afternoon, from a low hill near the river, we sighted the stockade and north bastion of Fort Standish. We halted there, each of us aching with some personal affliction from the strain of the journey, all of us victims of frost that had burned our skins and eaten at our fingers and toes. We suffered from mental exhaustion also, a torment that can be more damaging to the spirit than physical distress."

Selkirk paused in his narrative, listening, and then I heard the wild geese high above Fort Rawley, thousands of them following the river northward, filling the air with their honking. He raised up from his improvised seat on the horse blankets and walked past me to the open door of the livery stable. "Reassuring," he said. "That sound. A signal, a promise that the world will go on as it always has."

After the flight had passed over, he slapped his hands against his thighs. "I wasn't trying to justify myself," he said almost apologetically, "when I told you how I — how we all were suffering from exhaustion. I remember in that last hour of our ordeal the wind was especially keen, cutting like cold steel into our faces. Fromboise had already started along the narrow river trail. Towanjila was waiting beside her horse. We had lashed her father to the dogsled again and fastened it to her horse. Sergeant O'Hara and Nettie Steever were resting on two flat-topped rock outcroppings, waiting for me to start the last painful stage of our journey.

"I turned to Towanjila's horse and unfastened the bag I'd attached to her saddle, Shanks's canvas bag that still contained much of the gold he'd taken to Canada. Slinging it across one arm, I walked over and stood between Nettie and O'Hara. 'When I deliver that Indian to Colonel Herrick within the hour,' I said, 'he'll be Spotted Horse. Otherwise, everything we have done will have no meaning.' Nettie and O'Hara both stared at me as if I had gone mad. Perhaps I had. I said that since Antoine would not question his identity, only the two of them could raise doubts. Towanjila might try, but she would never be listened to. With the delivery, my duty at Fort Standish was finished and I'd leave as soon as a thaw brought us a steamboat. I told them that after I'd gone, they could say what they pleased about Sun Pejuta or Sun Gleska. Or whoever he may be."

Selkirk stopped talking again; then he turned and walked past me to the horse blankets, but remained standing. "Even as I said the words — that I'd be leaving — I was looking at Towanjila and the man strapped on the sled, and I knew in my heart that I could not. But I went through the motions, yes, I went through the motions."

"You gave O'Hara and Nettie Steever the gold? To keep them quiet?"

He laughed. "What do you think?" He turned and started into the gloom of the stables, as though dismissing me.

"Wait," I called after him. He stopped still for a moment as I almost shouted: "You're Drew Hardesty, aren't you?"

If he was startled, he gave no sign of it. "What do you think?" he countered again.

"I want you to go back with me to the hotel."

"My Good Samaritan again, eh?" His voice was almost scornful, the words fading as he moved away. "Can't you let a man ease himself?"

I waited for ten minutes, maybe a quarter-hour, then took the lantern from the rafter and started in search of him. He had gone out a side door, and I could not find him in the privies, or anywhere in the deserted alleys and streets of the town of Fort Rawley.

11

I awakened the next morning so drowned in sleep that a full minute must have passed before I realized that I was in Kathleen Hardesty's room. Then I remembered coming back to the Hotel Como in the late hours of the night, noticing the spray of light along the crack at the bottom of her locked door, thinking surely she had fallen asleep during my prolonged absence. But while I was fiddling with the key in my own door, hers opened behind me and she whispered my name, motioning me to come in.

"Where is he?" she demanded, at first almost angrily, then teasingly: "You promised you would bring him here to expunge my ghost."

She was quite excited, and some of this was communicated to me while I lamely tried to explain how Selkirk had eluded me. I muttered something to the effect that probably he *was* a ghost, which was the wrong thing to say to her. She was still apprehensive, and her fears drove her to me as the only staunch protector in reach. After a long day with the ghosts of Major Charles Rawley, Alex Selkirk, and Drew Hardesty I was in a state of indefiniteness. I had taken on some of the attributes of each ghost, had become an amorphous shape myself, like the river fog that drifted into the window of that cramped hotel room. So I was not much of a guardian for her, falling asleep on the uncomfortable hotel chair that left me feeling as if I'd been trampled by a horse.

When I awoke she was holding a mirror in which she could see me rising from the chair. She was wearing the tight-waisted green dress that set off her fine figure and complexion. She turned and smiled and said: "Make yourself presentable, Sam Morrison. You're going with me to see the fort commander. I must verify Joseph O'Hara's arrangements for the disinterment tomorrow, and I'm following your advice and returning the locket that I showed you last night."

I wouldn't have missed going with her, although I disliked her peremptory manner, and told her so. After a splendid breakfast in Signora Martini's dining room, we walked in the coolness of the morning up the hill to the gate of Fort Rawley.

Obviously Senator Rawley had seen to it that

the U.S. Congress was generous in its appropriations for construction of the new fort that was to honor the name of his son. Although not yet completed, because most of the designated materials had to be shipped upriver by boat, the north façade was solid and imposing. Roughhewn oak slabs that must have come all the way from Missouri formed an impenetrable stockade divided in the middle by a wide sallyport. From towers at each end, large flags flapped in the wind, and after we entered we were greeted by the most resplendent array of red, white, and blue banners, gonfalons, pennons, and oriflammes that I had seen since the day I'd watched the Union army celebrating the ending of the war in a grand march up Pennsylvania Avenue in Washington City.

The headquarters building was to our right, faced with stone and Saint Louis red bricks, and the interior was luxurious in comparison with those of other frontier posts. The floor was made of tongued and grooved pine, the walls and ceilings lath and plaster. The acting commander, Captain Lowe, had been expecting Kathleen, and he received her warmly, but when he learned that I was a newspaper correspondent he became suspicious of my presence. I was not surprised. Three years of following the war for the *Herald* had taught me that military men distrust the press, perhaps with good reasons.

"I very much regret," Captain Lowe said to Kathleen, with a slightly hostile glance in my direction, "that the arrival of the permanent commander, Colonel Herrick, has been delayed."

I could not restrain myself from breaking a self-imposed silence. "Colonel Herrick?" I asked. "The same Colonel Herrick who commanded old Fort Standish?"

Captain Lowe admitted they were the same, and added somewhat enviously, I thought, that the rank was now permanent. Herrick had been rewarded for his zeal in capturing Spotted Horse and was no longer a brevet colonel of Volunteers. His duties at the War Department in Washington were of such importance, moreover, that he had been delayed in reporting for duty. Naturally, Senator Rawley was most fretful over the colonel's failure to be present for the commemoration. "In the matter of recovering the remains of your husband, Mrs. Hardesty," he went on, "it would be expedient for you to await the arrival of Colonel Herrick."

Kathleen politely objected to any further delay, reminding the captain that she had an arrangement with Joseph O'Hara to disinter her husband's remains on the next day. Captain Lowe agreed that he had granted permission to Mr. O'Hara, but he had meant for the affair to be kept confidential. I got the drift of his meaning immediately and hastened to assure him that the *Saint Louis Herald* would receive no intelligences from me about the matter. I was at Fort Rawley for the purpose of reporting the dedication ceremonies and was present in his office merely as an escort for Mrs. Hardesty. His response was a rapid nodding of his head to indicate his relief.

"I have a locket, captain," Kathleen said then, "that was sent to me from Fort Standish with some of my husband's personal effects." She took the small heart-shaped case and its gold chain necklace from her handbag and placed it on the commandant's desk. "I am certain that it was not Drew Hardesty's."

Captain Lowe picked up the locket. "Odd, extremely odd," he said. "Not so much that you received it in error, Mrs. Hardesty, but that it was recovered at all. When opportunity affords, as it must have on the Malpais, the Indians always strip bodies of such jewelry as this."

"There's a portrait inside," Kathleen said.

The captain carefully opened the small hinged case. "Yes." He frowned at the portrait.

"Do you know who she is, ma'am?"

Kathleen shook her head.

"Well, there's no doubt in my mind whose portrait this is. It's Miss Lydia Rawley."

"The late Major Rawley's sister?" Kathleen asked in surprise.

"Absolutely. She arrived at this post with her parents, Senator and Mrs. Rawley, on the *Deer Lodge* just three days past."

"Then it must be given to her." She drew a deep breath of relief. "I trust you will do this for me, Captain Lowe. Miss Rawley should treasure it."

He smiled. "I suggest that you make the presentation to her yourself, Mrs. Hardesty. You can better explain how it came into your possession." He leaned to one side, pointing out the window of the office. "Across the parade ground there, in that neat building we've just completed, the Rawley family is gathered with the others who are to take part in the commemoration ceremonies. I am just about to go there myself, ma'am, and shall be pleased to introduce you to Miss Lydia."

We went, of course, following the captain along a series of wide planks that had been put down for use as pathways across the unsodded parade ground. On our right, toward the river, no stockade had yet been erected, and through

291

the opening I could see rows of temporary wooden benches rising in tiers, a sort of natural amphitheater on the edge of the river bluff. Facing the benches was a reviewing stand built of new pine lumber, liberally decorated with bunting. Beside the stand was a large granite marker that had been brought up the Missouri on the *Deer Lodge.* "Major Rawley's remains were moved there yesterday from the cemetery at old Fort Standish," the captain informed us.

The new building into which Captain Lowe ushered us appeared to be designed for recreation, with a few bookshelves, a Catlin painting of a buffalo herd on one wall, small tables for games and reading, and a long table in the rear, around which were seated at that moment about a dozen people, all of whom appeared to be talking at once. My old friends, Emilie and Konrad Lieber, saw us first, and he came bustling to greet us. Nettie Steever, Towanjila, Joseph O'Hara, and Lieutenant Colonel Harris were all there, and also a large white-haired man wearing a frock coat and wing collar who could be none other than the great Senator Rawley. With him was a plain-faced young woman who was his daughter Lydia. I had met numerous politicians of the Rawley stamp during the war, perhaps none as imposing as he, but all coated with artificial veneers of affability and volubility that barely concealed the scoundrels beneath. His daughter impressed me as being a female replica struck from a similar mold. It was plain that she was quite in charge of the day's activities, and also that she had made an unwilling prisoner of Lieutenant Colonel Harris. That horse-faced emissary of the President was as delighted to see Kathleen as he was unhappy to see me, but Miss Lydia Rawley had him so thoroughly bridled that he was given little opportunity to resume his interrupted pursuit of the green-eyed and much more buoyant young widow.

Needless to say, there was quite a commotion over the locket containing Lydia Rawley's portrait. To express her gratitude, the senator's daughter invited Kathleen to remain on the post for a late morning tea she was giving for the officers' wives. This move effectively separated both Harris and me from the company of Mrs. Hardesty.

As this informal meeting of the commemoration participants was breaking up, Dr. Lieber asked if I would care to accompany him on a walk. "My blood's a bit sluggish," he said. "Besides I'd like to revisit the site of old Fort Standish."

After we left the sallyport, he led the way around the stockade to a winding pathway that led down a slope until we were soon almost on a level with the river. "The old fort flooded once or twice while I was surgeon here," he reminisced. " 'Twas a sensible plan to build the new one on the bluff."

About all that remained of Fort Standish were a few rotting stakes of the old stockade, stone foundations of structures that had been razed, and the blackened remains of two buildings that Dr. Lieber identified as the site of the tragedy that took the life of Major Rawley. "The guardhouse was there, and that deep hole beyond was the powder magazine. A considerable amount of gunpowder and other explosives were stored in the magazine, and when the fire reached them, there were three or four powerful blasts, the first one awakening most of us around midnight. The hospital was straight across what was the parade ground there, my quarters being adjacent to it." Lieber adjusted his hat to shade his eyes as he pointed across the weed-grown sward.

"What started the fire?" I asked.

"An official inquiry reached the conclusion that the Indians started it in their attempt to break Spotted Horse out of the guardhouse."

"And Spotted Horse did escape?"

"Yes. Supposedly he's still alive, someplace across the line in the British possessions. I was told last evening that efforts are still being made to have him extradited. Seems the Canadians pretend they can't find him."

I walked closer to the charred beams of the old guardhouse. "So Major Rawley died here while attempting to stop the escape of Spotted Horse. How was it that he failed?"

Lieber shook his head. "I suppose no one will ever know. We found his body right about there. Beside that stone abutment, near the heat-twisted iron bars. One of the guards was lying a few yards away, partially burned, but he'd been killed by an arrow driven deep into his chest. The adjoining magazine was filled with niter, portfires, fixed ammunition, and barrels of gunpowder. I believe a burst of fiery explosive literally enveloped the major. His body was seared and shriveled beyond recognition."

"How did you identify him?"

"That was my grisly duty, yes. By the pistol that had been issued to him, a barely recognizable crossed-swords insignia that he wore on his hat, and a half-melted watch bearing his initials." Lieber sighed. "A ghastly business." He turned as though to start back toward the new fort.

"You were here when he returned from Canada. What was his condition then, his attitude?"

"Physically he was not as badly damaged as some of the others. Mild chilblains on his hands and feet, a bit of frostbite. Mentally he seemed elated. During his absence, papers absolving him of censure for the Killdeer Mountain affair had come overland through Fort Ripley. After his return Colonel Herrick praised him daily, and informed him that he was sending a recommendation for promotion to headquarters of the Department of Dakota. To be brevet lieutenant colonel. At first Rawley spoke frequently of his eagerness to see his family, of returning to Ohio for a short furlough, of his hopes for a new command somewhere in the East."

Lieber paused as though aware that his accent had begun to thicken. "Then something happened to him, soon after Colonel Herrick appointed a military commission to try Spotted Horse for his crimes. The colonel chose two of his captains and a lieutenant, with the regimental adjutant serving as judge advocate. Major Rawley became more and more critical of the colonel and disagreed strongly with the commission's charges against Spotted Horse."

"What were the charges?"

Lieber stopped his slow pace, squinted at me, and muttered something about "damned newspaper scribblers." After he'd thought a moment he said that the main charge was murder of white settlers. "One of the specifications accused him of shooting settlers in their wagons near a certain town, another of shooting and killing soldiers sent against the Sioux, another of discharging guns with intent to kill. I think it was the last that angered Major Rawley the most. In a war, I recall him saying, you always discharge your guns with intent to kill, and the Sioux were in a war.

"With our weekly overland mail service from Fort Ripley, we received copies of the Saint Paul newspapers, and they carried reports of the capture of Spotted Horse, the forthcoming trial, and a prediction of a probable hanging which might be carried out in Saint Paul. Major Rawley always read these papers, and it occurred to me that he may have been resentful because all the credit for the capture of Spotted Horse was given to Colonel Herrick, who himself was sending this information to newspapermen he knew in Saint Paul. This may or may not have been true. I am only guessing. Yet I am certain that he was perturbed by some of the newspaper reports.

"About this same time Rawley began making frequent visits to see Mrs. Steever and the Indian girl, Towanjila. They were staying in a loft above Antoine Fromboise's trading post, a log building down near the boat landing. I believe both Herrick and Rawley had asked them to remain nearby so that they could appear as witnesses in the trial, and they had no place to go anyhow. Strangely, however, neither was allowed to give testimony during the trial.

"Another strange thing I noticed at the time. For days Rawley had been looking forward to arrival of the first steamboat, but when the first boat arrived he did not take passage on it, nor did he do so on the second and third. He also rejected opportunities to leave by the overland route. When two correspondents from Saint Paul newspapers — escorted by our overland messenger service — came to report the trial, Colonel Herrick suggested that Rawley use one of their sleds to travel to Saint Paul, from where he could easily reach his home in Ohio. Herrick obviously wanted him out of the way. Rawley was becoming a threat, don't you see, to a sure and unencumbered conviction of the Indian he'd brought back from Canada.

"After the trial started, Rawley became more and more morose. I was not able to attend some of the proceedings because of an epidemic of intermittent fever that swept through the enlisted men's barracks, but I was told by some of the officers who were there that Rawley was behaving badly in the court-room, interrupting and challenging testimony, and on at least one occasion was ordered out of the court by the judge advocate. Most uncharacteristic of him.

"Colonel Herrick was especially angered when Rawley prepared a report for submission through military channels to the Secretary of War. In his statement Rawley claimed that the Sioux captive known as Spotted Horse had never been satisfactorily identified as the war chief Spotted Horse, and that although he was sometimes known as Spotted Horse by white men, he was known among his own people as Medicine Horse. Furthermore, the major additionally stipulated that the Spotted Horse on trial had been living in Canada during the Sioux War and could not have been a participant. Rawley also claimed that the captive Sioux had been illegally kidnapped from a foreign state where the United States had no right to seize him, to drag him by force from the protection of the British government.

"He showed me his statement before submitting it to Colonel Herrick. I asked him how he could prove that Spotted Horse was living in Canada during the war and he replied that Towanjila had sworn these things to him. 'Spotted Horse went to Canada to be away from the warlike members of the tribe,' Rawley contended. 'He has never killed a white person, or been a member of any war party against them. He is Sun Pejuta, Medicine Horse.'"

We were beginning to climb the steep pathway to the new fort. The sun felt excessively warm against our backs. On the grassy flat behind us meadowlarks started to sing. "What effect did Rawley's statement have on the trial?" I asked.

"I am of the belief that his deposition never left Colonel Herrick's headquarters. Most likely it was held there and then destroyed after Rawley's death a few days later."

"The court found Spotted Horse guilty before Rawley's death?"

"By one day. The commission found the old chief guilty of all charges and sentenced him to death by hanging, the time and place to be determined later by the judge advocate. That meant Colonel Herrick would decide, the judge advocate being his adjutant. I remember well how old Spotted Horse received the sentence of death. Antoine Fromboise was interpreter, and Spotted Horse answered the court's sentence through him. 'I am no coward,' he said. 'I can die whenever the white man wishes.'"

Lieber was breathing hard from the climb to

the top of the bluff. Somewhere beyond the stockade, the post musicians were tuning their instruments, creating an absurd cacophony to drown out the calls of the meadowlarks.

"Do you believe he was guilty?"

The doctor shrugged. "I don't know, Sam, honestly I don't know. Whether he was Spotted Horse the Bad, or Spotted Horse the Good, or Medicine Horse, it is my belief that no white man could have been sentenced to death upon the testimony I heard in that court. The evidence given was mostly hearsay, and when you add to that the violation of international law that brought him to captivity — well, I must agree with the late lamented Major Rawley that it was a flagrant outrage to law and justice."

At a shouted command, the band burst into a brassy "Hail, Columbia," the sound surging upon us through the sallyport. Lieber said something, but his words were drowned by the music, and I could tell from his wincing grin that he knew I had not understood.

The music stopped as abruptly as it had begun. The bandsmen, in bright blue uniforms, were practicing for the ceremonies that were yet almost an hour away. They were formed on the slope of ground between the platform and the spectators' seats.

"Odd about that locket of Major Rawley's," I said. "That it should've been sent to Mrs. Hardesty by mistake."

"No," he replied. "Easily explained, even to a skeptical scribbler such as you, Sam. The major had dropped his locket, I think, probably when he removed his clothes to bathe in that creek on the Malpais, a few minutes before they were attacked by the Sioux warriors. When Hardesty was killed, he fell on the locket. That's where we found it. Under his body."

I nodded, pretending that I understood. "Hardesty's body was some distance from the others?"

"Yes, he and one other man. About a quarter of a mile from the others. The second man was a few paces from Hardesty's body. They were killed in the first attack. Major Rawley and the others tried to escape in the brush along the creek."

When I looked at Lieber my face must have shown my incredulity. His account was the reverse of the story I'd heard from Alex Selkirk alias Charles Rawley.

"In the first attack?" I repeated. "Is that the way it happened?"

He seemed surprised that I would have thought of the Malpais massacre in any other way. "They were far outnumbered and without horses," he said.

"Yes. Did the major go back with you to search for the bodies?"

"No, he was very feverish that morning, almost blind, wound infected."

"How did you identify the dead?"

He shook his head, trying to remember. "We identified only two for certain. Hardesty because of the location of his body, and the second man. Major Rawley helped us draw up the casualty list."

We were halfway across the parade ground, walking on the loose planks toward the recreation building, Lieber ahead of me so I could not hear him plainly, with drums beating ruffles only a few yards away.

"Was the name Alex Selkirk on that list?" I asked, raising my voice.

Lieber stopped abruptly and turned to face me. "How did you know that name?"

"Prying scribbler," I replied with a grim smile.

"Major Rawley told us it was Hardesty's enlistment name. He was ashamed of being in the Galvanized Yankees, Rawley explained, and he asked me to set the name down on the casualty list as Drew Hardesty to make it easier to trace and inform his kin."

"One more question, doctor, and I'll shut up. Do you remember the name of the second man killed in the first attack?"

Trumpets blared in a flourish to accompany the drum ruffles, and I could not hear his reply clearly.

"Did you say it was Tharp?" I yelled.

He nodded briskly. "Tharp, yes, a little man. Private Tharp."

12

In Dakota the weather leaps back and forth from winter to spring for a few days and then it is summer. As the hour for Fort Rawley's dedication ceremonies drew closer, the sun burned like a summer sun, so brilliant the sky was drained of color. I sat on one of the front benches surrounded by a gathering crowd that was mostly males, many carrying bottles of whiskey with which to fortify themselves against the oratory that would soon engulf them. Occasionally a group would stroll across to the granite monument and read the simple epitaph:

MAJOR CHARLES RAWLEY
HERO OF THE UNION
He Behaved Himself With Honor
and Died in the Flower of His Age.

I pulled my hat brim low, watching the honored guests approaching from the incompleted fort to file past the memorial to Major Rawley and then up the steps of the reviewing stand. Parasols had been found for the women, and after they reached their chairs they kept the black shields raised against the glare.

Kathleen Hardesty was one of the last in the line. She gave a quick nod and a smile to Miss Lydia Rawley, and then came on toward the spectators' seats, her body swinging in that sensual gait that distinguished her from all other women I have known. She had no parasol. I stood up and waited for her. When she saw me, she smiled with relief, aware that the eyes of a hundred or more frontier ruffians were fixed upon her instead of the notables in the reviewing stand.

"Look," I said, "there's a bit of shade up there along the top rows. We'll fry in the sun down here."

"By all means, Sam. I have no desire to turn to a crisp."

We made our way up a narrow passage of earthen steps that were surfaced with powdery dust. The female-starved spectators watched us boldly, envying me for my good fortune. I recognized the faces of several passengers from the *Roanoke;* some greeted her politely. Very near the top, in the irregular fringe of shadow cast by a clump of new-leaved basswood trees, sat Captain Adams and Mr. Allford, both grinning like pleased tomcats, rising to greet her with courtly bows, totally oblivious to my presence until they had finished with their pleasantries.

The bench behind them in the last row was unoccupied, and we took it, grateful for the comparative coolness of the shade. Captain Adams pulled out his curved-stem pipe, charged and lighted it, and slowly turned to look upon the proceedings below with his usual inquisitive eye. Mr. Allford's lean face lapsed into its normal doom-ridden expression. And then the band began playing "Listen to the Mocking Bird."

To make herself heard above the din of shrilling flutes and blaring horns, Kathleen spoke close to my ear: "Lydia Rawley told me that piece of music was her brother's favorite."

"What are they like, the Rawleys?"

"Rather stuffy," she answered with a loud laugh. "The senator is quite a ladies' man. Mrs. Rawley and Lydia are reserved, not unfriendly, but distant. They keep you reminded of their station in life, the old family name." She waited for the music to grow softer. "They pretended to remember meeting my late husband, but I don't believe any of the three have the faintest recollection of him."

"When did your husband know the Rawleys?" The last words of my question must have been heard for some distance because while I was shouting my astonishment the band music came to an abrupt stop.

"Drew knew Charles Rawley sometime before our marriage. He was planning to take me to visit the family just about the time the war broke out."

My memory whirled with a confused juxtaposition of past incidents. "Why didn't you tell me this?" I demanded in an exasperated tone.

She gave me a wide-eyed questioning childlike stare that might have been feigned, might have been genuine. The band began running through a medley of gay quick-steps and schottisches, waiting for the crowd to settle. I think I would have kissed her right there had Captain Adams and Mr. Allford not been constantly turning their heads to make some trivial comment or other.

In the lull between the band's bugler playing assembly call and the beginning of the oratory, she told me that Major Rawley and Drew Hardesty had been leaders of rival mounted militia companies on opposite sides of the Ohio River. They met in occasional friendly riding competitions. That was all she knew.

Captain Lowe, the fort's acting commandant,

resplendent in dress blues with elaborately braided sleeves, stood behind the unpainted pine-board speaker's stand, a gloved hand upraised to silence the murmur of the crowd. He had two or three announcements to make, among them the departure times of the *Roanoke* and the *Deer Lodge*. Both would be leaving one hour after the conclusion of the commemoration exercises, the *Roanoke* bound upriver, the *Deer Lodge* downriver. Staterooms were available on both steamboats for those who had not yet booked passage. I let the details flow by me; I was committed to remaining another day for the disinterment of the bones of Drew Hardesty, U.S. Volunteers, and hoped that another downriver boat would soon be stopping at the Fort Rawley landing.

After a lengthy prayer by the post chaplain, Captain Lowe introduced our peerless speaker of the day, the renowned Senator Rawley, whose mere presence in that remote outpost of frontier America brought the crowd to its feet with shouts and whistles and loud huzzas before he'd even opened his profluent mouth. He stood there letting the applause wash upon him, smiling and nodding, until he sensed the exact moment to use his sonorous voice to keep both the sober and the inebriated among his audience expectant of his golden phrases.

Senator Rawley was practiced in the art of transfixing a crowd with his vocal cords, and like most men of his profession overlooked no opportunity to create an image of himself as a national leader, a man suited for the highest political office in the Republic. He spoke of the great territory of Dakota, the blue vaults of heaven above us, the tree of liberty that had been bent by the tempests of war and drenched in blood. He spoke of his noble son, a soldier of the Union, of his bravery, and then he stood silent while another wave of applause swept over him.

He came then to what he described as Major Charles Rawley's "holy crusade," the journey to Canada to capture that villainous murderer of helpless women and children, the black-hearted Spotted Horse. He mentioned Colonel Herrick and expressed regrets that the gallant commander of old Fort Standish could not be present to narrate the stirring events in which Major Charles Rawley had been the prime mover. His valiant son was not alone in his holy crusade, he conceded. No, there were four courageous souls to give him aid. Antoine Fromboise, who recently had passed away; a stouthearted sergeant, Joseph O'Hara; a noble daughter of the frontier, Mrs. Nettie Steever; and a young Indian woman who had rejected the evil barbarities of her people and cast her lot with civilization, Towanjila the Blue Sky Woman.

"Three of them are here today," he cried, "to join us in honoring the memory of my brave son." He turned with a dramatic flourish, the long tails of his coat flowing with his movement. He asked the three to stand, and introduced them again by name. Nettie stood with her arms folded, her face stern as if she were daring the spectators to challenge her presence. O'Hara, his hair parted in the middle and water-plastered to his skull, stood to attention with his chin angled so that I could not see the expression on his face. Towanjila, obviously frightened and struggling to keep from casting her glance downward, was the most appealing of the three — a slender beauty with her dark hair shining in the sunlight, the tint of a red shawl reflected against her tawny skin. It was easy to understand how Major Rawley had lost his heart to her.

After each introduction the crowd applauded politely, and then with a few flowery phrases about the evermoving tide of time, the fire of battle, and the blood of patriots, Senator Rawley launched into a lurid narration of Major Rawley's holy crusade to capture Spotted Horse. He had scarcely begun when I heard a strange moaning nearby. I looked to the right and left. Kathleen stared hard at me, puzzled, anxious. The sound continued, muffled now, a desolate sobbing, and then it turned feral, like the subdued cry of a wounded animal in the wild. I swung around on the bench, and through an opening in the pale green leaves saw his face, the long scar slanting across his dark beard, the eyes sunken and dead. I do not know whether he recognized me or even saw me. An instant later he pushed through the brush and stepped upon a clump of rocky earth behind an adjoining bench. I felt as though I were under the spell of a mad giant rising from the earth, his deep hollow voice challenging the senator on the platform below: "False witness! False witness!" he cried. "He that speaketh a lie shall perish!"

The silence that followed was like suspended time. Perhaps only a moment or so passed, yet it seemed forever, the members of the crowd frozen in wonderment or dread. Senator Rawley's arm, uplifted to emphasize a point, dropped slowly to his side. He stared straight forward into infinity. A rush of wind caught at the flag above the platform, and its flapping was like the sound of a slow-lifting bird. Joseph O'Hara's face was a distant caricature of terror. Nettie Steever was halfway out of her chair, one hand gripping Towanjila's arm to restrain her. Heads began turning below me. Captain Adams, his gray hair splaying from both sides of his cap, swung around with a stare of accusation as though for a moment he suspected me of the interruption. I motioned silently to my left, but the man was gone, vanished with the echoes of his powerful voice.

"Drew! Drew!" Kathleen's painful cry was almost a whisper; I think that only I heard her. Below us the senator was rapping for order, his words lifting again as though nothing had happened.

Kathleen was trying to rise from the bench, her body half turned, her arms reaching desperately toward the river. She repeated her dead husband's name again, and then slumped toward me, her fingers clutching at my shoulders. "Go find him, bring him back to me, for God's sake," she pleaded. I could feel the pressure of the bones of her fingers. Pulling away from her, I hurried around the bench and past the brush until I could see the river flowing below. I caught a glimpse of him through the sundappled foliage, and started in pursuit.

By the time I reached the sandy bank of the river I had lost sight of him. Between me and the steamboat landing the hard sand was marked by hooves and boots and wagon wheels, but only a few hoofprints led off down-river. I hurried on to the *Deer Lodge.* A rousta-bout lazing on the lower deck watched me approach. "You see a man come by here?" I asked.

"Runnin' like the devil was after him," he answered.

I waved my thanks to him.

"What'd he do, mister?" he asked. "Steal your purse?"

I shook my head and went on to the *Roanoke.* I found the gangplank watch asleep; he could not say for certain whether anyone had come past him. The only others aboard were an engineer and Mr. Allford's number two pilot. They had neither seen nor heard anyone since the crew and passengers departed for the Fort Rawley ceremonies. After I explained the reason for my being there, the pilot went around with me to make a search, but I performed the task rather halfheartedly, knowing from experience the difficulty of finding anyone as clever at concealment as was my quarry.

While we were circling the hurricane deck, band music drifted down from the fort, one of those dirges the military like to play for their departed, and then the rousing drums and brass of a march in review. A few minutes later the vanguard of returning spectators appeared on the fort road. The commemoration ceremonies were ended. Thanking the number two pilot for his cooperation, I hastened ashore and began the same tedious inspection of the *Octavia*. The boat's engineer, a swarthy piratical sort from lower Louisiana, had steam up in his boilers and was impatiently awaiting the return of his captain. He insisted that no scar-faced bearded man had come aboard and was reluctant to allow me to rummage about through the stacks of buffalo hides on the main deck. He might have ordered me off the boat had not the captain arrived.

"That gent who railed at Senator Rawley, eh?" he replied to my request, while giving me a rather sharp stare. "He was drunk as a lord, for sure, unless he's clean daft. Is he a wanted man?"

"You might say that, I suppose," I replied.

He gave me another intent study. "You're the gent was with that handsome lady at the ceremonies. What's your concern?"

After I'd given him my particulars, he granted permission for a search of his boat, with a warning they'd be shoving off for Saint Louis in a matter of minutes. The *Octavia* was an evil-smelling old craft, its planking soaked with manure and hide droppings and heaven knows what else. Its cargo provided numerous places for a fugitive to hide, but it had no cabins except for the crew's quarters. By the time the bell gave the signal for starting, I'd finished a cursory search and managed to clear the gangplank before the roustabouts pulled it aboard.

I was standing on the riverbank, considering whether or not I should pay a visit to the livery stable where the man I was looking for had told me the tale of his harrowing journey from Canada. A moment or so later, I glimpsed a familiar figure leaving the nearby *Deer Lodge*. Joseph O'Hara was in a hurry, moving in a kind of military doubletime as though he could not wait to reach his hotel and settle down to a drink to steady his nerves. His face held a haunted expression, the skin paler than usual. When I shouted his name, he did not respond, continuing his rapid pace along the slant of ground that led to the livery stables behind the Hotel Como. I had to jogtrot to overtake him.

He turned like a skittish pony to face me. "Oh," he said. "She asked me to tell you he's gone."

"You've seen Mrs. Hardesty?"

"Yes, sir. I just put her trunk aboard the *Deer Lodge.*"

"She's leaving?" I felt as if events were eluding me. "She's not going with you to the Malpais tomorrow?"

His blue eyes shifted under my direct gaze. "That's done with, sir." He sighed. "She believes that man — the one who interrupted the ceremonies — is her husband."

"But where is he? She asked you to tell me he's gone. Gone where?"

"Downriver." O'Hara's mouth twisted. "He took my best rowboat. Blacksmith saw him from the livery stable. Just jumped in it and hovered close to the steamboats. Last the blacksmith saw of him he was hightailing it in the bank current."

"Damn!" I cried. "Right under my nose while I was searching the steamboats."

He forced a rueful smile to show his sympathy.

"You saw him," I said. "Is he the man you accompanied across the border to bring out Spotted Horse?"

Only his eyes revealed the shock I'd given him; they flickered as though he'd received a hard blow to the head. He must have had words prepared for the question, however, because he answered without hesitation, almost mechanically: "Major Rawley died in the fire, sir."

"Yes. Then who do you think the bearded man is, O'Hara?"

He shrugged and looked away toward the river. "Perhaps he *is* Mrs. Hardesty's husband."

From behind us came the blast of a steamboat whistle. I turned and saw the *Octavia's* paddle wheels flashing in the late afternoon light. In moments the vessel would vanish around the first bend. A second series of short blasts followed, steam jetting above the pilothouse of the *Deer Lodge*. "That's the ten-minute whistle!" I cried. "I'd damn well better get my traps from your hotel and run for it if I'm not to be stranded here."

"You're going back to Saint Louis?"

"Yes." As we hurried up the alleyway beside the hotel, I saw some of the anxiety leave his face at my reply. Most of it returned, however, when I added: "After a stop at Bell's Landing."

I barely made it aboard the *Deer Lodge* before the plank was pulled up. Amidst cheerful shouts from army people ashore and gay laughter aboard, ropes were loosened hurriedly, paddles churned, the boat vibrating until it moved into midstream and began riding easily on the full current.

With my usual traveler's luck I was too late to obtain a decent stateroom, and had to settle for a dingy kip on the boiler deck. The fare for the accommodations was quite low, however, leaving me with a lagniappe of cash to invest in a bottle of first-rate Kentucky bourbon that I hoped to put to good use before the evening ended.

At dinner hour I waited near the the main entrance to the *Deer Lodge's* dining room, hoping to join Kathleen Hardesty. She did not appear, however, and my table companions were Emilie and Konrad Lieber. They wanted to talk of nothing but the curious affair of the bearded stranger shouting his biblical admonitions in the midst of Senator Rawley's speech. "The voice out of nowhere and then the blur of that figure, rushing by. Haunting," the doctor said in an unusually somber tone for him. "Most unsettling, I must say. Its effect upon poor Mrs. Hardesty has been devastating. Of course she was so close by that madman."

"Perhaps I should have stayed with her," I said. "Yet she was insistent that I pursue him. 'Bring him back to me,' she kept pleading. 'Bring him back to me!' "

"A hallucination, I'm convinced." Dr. Lieber rubbed a finger across the neatly trimmed beard on his chin, frowning. "Brought on, I would guess, by her willful determination to be present at the exhumation of her husband's bones, a grisly business that was to take place within hours. Fortunately a project that she has now wisely abandoned."

"Only because she believes the mad stranger to be Drew Hardesty," I reminded him.

"Ah, yes." He shook his head and turned to his food.

"As you both know," Emilie Lieber said, "I have no liking for Kathleen Hardesty." She hesitated a moment. "I felt sorry for the creature, though, and gave her some of Konrad's headache powders. I'm sure that after a good night's rest, she'll be her usual pretentious self." She smiled and put on a jolly and agreeable front in an effort to bring some cheer to our dinner table. Like many frail persons, Emilie Lieber was always at her best when she was placed in a position to aid those stronger than herself.

"Have a look across there at the Rawleys' table," she whispered. "The senator is as merry as a racetrack winner, and if anyone should be aggrieved it should be he. To be interrupted at the climax of his brilliant oration, ah, that's an unforgivable outrage."

The Rawleys and their guest, Lieutenant Colonel Harris, were indeed a picture of conviviality. But I was more interested in Nettie Steever who was dining at an adjoining table. She sat between two gray-bearded traders, one of whom kept nudging her with his elbow and breaking into bursts of coarse laughter. Nettie was not amused, and was evidently more intent upon emptying the wine carafe than in consuming food.

As soon as dinner was ended and the crowd began dispersing, I followed her to the outer lounge and trapped her before she could retreat to the ladies' cabin. Any doubts I may have had about her willingness to submit to the seduction of my bottle of gilt-edge Kentucky bourbon were quickly dispelled.

"Bygod, yes, scribbler, tonight I'd get drunk with a polecat if I had no other choice." She spoke softly so as not to be overheard in the crowded lounge. "You're not such a bad sort, scribbler, even though I know you're after something, something more than whiddling, I'll wager." She grinned, showing those remarkable white teeth of hers. She was already slightly tipsy from the dinner wine. She had exchanged the fancy dress and shoes she'd worn at the commemoration for her plain black woolen skirt and rough brogans.

An hour or so later she met me at the front of the companionway on the main deck, and I led her past the boilers to my dingy cubbyhole. I lighted the oil lamp hanging from a nail in the low ceiling. The place was not dirty, just shabby and cramped by comparison with the staterooms on the saloon deck above. Nettie obviously did not mind. She propped a pillow against the wall and made herself comfortable on the narrow bunk while I sat in a sagging canvas chair facing her.

When I took the bourbon bottle out of my bag, she whistled — the way a mule driver would — and gave me a conspiratorial wink. "Are you buying me or my company with that honeydew, scribbler?"

"I just want you to tell me who he is," I replied.

"You won't let it go, will you?" Her tone was scornful. "Like a cur dog sneaking around the back of a wagon for a thrown scrap. She won't let it go, either, the henhussy. Are you following her to Bell's Landing?"

"Mrs. Hardesty? She's stopping at Bell's Landing?"

Nettie grimaced. "I thought you knew. She pried it out of poor Towanjila. That he lives with her at the woodyard. Now Towanjila is dog-sick over it."

"Kathleen Hardesty believes him to be her supposedly dead husband," I said. "Is he?"

"Only God knows." Her eyes were on the

bottle I still held in my hands. I gave it to her and she tipped her head back, letting the liquor gurgle into her mouth until she almost choked.

"Is he the man who brought you back from Canada?"

She nodded. "Yeah." She wiped her lips with the back of her hand. "I reckon it don't matter if you know. Now that Major Rawley's been properly buried – with honors by his folks and the army. Nobody would believe you if you tried to make out he's alive and a squaw man."

"If he is Major Rawley," I asked, "why does she believe he's Drew Hardesty?"

She spread her hands. "Maybe she's not right in the head."

"He told me he was Alex Selkirk. That was the name Drew Hardesty used when he enlisted in the Galvanized Yankees."

She tipped the bottle again, shuddering under the potency of the whiskey. "Believe what you like, scribbler." She gasped for air, and then went on in a less contentious voice: "When I was a bound girl in Philadelphia, there was a neighbor woman in the house next door who would be kindly and winsome one day, but hateful and thievish the next. Sometimes she would change right in front of your eyes, like a skink turning from yellow to green. We called her the Two-Hearted Woman. I reckon Major Rawley is a two-hearted man."

"From what I've been told he was not like that in the beginning."

Her face turned serious. "No. Maybe it started at Killdeer Mountain, when he saw me a captive and refused to believe he saw me. Before that, while he was escorting the wagons, I'm sure he loved me. We were going to run off together. When he found me in Canada I reckon he could not face the fact I'd bedded with an Indian." She leaned back and stared at the rough boards of the ceiling just above her head. "He talked about Killdeer Mountain a lot. But I guess the big change in him started that day in the snow — at La Petite Mauvais — the morning that Sergeant O'Hara and I told him he'd captured the wrong Indian. It was like we'd stabbed him in the heart. He was still full of pride then, you see. He'd paid for Killdeer Mountain — or thought he had until we told him he'd brought out Medicine Horse instead of Spotted Horse."

"You're convinced of that — that the old chief was Medicine Horse?"

"Towanjila could not tell a lie, would sooner cut out her own tongue than tell a lie. The Indian was Medicine Horse."

I reached for the bottle and had a long swallow myself. "Who died in the fire?" I asked.

She grinned, almost shyly, like a schoolgirl resisting the telling of a secret.

"Nobody would believe me, you said so yourself," I reminded her, "if I tried to tell the world that Major Rawley is alive. He's well buried under that granite monument we left back there beside the fort they named for him."

As I had hoped, liquor loosened Nettie Steever's tongue and weakened whatever constraints she may have had about revealing the major's relationship with Medicine Horse, Towanjila, and herself. Until the trial of Medicine Horse began, the major remained aloof from Nettie and Towanjila. He was torn between a desire to leave Dakota Territory forever and a painful self-reproach for concealing the probability that his prisoner was not Spotted Horse. If the military court accepted the prisoner as Medicine Horse and released him, then Major Rawley would be declared a blundering failure, which to his mind was almost as bad as being a cowardly failure. Killdeer Mountain would not be forgotten; instead it would be recalled and compared with the failure of his mission to Canada. Yet, if the prisoner was decided by the court to be Spotted Horse, then a great wrong would surely be committed against an innocent man.

After the trial began, the major went to see Nettie and told her of these apprehensions in his mind. "At first he was like a child," she said. "He leaned on me, drew on me, fed on me. He began coming to Antoine Fromboise's place every night — Towanjila and I stayed in the loft there. Right after dark, he'd come, always bringing bread or beans or salt bacon, some kind of little present from the fort's supplies. We'd talk, the major and me, Towanjila seldom speaking a word, but I could soon tell there was something growing between them. It showed in their eyes. They'd touch each other, secretly they thought, but I noticed."

At last the attraction between the major and the Indian girl reached such a passion that Nettie felt compelled to give them the privacy of the loft room. She would go and walk along the riverbank, leaving them alone there. Nettie was quite frank about the details. As I have said, she was an elemental woman with elemental attitudes, Nettie Steever. Yet she evidently held no emotion of jealousy in the matter. She had learned to accept the fevers and rebuffs that flow from passions. I also suspect that for the first time in her life she was buoyed by a sense of independence, a self-sufficiency provided by the gold coins with which the major had bought her silence. She would never tell me of the gold, how she guarded it, how she later used it. Not even when she glowed with the enchantment and false confidence brought on by the drink I gave her did she relax her vigilance over the secret of the gold.

Ironically, by this time the major no longer desired her silence, but quite the opposite, in fact. He desperately attempted to force the military court to call both Nettie and Towanjila to testify that the prisoner was Medicine Horse, not Spotted Horse. Colonel Herrick, of course, had no intention of jeopardizing his goal — the conviction and hanging of a Sioux Indian known as Spotted Horse. The two women were never summoned.

After the major realized that Medicine Horse was going to be tried as Spotted Horse, he began to lean more than ever upon Nettie. "He was like a little boy," she said, "who has done a bad thing and wants to atone for it. Once, a long time ago, I was driving a buggy drawn by a slow horse, unfamiliar to me. I lashed the animal sharply with a whip. It leaped into a run, and no matter how hard I pulled on the lines the faster it ran, faster and faster. The major was like me and the horse. He'd got something started, something evil started by his own acts, and he could not stop it. I was luckier. The horse came to a barn gate and had to stop. The major foresaw the only stop for Medicine Horse was a gallows."

With the first warmth of spring, while the military trial continued its slow progress, a number of Medicine Horse's relatives and friends began coming down from Canada, singly, in pairs, more sometimes. They did not show themselves at Fort Standish, but set up camp in a wooded area downriver. Major Rawley was the only person in Fort Standish who knew they were there. At Towanjila's urging, he slipped away with her one night to visit the hidden camp.

He returned from the visit, Nettie said, as full of himself as a sinner converted to some primitive religion. No longer could he sit quietly with her and Towanjila in the loft room; he paced back and forth nervously, his eyes shining with a strange self-conceit. Through Towanjila the Indians accepted him; indeed, they literally compelled him to become the leader in their mutual objective.

From Nettie's artless viewpoint the change in Rawley was the result of another effort to redeem himself, but not for Killdeer Mountain this time. This was an act of propitiation for the wrong he had committed against Medicine Horse, a wrong that also affected Towanjila, the old man's daughter. In the expiatory actions of Charles Rawley, however, there was always a struggle between two kinds of innocence. His was not the innocence of unknowing, but was a fearful innocence that imperiled all within range of his deeds. He simply did not know how to come to terms with himself.

On those rare occasions when he was alone with her, Nettie said, he would confess that the little band of Sioux who had chosen him to lead the rescue attempt was a burden, bringing on agonies of indecision and foreboding. The responsibility he had not sought, yet he was committed to it, and never in the presence of Towanjila did he reveal any doubts that Medicine Horse could be delivered, snatched by force if necessary from the solid wood and iron of the seven-by-seven foot guardhouse cell where he was confined.

Being without any military assignment — while he ostensibly awaited the arrival of a southbound passenger boat — the major was free to attend the daily sessions of the "Spotted Horse" trial. He soon perceived that the proceedings were being deliberately prolonged by Colonel Herrick so that the correspondents present could write daily dispatches for their Saint Paul papers. Rawley also visited Medicine Horse in his cell, remaining only long enough to examine the arrangement of the guard post and to note the location and size of the single wall vent secured by the square of iron bars. The opening was much too small for the passage of a man's head and shoulders even if the bars could be removed.

After that visit, he began preparing his plan for rescuing Medicine Horse. One evening while visiting Nettie and Towanjila he showed them a diagram he had penciled on a sheet of foolscap. It was probably drawn to scale, indicating the guardhouse, the location of Medicine Horse's tiny room, the height of the barred window, the distance from the stockade to the guardhouse wall, the adjoining powder magazine, and a small shed between the guardhouse and the magazine where tools were kept for maintenance of the parade ground. The major's plan was to set fire to the shed very late at night when the alertness of the guards would be at lowest ebb. As soon as their attention was drawn to the fire, he would set free Medicine Horse and somehow get him outside the stockade. At the same time he was determined to protect himself, the name of Rawley, from any suspicion of complicity with the escape. Only after Medicine Horse was safely outside the fort and in flight to Canada would Major Charles Rawley himself be free.

For hours he discussed these plans with the two women, and then the three of them journeyed downriver to the hidden Sioux camp in the woods. Because of Whirlwind's intense loyalty to Medicine Horse, the major chose him as his lieutenant for the enterprise. Whirlwind sometimes acted foolishly and his knowledge of English was scanty, but Towanjila was learning words rapidly under Rawley's tutelage and she was helpful in explaining the rescue plan to Whirlwind and the dozen or so other Sioux, both women and men, who were resolved to risk their lives to liberate Medicine Horse.

They had a fierce argument over whether bows or rifles should be used as weapons. The major expressed his hope that violence might be avoided if everything was properly planned. In case something went wrong, he said, he favored arrows because they were silent weapons. Guards and sentinels could be put out of action without alarming a sleeping garrison. Whirlwind supported Rawley in this, but several of the others – especially those who were to wait outside the stockade on the open prairie to act as a rear guard if the soldiers pursued — were strong in arguing for rifles, better rifles than the old trade guns they had brought down from Canada.

"I reckon Major Rawley finally decided in his mind that those Sioux who would be chancing their lives to cover the escape deserved to have at least two long-range faster-shooting guns," Nettie said. "He bought a hunting rifle from Antoine Fromboise and ordered me to do the same. We made a show of crossing the river to hunt antelope, but we come back in after dark — without the rifles. We'd passed 'em to the Sioux.

"Then he and Whirlwind went about trying different ways of setting fire to wooden walls. We found some pieces of weathered shakes and clapboard behind the trading post and floated them down to the camp in a borrowed bull-boat. We fixed this wood up like a slanting wall, and Whirlwind tried shooting at it with fire-arrows. These Sioux Indians had never done anything like that, and all Major Rawley knew about fire-arrows was what he'd heard others tell. We tried tying rags soaked in lamp oil to the shafts, but they'd spoil Whirlwind's aim, and most times the fire went out in flight, and if he did hit the target there was only a smoldering rag making smoke instead of fire. The major finally gave it up, said he reckoned fire-arrows was something the tribes back east could handle, but they wasn't meant for the western country."

Nettie laughed, low in her throat, and leaned back against the bunk pillow. "God, what fools we acted, and what a sportive way we went about that earnest undertaking. The major said he would need at least one of the Sioux inside the fort with him, anyhow, and if it was Whirlwind he might as well fire the shed after he got over the stockade with a rope ladder. A double rope ladder, one side to climb in, the other to climb out. Towanjila and I fashioned it out of strong cordage we bought from old Antoine.

"And then late one evening, the major come to our loft room, knocking hard on the door, very excited he was. He said the Fort Standish court had sentenced Medicine Horse to die by hanging — only they named him Spotted Horse. 'Tomorrow night,' the major said, 'we must free him tomorrow night, Nettie. They'll be hauling him off to Saint Paul any day soon, and we could never take him from a soldier escort.'

"So that night we went down to the Sioux camp and made everything ready. I'd collected a bunch of old rags and a supply of lamp oil for Whirlwind to set the shed afire. We tested the rope ladder over a big cottonwood limb. All of us knew what we were supposed to do." She stopped talking and reached for the forgotten whiskey bottle. Holding it up against the lamplight, she measured the remaining contents with the thumb and forefinger. "About one drink apiece left. You go first, scribbler."

I deferred to her. She very carefully left half of it for me. "Say, do you have a cigar somewhere about you?" she asked. I had only one remaining, but I handed it to her. She bit the end off with her perfect teeth, and I brought the lamp down so she could light it easily from the wick. After she'd blown a circular cloud of blue smoke against the low ceiling, she stretched out on my bunk and told me what happened that night at Fort Standish.

Soon after sundown the Sioux, with Nettie Steever, left their camp and started north along the river trail. By midnight they were in the last fringe of woods, a quarter of a mile or so below the southwest corner of the fort's stockade. They waited until the half-moon dropped below the horizon, and then the first group began crawling across the grassy flat. The major had assured them that sentinels would be stationed only in the parapet above the northwest gate, and that if the Indians made no silhouettes against the sky, they could reach the south stockade without being observed.

Whirlwind, Towanjila, Nettie, and two young warriors were in the first group. Nettie's particular duty was to count off forty paces along the stockade from the southwest corner. This would bring them to the most suitable spot to position the rope ladder. There its inside overhang was unlikely to be visible from the parade ground, and it would be only a few steps from the small shed adjoining the powder magazine.

Keeping within the dark shadows of the stockade, she stepped off the forty paces, the others following her silently. The sleeping fort was soundless; not even a dog barked. Whirlwind cupped his hands over his mouth and blew the soft call of a nighthawk. A few moments later they heard a light rap from the other side of the stockade. Major Rawley was there. Nettie unrolled the rope ladder, stepped back, and tossed one end over the high stakes. She felt a tug that reminded her of a fish taking a hook, and then the middle segment of rope tightened against the irregular tops of the stockade posts. Towanjila was carrying the rags soaked in lamp oil in a folding parfleche case. With one swift motion she removed the rags and thrust them inside Whirlwind's loose buckskin shirt. He sniffed and turned his head quickly, holding one hand over his eyes and nose to protect them from the sudden pungency of the fumes. Nettie pushed a block of wooden matches into his hand, and slapped him on the shoulder, motioning silently to the rope ladder. In the starlight she could see his foolish grin given in response, and then he was climbing, nimble as a young boy, noiseless as a stalking cat.

Nettie found a slit between two stakes. Recent rains had swelled the wood so that her field of vision was narrowed, but she could see the black shape of the small shed, and beyond it a strip of starlit parade ground. Major Rawley was somewhere in the hushed shadows, waiting with her and the others for the first blaze of Whirlwind's fire. A match flared and died. She had a dreadful presentiment that dampness might have reached the matches even though she'd kept them in a metal case. At last another tiny flare broke the blackness and spread into a reddish glow that came from the lamp oil in the rags. The flambeau appeared to be moving aimlessly, darting and circling like a mindless firefly, and then it vanished. Nettie heard Towanjila whisper a sharp Lakota malediction, and then suddenly the girl was on the rope ladder, climbing swiftly. Almost too late Nettie stifled the warning cry in her throat. She reached out in a desperate try to stop Towanjila, catching a boot moccasin in one hand only to have it slip from her.

Everything happened very fast after that. Towanjila went over without a sound, and as her feet touched the ground inside she saw that Whirlwind had moved to his right and was applying a freshly lit torch to the edge of the powder magazine. Nettie also could see this, and again she had to repress a cry of warning. She remembered Major Rawley mentioning the magazine, cautioning them about an explosion if the fire spread to that structure. He had said he was counting on the proximity of the shed to the magazine to draw the full attention of all the guards, thus giving him the few moments needed to remove Medicine Horse from the guardhouse. Whirlwind may not have heard or understood Rawley's warning. Anyhow, after he found the rough boards of the shed were difficult to set ablaze he had turned in search of more flammable wood and discovered it in the corner of the magazine, a slant roof that came almost to the ground. As Nettie watched in helpless panic he not only set fire to the corner of the magazine, he found a small venthole through which he dropped a blazing oil-soaked rag.

Meanwhile Major Rawley had withdrawn to the farther side of the guardhouse and was pacing slowly back and forth along a wooden sidewalk. Had any of the guards chanced to see him there, he would have been accepted as a duty officer going about his rounds. When Rawley glimpsed the first flames rising in a swirl of black smoke, he assumed that Whirlwind had successfully ignited the small shed. In the darkness and from his angle of vision, as well as from the expectation in his mind, this was an error of observation that anyone could have made. He waited a few seconds to be certain the fire would not burn itself out, then dashed up the steps of the guardhouse, flung the door open, and shouted to the startled guard on duty that a fire was blazing in the shed next door. "Wake your guards, corporal! Tell them to take their blankets to smother the flames, and whatever water containers are at hand. Not a moment to lose! The powder magazine is hard by. You take charge, corporal. I'll stand by here until you return."

The soldier of course questioned nothing. He sprang up and dashed into the adjoining sleeping quarters. Rawley waited beside the rough table, listening for the confused sounds of awakening men, heard their hurrying footsteps and shouts as they ran out a side door. Then he reached across the table, lifted a large key hook from a nail in the wall, and strode down the narrow passage to Medicine Horse's cell.

The old man was awake, his head silhouetted against the small barred window illuminated by the glow outside. He evidently heard the key in the lock, the light clang of metal as Rawley drew the door back. His head turned for only a second; he remained fixed at the grille, peering desperately through a whorl of smoke that forced him to shield his eyes momentarily. "Hiyu!" Rawley shouted. "Kokela!" He hoped the words that Towanjila had taught him sounded right. "Come quickly," he added in English.

Medicine Horse coughed, and motioned outside through the barred smoke-filled window. In two strides Rawley reached him, caught at his shoulders. Then as the smoke rolled clear for a second, Rawley saw what Medicine Horse had been straining to see. "Towanjila!" In a sudden burst of firelight, she stood totally revealed in her quilled and beaded buckskins, an alien on forbidden ground, searching for her father.

One of the guards must have seen her at about the same moment that Rawley and her father sighted her through the barred window. The guard got his pistol out and fired once; the noise was no louder than the explosive crackling of the fire. Before the guard could fire again, Whirlwind — who was watching from somewhere in the shadows — drove an arrow, silent and deep, into the man's chest.

Seconds later came the first explosion. "Ihakabya!" Rawley had barely shouted the Lakota word, commanding Medicine Horse to follow him out of the guardhouse, when the building rocked under the blast. The old Sioux staggered in the narrow corridor; the thin wall boards cracked and split apart. The lantern on the guards' table struck the floor with a thud and a tinkle of glass. The smell of oil and woodsmoke and acrid gunpowder was over-powering. When he reached the table, Rawley saw that the door into the guards' sleeping quarters had been flung open by the explosion. Oil from the lantern had run along the slant of wrecked flooring into the room and was beginning to blaze under the wooden bed frames.

He hurriedly opened the front door. The magazine fire now lighted the edge of the parade ground and he could see several men running out there; some were in night robes, some half dressed. If Medicine Horse walked outside and down the steps to the wooden side-walk, he would stand forth like an actor entering a brightly lighted stage. Rawley closed the door quickly and turned back to Medicine Horse, motioning him to shed his fringed shirt. The old man did not understand, and he could not see clearly in the smoke and flickering fire-light. Unbuttoning his uniform frock coat, Rawley offered it to Medicine Horse, at the same time tugging at the Indian's shirt. At last Medicine Horse understood. While the Sioux was getting into the oversized uniform coat, Rawley clapped his yellow-corded cavalry hat upon the man's head. He then took his service revolver from its holster and handed it to him. "Use it if you must," he said without thinking of the barrier of langauge. The brim of the hat had dropped almost to the old Indian's eyes. The incongruity of the hat's size, the gray-streaked black hair falling below it to the shoulders, the expression of puzzlement on the dark wrinkled face, all gave a comical air to the hasty disguise. For a fleeting moment he looked into Medicine Horse's eyes and lifted a hand to indicate that the Sioux should wait there while he went to open the door again to survey the outside. That was the last he saw of Towanjila's father. "Ihakabya!" he called. "Follow me!" And as if those syllables held some demonic power of destruction, a second and more violent detonation overrode the echoes of his voice. He felt rather then heard the enormous blast that hurled flaming explosives into the smashed walls and roof of the guardhouse. The impact pitched him to the floor and one side of his face was covered with fire that clung to his skin like a slimy burning incubus. He crawled down the broken steps, beating at the pain with one hand.

"The stockade posts shook under my hands and the earth trembled," Nettie said. "We could see nothing in the smoke. One of the boys climbed the ropes, but the choking smoke drove him back. I don't know how Whirlwind found his way to Major Rawley. Perhaps he heard the cries of Towanjila who was searching for her father. She also had been burned, on the neck and one hand, but not nearly so bad as the major. In a way the smoke was a blessing. The soldiers in the fort could see only shadows. If they had recognized Whirlwind and Towanjila as Indians they would have killed them there. Some soldiers were already shouting about an Indian attack. The guards knew that one of their fellows was dead from an arrow at close range. They were confused and fearful of the explosions and an attack by

Indians. In the confusion Whirlwind and Towanjila got Major Rawley over the stockade. Whirlwind carried him on his back all the way to the river."

The *Deer Lodge* was slowing and turning, the throbbing engines making the walls of the tiny cabin vibrate with popping noises. "They're stopping," I said. "You want to go ashore if they put out a plank for wood?"

She yawned and stretched herself like a cat. "This time of night? You go and have a look. Maybe I'll join you if they do stop."

When I stepped outside the narrow door I was standing only a few yards from a land flare — an iron bucket packed with brightly burning rosin and pine knots, fastened to a pike thrust into the riverbank. The roustabouts eased the gangplank ashore; the loaders at the woodyard were already lined up like shadow figures, billets resting on their shoulders.

I was disappointed that Nettie did not come out to keep me company. I wanted to ask her when she started the Steever House at Bell's Landing, and when the major started that woodyard with the Sioux somewhere near Dutchman's Landing. After the *Deer Lodge* shoved off into the current again I went back to my cabin. Nettie lay curled on the bunk, abandoned the way children sleep, tiny drops of moisture on her upper lip. A slight sibilation accompanied her breathing, not a snore but a gentle soughing like wind in needled trees, or whispers of the innocent. I turned down the lamp wick, closed the door quietly behind me, and strolled toward the nearer boiler. A pile of gunnysacking lay nearby and I made myself a pallet of the fishy-smelling stuff. I had a hard time getting to sleep for thinking of the comic irony of that expensive granite monument at Fort Rawley standing for eternity above the bones of Old Medicine Horse.

13

At first daylight I opened my eyes to see a crane in flight, stark white against an amaranth sky. A graceful bird, the crane, but only a minute feature of landscapes that constantly lure artists into the mysterious reaches of the wide Missouri — Catlin, Bodmer, Miller, Kurz, the birdman himself, Mr. John James Audubon, a dozen more as good as any of the aforementioned, and a hundred lesser lights. At that time of day, that moment, however, I'd had enough of the Missouri River and Dakota Territory. I felt an aching in my soul and body for my pretty German girl out at Belle Fontaine and a longing for the sights and smells and sounds of old Saint Louis, the tastes of strong dark beer and sausages, good music in the twilight, soft voices on the riverfront, even the smothering warm humidity of the coming summer nights.

I knocked at the door of my cabin, but there was no answer. Nettie had gone, the bunk still warm where she had slept, and a faint scent of her still lingered, a primitive and indefinable fragrance. There was something about Nettie that was akin to that hollow-eyed, hollow-voiced man we called Major Rawley, a duality of attraction and repulsion, like the negative and positive mysteries of electricity that a Signal Corps telegrapher tried to explain to me one day on the heights above Chattanooga. Perhaps I confused her with Cybele, the Great Mother of the Gods. I had to see the ending of it.

Down the railing from my cabin one of the engineers was wiping his sweated face with a white-dotted blue bandanna. He was watching, but probably not seeing, the full muddy flow of the river fed by snow melts from mountains hundreds of miles upstream.

"What's your guess as to when we'll see Bell's Landing?" I asked him.

He glanced sidewise at me from under his cap visor, leaned over the rail, and released a spout of tobacco juice. " 'Bout duskfall, mebbe. If no troubles beset."

We had troubles with snags and sawyers, and did not reach Bell's Landing until nearly midnight. All that day I'd been keeping a sharp watch out for Kathleen Hardesty, meaning to make a hard try at convincing her to remain on the *Deer Lodge* until its run ended at Saint Louis. She did not leave her stateroom, however, evidently having her meals sent there. The first I saw of Kathleen was when those of us who were disembarking at Bell's Landing began gathering on the boiler deck with our luggage – Nettie, Towanjila, a pair of wagon-transport contractors, a Portuguese buffalo hunter, and I. Lighted lanterns had been swung above and around us, bathing everything in a yellow glow. Towanjila kept peering fearfully over her shoulder at the steps to the saloon deck, and sure enough, just as the *Deer Lodge* eased in beside the crude log deck, Kathleen appeared in company with a roustabout who was carrying her dome trunk on his shoulder. She walked with her usual sensuous stride, one hand on her side to lift slightly the hem of her rich emerald dress. She knew we had all turned to stare at her; she nodded and smiled but kept her green eyes from looking at any one of us. Except for an insignificant puffiness below her eyes, her complexion was as lovely as ever. She stopped beside me, whether purposely or by chance I do not know.

"I expected you would be stopping here," she said, her voice low and controlled.

"Are you sure that *you* should stop?" I asked her.

Her eyebrows raised slightly. "I have stronger reasons than you." She looked away for a moment. "You tried to tell me – that night in the hotel. I could not accept it then, that he was –" Her voice broke off huskily, and then she added in a whisper: "I betrayed him. He was trying to reach me, the night you came to my room."

The deckhands were swinging the plank out with their ropes, lowering it skillfully until the farther end dropped with a soft thud upon the log dock. Two men hurried ashore with lanterns.

"It's not too late," I said urgently. "If you'll stay on board so will I."

She looked at me curiously, almost pityingly. "I *must* go ashore, Sam. Surely you understand that. He expects me."

The others, laden with their belongings, were already moving along the gangplank. She turned to the roustabout, beckoning him politely to follow her with the trunk. When he set it down on the landing, I was there beside it.

And so for the second time I carried Kathleen Hardesty's brass-ribbed trunk up a hill to a hotel, while she silently walked alongside with my bag. The darkness was dense, the road uneven, and when Nettie let us into her

Steever House, the place was cold and damp and rustling with mice. She tried to cheer us with a crackling blaze in the entry fireplace, but most of us went off to our assigned rooms to crawl into our clammy beds.

To my surprise Nettie had breakfast on the long dining-room table by sunrise. She must have stayed up all night, getting supplies in from the nearby trading post. She had three girls helping her though, not especially pretty, but lively, with ready smiles. She introduced them to us as Matty, Kitty, and Essie, if I remember correctly. I've often wondered where such girls come from to the frontier, and why they stay in such wretched backwaters as Bell's Landing. Perhaps they have a sixth sense for locating the loneliest points of convergence for transient well-heeled males. At any rate, the two prosperous wagon contractors and the Portuguese hide hunter each showed signs of negotiating some kind of temporary or perhaps permanent alliance with Matty, Kitty, and Essie before they departed Bell's Landing.

As we were pushing our chairs back from the table, Kathleen Hardesty suprised me by appearing in the entrance door of the Steever House. I had thought her absence might be a continuation of the indisposition that had kept her confined to her stateroom on the *Deer*

Lodge, but instead she had risen early and gone outside. Her rosy cheeks and flashing eyes indicated either a vigorous reaction to a briskness of air and exercise, or repressed anger. It was mostly anger. She demanded to know where Towanjila was, and why the livery stable keeper would not tell her how to reach the Sioux woodyard.

Nettie calmly set her down in a rocking chair, ordered one of the girls to bring her a cup of tea, and patiently began explaining that a messenger had come with a riding horse for Towanjila soon after the *Deer Lodge* landed. Towanjila had gone to rejoin her husband and child.

"He cannot be her legal husband," Kathleen retorted. "The child is a bastard."

"The man is not who you believe him to be," Nettie said with continued forbearance. "You ought not to meddle in this."

"The man I saw and heard at Fort Rawley is Drew Hardesty. He's been through some terrible trial, but when he sees me, he'll remember me."

Nettie folded her arms and continued in the same mild tone: "The messenger he sent told me he does not wish to see anyone from outside."

Kathleen set the teacup down hard so that it

splashed on the tray. "You've conspired to ostracize me," she cried accusingly. "You and that Indian girl, the livery stable man, and God knows who else. Just now that livery stable oaf said to me" — and she mimicked the stable-man's voice with a furious but controlled anger —" 'I don't know his name. He's a furtive sort. Some say he's a squaw man from somewheres back on the Dutchman. He only shows up here after long absences. Stays at the Steever House.' "

Nettie could not help but smile at the mimicry, and this further infuriated Kathleen, who shouted: "Just what is Drew Hardesty's business here, Nettie Steever, what has he to do with you?"

Nettie shook her head calmly. "You're all mixed up, Miss Kathleen."

"Not *Miss* Kathleen. *Mrs.* Drew Hardesty."

"Very well. Nobody's trying to send you to Coventry, Mrs. Hardesty. But for your own sake, I beg you to please take passage on the next steamboat at Bell's Landing."

Eventually Nettie must have realized that she was not going to be rid of Kathleen Hardesty by use of words, and so she tried to strike a compromise. She asked Kathleen if she would accept me as her agent, a go-between to

351

deliver whatever oral or written communication she might wish to send. At first Kathleen was reluctant, but after turning the offer over in her mind I suppose she must have accepted it as an entering wedge rather than as an evasion.

"Just tell him I'm here at Bell's Landing," she declared. "He'll come."

I had meant to search out the man, regardless, and Nettie surely knew that. Perhaps the arrangement was one that she saw as inevitable.

Nettie and I left the Steever House after a hasty noon meal, riding on a pair of bay horses hired from her friend at the livery stable. The distance was less than I'd imagined, but the route there was circuitous, to say the least. Had I tried to find the woodyard on my own, and without directions, I might never have arrived there through the maze of crooking pathways and thorn thickets and muddy bottoms. The only easy route in or out must have been the creek that flowed lazily to the Missouri and served to float small boats and billets that had been cut for steamboat fuel.

Forcing our horses up a sort of natural levee, we came suddenly upon the place, and there on high ground set among several gigantic cottonwoods were a dozen small log cabins. To our left was a wide arm of the creek, a bayou, it would have been called in the South, the water almost as dark as ink. Floating in the still water were a number of logs. Three or four men were wading among them, guiding them with crudely made canthooks. The men appeared to be Indians, but the nearest one turned at the sound of our horses, and although he wore a Sioux hunting jacket and a faded scarf around his head, he was the man we had come to see.

He waded slowly toward us as we dismounted, his expression grim and resentful, his scar inflamed against his beard. I remembered Kathleen's remark about our similarities. Our eyes, she said, were of the same shade of brown. I studied his eyes, deep in their hollows, as he strode out of the water; they were neither brown nor blue; they were dead, ashen.

"You did not keep your promise to me, Nettie," he said sternly. Rivulets of watery mud ran down his ragged brown jeans, leaving black streaks across the tops of his bare feet.

"The thing has to be settled," she replied firmly. "Until it's done, she will not leave Bell's Landing. Sam Morrison will tell you that."

He shook his head at me, and I knew he disliked me now as much or more than I was repelled by him. "Men have killed for less persecution," he threatened me in that hollow way he had of speaking under stress. He drew himself up straight. "All right. Let's go and sit. I'll tell you some things, Good Samaritan, I've never uttered to a living soul. Will you go back then and convince the Iron Maiden to show this godless place her fair heels? Tell her to run while she can?"

"I'll do my best," I promised.

He led the way to the only cabin that boasted a covered porch. It was roofed with bark slabs. Log benches and chairs hewn out of huge sections of tree trunks crowded the sandy porch floor. From the gloom of the interior Towanjila appeared in the doorway. She was carrying a sleepy child in her arms. She was not pleased to see me, but murmured a few words of greeting.

"Coffee for us," he commanded her brusquely. The child began crying. Nettie followed Towanjila back into the cabin, and he and I sat down facing each other, no more than a yard separating us.

"I might have known you would guess my secret," he began in a deliberately disarming manner. "You remind me of a persistent dog that's chased a coon up a tree. Of course no one would believe you now, Mr. Morrison, if you catch the coon."

"If *you* are the coon," I replied, "why do you call Mrs. Hardesty the Iron Maiden?"

He looked offended. "Because that's what Drew always called her." He laughed but not with amusement, the sound dry and brittle in his throat. "Drew and I knew each other long before he ever met her." Something in my expression must have disturbed him. "Look here, Mr. Morrison, you don't believe that cock-and-bull tale I related in your stateroom on the *Roanoke*, do you? Good Lord, man, Drew Hardesty would not have hung about Fort Standish all those weeks, risking discovery. Too many officers from the Galvanized Yankee battalion at Fort Rice were coming and going along the Missouri. No, sir, he'd've found a way to 'scape off to Canada. And once he got across the border on that crazy jaunt to capture Spotted Horse, hellfire, old Drew wouldn't have come back. Never, never! Only Charles Rawley would be compelled to do that. Clear the family escutcheon, don't you see?

"Even so, Drew was a far better man than I. Better at everything. When we had our mounted militia companies, he and his Kentucky boys never failed to outride and outshoot us Ohio boys in the meets. Couldn't help but envy him, but not enough to let it spoil our friendship. After the war started, I envied him again when he threw his militia company in with General John Morgan's cavalry. God, how I wanted to be in that regiment! Not that I had any feelings for the southern cause. To me horse soldiering was all delightful derring-do, and the Kentuckians were always the best. I could have crossed the Ohio River any morning and joined on with Morgan's men, but I was a Rawley, Senator Rawley's son, and Senator Rawley was a symbol of the Union. Couldn't stain the family honor, now could I? My father got me my major's rank in the U.S. Volunteers."

He'd found a cloth under the bench and began cleaning his feet with it. He squeezed muddy water out of the lower parts of his pants legs. "You saw him and heard him at that sanctimonious commemoration the other day. All lies, as I tried to tell him. I could never return to that, Mr. Morrison. I am well out of it, buried with old Spotted Horse under that granite monument which was put there more for Senator Rawley than for Major Rawley.

"My life was a series of failures until I came to this place." He moved his hands, palms down, slowly in an arc as if blessing the point of land, the backwater, and the weather-faded log cabins. "We do what we please here. Trap a little, hunt a little, cut wood for the steamboats. Of course it won't last much longer, the wood. Some of the Sioux want to stop cutting now before the trees are all gone.

"I could not endure another defeat. Immediately after what happened on the Malpais I was so overcome with the humiliation of failure that I could not bear to be Charles Rawley. No gratification, you understand, that Providence had spared me, spared me alone of the others, the men under my command, but only mortification for the dishonor that I'd brought upon a Rawley. I had to lay the responsibility for it upon one of my betters, and so I became him, the old friend I'd envied. And then Killdeer Mountain. Cowardice they said. Killdeer Mountain. I was too much of Drew Hardesty there.

"He was dead, out there in that alien land, the Malpais. He was dead, after giving his life to save mine, old Drew was."

"What do you mean?" I asked. "Gave his life to save yours?"

"He threw himself between me and Private Tharp." He stopped suddenly as though startled by the sound in the shadowy doorway behind him. Towanjila was bringing the coffee, in metal cups on a flat board tray.

Somewhere back in the cabin the baby was crying again, with Nettie's voice trying to soothe it to sleep. I thanked Towanjila for the coffee, but the major took his cup without a word.

"Lukewarm," he said after she'd vanished through the doorway. "You'd think — Oh, well. There was never much humanity in me — in Charles Rawley. I had no feeling for other human beings. Drew Hardesty was all the things I was not. Everyone liked old Drew because he liked everyone. I tried to become Drew Hardesty, you see, after that disaster on the Malpais. Became too much of him at Killdeer Mountain."

He drank half the coffee in his cup in one nervous gulp. I followed his gaze down the point of land to one of the smaller log houses. A man and a woman were stretching hides on pole frames. "They make the finest moccasins and leggings you'll find anywhere, Mr. Morrison."

Was he finished with his explanations, I wondered. "How did Drew Hardesty come to be in your battalion?" I asked.

"Ah, yes. He was one of the Morgan men captured during their wild raid across the Ohio. I'd lost track of him by then. Had no idea if he was dead or alive. After I'd got my major's commission they sent me down to Saint Louis to take command of the battalion on the *Effie Deans*. Made up my mind to put up a strict disciplinarian front, regular martinet, don't you see, to cover the fact I didn't know a damned thing about soldiering. Had them out on the hurricane deck, platoon by platoon for inspections. Drew was a platoon sergeant. He recognized me before I did him. Had a droll owlish expression on his face when I came to him at the end of the first rank. I'll say this for old Drew. He held it all in, never blinked when I made a derogatory remark about his stance. That evening I summoned him to my quarters on the steamboat. We had to talk in whispers, and both of us agreed right off to keep our former friendship a secret, for his good and my good.

"I let the impression get about that I'd chosen him to be my orderly. Actually when I'd summon him to my cabin we'd pitch in and clean the damned place together, reminiscing in low voices about the grand times we'd had before the war. On only one occasion did we come to a bitter disagreement. That was when I brought Private Noah Burkett to court-martial. Drew declared the man innocent and argued that any further attempts at desertion would cease because the *Effie Deans* had entered hostile Indian country. Then when Burkett was condemned to die, Drew refused any more conversations with me. He was right, of course, about the whole affair.

"He was surprised that I chose him to act as my sergeant when we started across the Malpais. He loosened up a bit on that hard and gritty march. We exchanged a few pleasantries, and when we stopped to rest and bathe along the sandy creek, just before the Sioux warriors struck us, he actually sang a song or two in that mellow voice of his."

" 'Pretty Betty Martin'?" I asked abruptly.

He stared directly at me, a faint smile showing through his beard. "He always sang it 'Pretty *Kathy* Martin.' "

"Yes. That's the way you sing it."

"Her name was Kathleen Martin," he replied, with a hint of annoyance in his tone, "before she married Drew."

Nettie Steever was in the doorway, cradling the sleeping child in her arms. She transferred it gently and somewhat reluctantly to Towanjila. The baby's skin was almost translucent, more olive than copper.

"If we expect to get back to Bell's Landing by sundown," Nettie said, "we'd best leave now."

I nodded my head to indicate that I was ready to go. "Let me repeat Kathleen

Hardesty's message," I said to the major. "She wants you to know that she is waiting at Bell's Landing."

He shrugged as we arose together. "You tell *her* this, Good Samaritan, tell her she is waiting for the wrong rooster. Tell the Iron Maiden to cut the tie and run."

Nettie was already tightening the saddles on the bays. I went out to join her. By the time we were mounted the major was entering the doorway of the cabin. I waved a farewell. He let his arm drop, and vanished, a shadow among shadows.

We turned the horses into the crooking pathway along the edge of the dark log-filled slough. The bright blue sky was filled with lazily floating pure white clouds, driven gently by a south wind. The entire outlook was most un-Dakotan, but it was springtime, a new beginning as they say. Nettie took the lead, leaving me to think on the obsessions and obstinacies of mortals.

Not long after the trail led us out to where we could see the Missouri running full, I sighted a steamboat. It was not a large vessel and its grayish appearance in the distance indicated it needed fresh paint. But the boat was heading south on those buoyant freshly melted waters from the north.

As we neared Bell's Landing the trail turned away from the river for a short distance, and then when we rode into view of the livery stable and the Steever House, the steamboat hove in sight, quickly drew ashore, and put down its gangplank. With a shout to Nettie that I was turning toward the landing, I slapped the bay into a lope.

The *Ben Jonson* had stopped to take on wood and some essential supplies from the trading post. It would be leaving in about two hours, bound for Saint Louis. I asked the captain to reserve two staterooms, one for me and one for Mrs. Kathleen Hardesty, and then rode the bay back to the livery stable.

As I was returning to the Steever House, Kathleen came outside to meet me, her hands clasped together and pressed against her breast, like a little girl awaiting a promised present. "What did he say?" she asked eagerly. "Nettie would not tell me."

"He swears he is not Drew Hardesty," I told her bluntly, as cruelly as I could, considering the pity I felt for her.

"But you made it clear to him that I'm here, that his wife Kathleen is here, waiting for him?"

I caught her by the shoulders. "He knows

362

that. He wants you to leave this place — now."

She shook her head.

"It's no use," I pleaded. "Look here, a boat, the *Ben Jonson* is at the landing. I've reserved a stateroom for you. Go and pack your things so I can haul that blasted trunk of yours aboard."

She drew away from me, her eyes filling with tears, her teeth biting into her lower lip in an attempt to stop the flow.

"Think on it," I said, "while I get my bag and say good-bye to Nettie."

When I came outside a few minutes later she was waiting for me there, the tears gone, her face almost serene, in full control of herself.

"Come on," I said, trying to put some cheer into my voice. "You still have time."

"He knows I'm here," she replied stubbornly. "He'll come for me."

I offered my hand. "Good-bye, Kathleen."

She smiled, her lips moving without sound. As I started to turn away she said: "Would you do a great favor for me, Sam?"

"Yes?"

"I'll need some immediate funds, to stay here. Could you —"

"I can only give you a draft on the Boatman's Bank," I said. "Nettie may refuse to accept it."

She lifted her chin. "She will accept it."

I opened my bag and wrote out a draft for her.

"I'll pay you back as soon as I can. Where shall I send the money?"

"In care of the *Saint Louis Herald*."

I told her good-bye once more, and hurried down the rutted and clod-filled road to the *Ben Jonson*, thinking once again on the obsessions and obstinacies, the self-deceptions and prevarications of humankind.

14

It must have been more than a year later; yes, I'm certain it was, because my pretty girl from Belle Fontaine had accepted me as a husband in spite of my poor prospects, and the *Saint Louis Herald* editor had taken pity and given me the waterfront to write about. Instead of traveling to faraway places in search of violence and gore, I reported on the comings and goings of steamboats, their captains and pilots, and sometimes their passengers.

With the passing of time, the events and human beings I had encountered on the upper Missouri gradually receded in my mind as had the excitements and horrors of the more distant war. Less and less often did I recall the puzzle of Major Rawley, the Malpais, Killdeer Mountain, Nettie Steever, even Kathleen Hardesty. Then one day a letter came addressed to me in care of the *Herald*. The envelope bore an Omaha postmark, and inside was a note scrawled across a sheet of ruled paper: *Thanks, many thanks. K.H.* The sheet was wrapped around the exact amount of the draft I'd given Kathleen the day I told her good-bye at Bell's Landing.

I'd never expected to see that money again, and somehow in my mind I'd placed green-eyed Kathleen back in Ohio or perhaps Kentucky, surrounded by suitors, perhaps already remarried. But no, she was in booming Omaha, railroad center of the vanishing frontier. For a day or two I itched for a correspondent assignment again, up the Missouri to Omaha of course, but the urge soon faded. Yet frequently for no reason whatever at almost any time of the day or night, visions of Kathleen would form in my mind and I'd speculate upon her fate, the enigma of her presence in a Missouri River town.

And then one day I learned the answer. I'd just made my daily call at the Eldridge House, a favored headquarters for rivermen, with its sedate lobby and comfortable bar. A late October day, halfway between summer and winter, it was. From the brick sidewalk in front of the Eldridge House was an open view of the Mississippi River waterfront, with its array of boats ranging from the shabbiest of crafts to the most sumptuous floating palaces. The air was especially clear that day. Above the

Illinois side of the river, rows of dark-bellied clouds were racing southward, signaling the first chill of autumn.

When I turned I noticed a man coming down the slant of sidewalk. From his gait he was surely a riverman, but to my eyes there was something more distinctive about him. He was wearing a plain black broadcloth suit and a wide-brimmed gray hat creased down the middle of the crown. It was the unfamiliar hat that threw me off. Having never seen him with any head-covering other than a steamboat captain's cap, I almost failed to recognize Enoch Adams. When I did so, I strode forward and we met with mutual cries of greeting. He had changed but little; his mustache drooped a bit more limply and the gray at his temples was spreading higher into his curly hair.

We went into the bar to celebrate our reunion. He was staying at the Eldridge House, he explained, awaiting a promised steamboat assignment. He had just returned from a holiday journey.

"Having never set my butt down in a railway passenger car," he growled, "I decided the time had come for Enoch Adams to beard the devil in his den. If those rattling contraptions hooting across the land are going to kill off our pleasantly appointed steamboats, I said to myself, then I want to know the reasons for it. Well, I can tell you, Sam, I've still got aches in the knees, kinks in the spine, and cinders lodged in my eyes. More'n once I was tempted to jump off the blasted monster and walk back to the nearest flow of water that could support a boat. Plain torture, Sam, pure agony."

"Perhaps it was worth it, sir, to be reassured that the railroad will never replace the steamboat."

He sniffed at the aromatic fumes rising from his brandy. "I'm not so certain of that. People are fools for the latest thing, you know, will endure torture and misery if necessary to be in the swim."

"Where did you journey for this adventure on the rails?"

"Took the new transcontinental. From Omaha to a dreadful placed called Julesburg. I've seen plenty of rowdy river towns in my day, but none to compare with Julesburg the railroad town." He took a bare sip of his liqueur. "Did have a strange meeting there — oh, yes, with someone you'll likely remember, Sam, for that last trip you made with me aboard the *Roanoke*. D'you recall the handsome widow, a Mrs. Hardesty? Played our melodeon and sang for us?"

"Yes, you held quite a passing fancy for the

lady, as I recall."

He nodded and smiled. "So did we all, Sam, so did we all. She was the soul of feminine beauty and vivacity. Admit it, you were smitten yourself. You were quite far gone the day you escorted her to that Rawley commemoration." His mouth opened wider as he drew in a sudden gasp of breath, his mild blue eyes brightening with excitement. "Good God! Couldn't be." For once the usually self-possessed Captain Adams seemed overcome with astonishment. "I've been racking my feeble memory to place that scarred and bearded fellow. How on earth could they have — well, you may know something of him, Sam. That mad son of the devil who interrupted Senator Rawley by shouting out at him during the speech. You went charging after him —"

"For God's sake," I cried. "Don't tell me you saw them together?"

"Cozy as turtledoves, yes, right there in Julesburg they were. Likely still there. I was strolling the town, waiting for train-departure time, when I heard this sweet melodeon music. 'Come where my love lies dreaming.' You know the ballad. 'Dreaming the happy hours away.' Drifting out through the canvas and wood walls of a place called the Alhambra. I entered and found myself in a combination saloon, gambling den, and dance hall. The music was still going, only by then she was singing, and the big man with the scarred face stood beside the melodeon to accompany her in a deep rich voice."

"A rather hollow voice," I said.

The captain nodded, and began humming a tune, then tried to sing the words: " 'Once I loved thee, Mary dear.' Hell, I can't come near the depth of his basso. Anyway, there they were, Sam. The place was crowded with case-hardened tracklayers, burned as dark as Indians by the summer sun. Tolerated the bass singer, they did, *worshiped* her as a goddess. As rough a collection of unwashed brutes as you could find anywhere on this earth, shedding a tear now and then when the songs turned melancholy."

"You spoke to her?" I asked.

"Yes, at first opportunity. She remembered me, all right. They call themselves the Selkirks, Alex and Kathleen." He turned to raise a hand in greeting to another veteran riverman who had just entered the barroom.

"How in hell did she do it?" I asked myself aloud. "The Iron Maiden. And he — He flim-flammed me in doubles."

"What was that, Sam? Tell me, who is that stern sadfaced fellow who calls himself Alex Selkirk?"

"If you do not know him, sir, I can't say for certain who he is. Truthfully I don't know, but if I knew and told you truth, you would never believe me."

"That's the case, eh?"

"Yes, sir, that's the case. Shall we have another brandy?"

THORNDIKE PRESS HOPES you have enjoyed this Large Print book. All our Large Print titles are designed for the easiest reading, and all our books are made to last. Other Thorndike Press Large Print books are available at your library, through selected bookstores, or directly from the publisher. For more information about our current and upcoming Large Print titles, please send your name and address to:

THORNDIKE PRESS
ONE MILE ROAD
P.O. BOX 157
THORNDIKE, MAINE 04986

There is no obligation, of course.